Skin and Bone

Gareth Creer was born in Salford in 1961, and brought up in North Manchester. He went to Oxford University and then into the City. In 1994 he abandoned his career to write full time, taking the Sheffield Hallam writing course. He lives in the North with his wife and daughters. His second novel, *Cradle to Grave*, is also published by Anchor.

D0967053

by the same author

CRADLE TO GRAVE

SKIN AND BONE

Gareth Creer

TRANSWORLD PUBLISHERS LTD
61–63 Uxbridge Road, London W5 5SA

TRANSWORLD PUBLISHERS (AUSTRALIA) PTY LTD
15–25 Helles Avenue, Moorebank, NSW 2170

TRANSWORLD PUBLISHERS (NZ) LTD
3 William Pickering Drive, Albany, Auckland

Published by Anchor – a division of Transworld Publishers Ltd

First published in Great Britain by Anchor, 1998
This paperback edition published by Anchor, 1999

Copyright © 1998 by Gareth Creer

Lyrics from Native Land by Everything But The Girl, 1984, WEA.
Courtesy of Complete Music. Written by Ben Watt/Tracey Thorn

The right of Gareth Creer to be identified as the author of this work has been
asserted in accordance with the Copyright, Designs and Patents Act 1988

A catalogue record for this book is available from the British Library

ISBN 1862 30024 0

All rights reserved. No part of this publication may be reproduced, stored
in a retrieval system, or transmitted in any form or by any means,
electronic, mechanical, photocopying, recording, or otherwise, without the
prior permission of the publishers

Typeset in 11/14pt Adobe Caslon by Kestrel Data, Exeter

Printed in Great Britain by Cox & Wyman Ltd, Reading, Berks.

Acknowledgements

Thank you to: Tony Devine, Lesley Glaister, Patrick Walsh, Sarah Westcott. And most of all, to my Mum and Dad.

You say we're in a different world now
Where money and love go hand in hand
But can't you see we share this town
So why should we fight on our native land

Can't you see we share this town
So why on earth should we tear it down

Native Land
Everything But The Girl

For Stefanie, with love.

Your name and your parents, where you're born and the friends who choose you, these are things you can't control. Delores O'Brien, my Grandma Delores, tells me 'it's how you adapt, the fortitude you show, that makes the man'. 'Fortitude', the way she says it, with cheeks drawn in and her chin in the air, smelling clean of old fashioned soap and with her real cracks far below the wrinkled surface. It's one of her words, from another language I don't speak, like 'faith' and 'forgiveness'. What she doesn't tell me, but which I've learned for myself, is that here and now, in Slipp, there's only so far you can get with fortitude.

The name is me and I am the name, and the same is true of the place, this Slipp I was born in and bred for. I've grown into them, let them shape me, like the slaps on unworked clay. It's almost complete, this shaping of me. It's gone as far as it can, I think. She'll leave me soon. Change her name, and break me, so I don't care about me any more.

*   *   *

Here comes Mrs Sellars, bang on time, and I'm having to rush her fillets. That's OK, I can do them quickly and still watch her stiff-limbed walk across the road, with her two bulging bags slowing her down, banging against her knees – a downshift warp of her breasts, heavy and dulled in her coats. The bell at the top of the door jangles, and in she trundles, bringing little bits of my past she doesn't know I know about.

'Morning Artie.'

'Morning Mrs Sellars. Nearly finished.'

I fillet as I speak, with a swipe and a jag and a flip and the same again. I look at her as I do it. Usually I like to watch the bones come away, like magic. I can amaze myself.

It's Friday, the last before Christmas. She's come for the four plaice fillets she always comes for. I'll let her have them for a fiver. I've been serving her for eight years. Dad for twenty years before that. Two hundred and fifty quid a year. For fish. That's seven grand she's spent here, in today's money. Can you imagine what seven grand of fish looks like? I can't and I work with them.

'You haven't done me four have you Artie?' She fiddles with her purse and looks across at me with a tired face – thin webs of blood vessels that have burst on her dry, winter cheeks. Her eyes are watery, from the wind. She is older than her years. Time's not been kind to her. Neither has having to live in Slipp. It can get to you, wear you down. Time and space. Bad news if they're both going against you.

I flip the plaice back over and enjoy its deep slap. The head and tail and bones go in my stock bin. Then she says it.

'I only want three today.'

After twenty-eight years, she only wants three. It's either none at all during Wakes when she goes to Blackpool, and the shop is closed anyway, or four. Never three. Three is an odd number. Three? She may as well have said 'the martians have landed', or 'the Russians are coming' or 'bring out your dead'.

'Our Kevin's off to London after Christmas.' Kev Sellars, a proper name you didn't have to say twice.

'I saw him Tuesday. He didn't say anything. Is he going for long?'

'Oh yes, he's got a job, with a big computer firm, come right out of the blue, it did. Good money too.'

Little Kev Sellars, with his shirt lap hanging out and smoking ciggies behind the gym, and the first in the class to get a bit – off Mandy Price. Mandy Price, the name of that kind of girl. Not like Madelaine, my Madelaine. Me and Madelaine, still here and with the likes of Kev on the move. We're together for now, but it's only a matter of time. Then it'll be me on my own, cutting fish on a slab, the way it seems I always will, like my dad always did.

I can see the envelope. It's sticking out of my jacket, on the back of the storeroom door. It's a week since I got it, or at least claimed it as my own. It's mocking me, sticking out past my lapel. I read it again this morning – scanning it for crannies of doubt or misunderstanding. There are none.

Next in is Mrs Hubbard. Can you believe it? Mrs Hubbard. That's her name, for real. Except she's not old or fat and drowned in skirts like you might imagine her, and she's not a mother. She's two years older than me, and with layered salt and peppered hair. They call it salt and peppered. Beth told me it's when they make your hair a kind of grey straw blonde. Beth used to own Candice, the hairdresser's down the street – before they closed her down. Moved her out. Some people thought she was called Candice, but she's not. Her name's Elizabeth, but she's got everyone calling her Beth. Good luck to her, getting the name to stick like that. Madelaine says they salt and pepper their hair so you can leave it longer before the roots show through. She says it looks cheap. It's for cheap people who want to look expensive. I don't know, but Madelaine wouldn't need it anyway, it's easy for her to say: with her perfect hair that's dark and thick and always with a sheen, easy to make look different.

But Mrs Hubbard, Karen Hubbard, doesn't just have expensive hair. She's expensive all over, expensive for Slipp – but 'obvious' according to Madelaine. At school she always had a boy with her, a different boy about to be swapped. Usually from St Peter's, the school down the road with the pink piping on their blazers. By the time I was doing my O'levels, and she'd left, it was men with sports cars. I'd see her in the precinct on Fridays, which was our wagging day, and she'd meet them in the Emperor's wine bar. They'd be much older than her, and married too was my guess.

One New Year's Eve she turned up, at the Masons. It was when Madelaine was at university. She wasn't actually at university, because it was the holiday, or the vacation as she called it, but she'd gone to a party, in Wales. I didn't want to go. I didn't really want her to go, but she insisted. So I didn't object. It's easy to see now that she would have known I wouldn't go when she invited me. Soon, it's going to be the eighth anniversary of when I didn't go.

I had the shop to look after, and other, adult, responsibilities. I didn't mind. I didn't see things changing, no dangers. Dad had just died, but it wasn't just that. I'd been down to Bristol to see her, once. That was all. Once was enough to see her with her trendy new friends. They were all right, but not like us – me and my friends. I had a different life, one that I couldn't resist. I was making the best of my lot. I can remember her meeting me from the station. I can remember every word, I've got the conversation catalogued in a way that would surprise her. I can even remember what she was wearing. I once got her to test me, on how I could remember her clothes, from every date we'd had. She couldn't fault me. This time she had a vest on, a singlet, too skimpy for the time of year, and with no bra underneath; and jeans that were too tight, so tight you could, well . . . you can imagine.

'Artie!' she shouted, excited, walking quickly up the platform.

'Hi.' I went to kiss her, but her eyes stayed wide.

'Come on. Come on. There's a party.' She was bouncing around. 'Everyone's going. We'll dump your luggage and go, it's going to be great.'

'I've come to see you,' I said.

'I'm here,' she said, tiptoeing up and kissing me, spinning round and leading me away by the hand, turning her back after a kiss that was only polite. I stopped, and let her arm go taut, gripping her hand tight and reeling her back towards me.

'I've come to see you.'

'Oh, Artie. It'll be fun. Come on.'

'I'm tired.'

We went to the party, and she introduced me to her friends. They seemed nice, safe. She was popular, and I was pleased for her, in the absence of threat. But I didn't feel as though I fitted. I was going a different way. After that, we just stayed in the room, that tiny room with the smells of burning toast and damp clothes, the smells of too much living in too small a confine. Sounds she shouldn't be living near and sleeping through.

From then on she'd come up here to see me. It was easier. I had the shop. I was turning it round, making it my life, or at least a foundation for a better life. She'd come every fortnight, then every month, then twice a term. That lasted for a year. Then we split up (her idea) the Christmas of her second year. I should have seen it coming, after she'd been round Europe during the summer – with a friend I never met. 'A friend', whose name I never discovered, never even pressed for. She asked if I would go with her, soothing suspicions I can't remember having. I couldn't have gone anyway, but she said she wanted me to. I believed her, and stayed in the shop I couldn't leave. The split lasted until the New Year, when we got together again. Then we got engaged. She started coming home every fortnight again, to help me with the house.

But that first New Year after she left Slipp, I stayed here while she went to her party in Wales. I knew she wouldn't get up to anything. I was sure about that. That left me and Karen Dugg, Mrs Hubbard, in the Masons – but not together. She was with some of the girls who'd been in her year. No men, which was strange, looking back on it. There was a gang of us, getting drunk in time for midnight. Kev was jumping off the bar. We formed two lines and held hands and he landed full stretch on our forearms. Then we tossed him in the air and he landed on us again. Someone threw beer on us and we laughed and sang a song. Only an hour or so to go until 1990. It was as good as it got without her.

Just before twelve I went to the toilet. When I came out there was Karen Dugg, just coming off the phone. I looked at her close up, and then at my feet as I passed her. I practically touched her. I could smell her expensive smell, like Madelaine's mum, a grown up smell, sophisticated. I'd gone through school two years behind her, but she had in most regards been more than two ahead of me, with her breasts that had always been too big, and her clothes too small, and her confident walk, the way she talked to the teachers, especially the men, as though they were no better than her. Even though she wasn't clever.

'All right?' she said, with a lick of the lips and a smile.

'All right,' I said, looking back down at my shoes and squinting sideways at her clothes and flesh and getting another waft of her. Nearly twelve and the place was heaving. I wanted to look up, to see what she really looked like, this close up. Her on her own, me on my own. I could see a chunk of nylon thigh, sheeny brown-black and jutting from a tartan skirt, split with no pin.

'Ten,' they shouted.

'Hey, Arthur,' she said – Nine – 'You on yer own?' – Eight

'Yeah, no' – Seven – 'Sort of' – Six – 'My mates, they're . . .' – Five

'Never mind yer . . .' – Four

'What?' – Three.

'C'mhere.' – Two – 'Happy New' – One – 'Year.'

Bedlam.

And now here she is. Mrs Hubbard, who I'd been with on New Year's Eve while Madelaine was in Pembrokeshire and Mr Hubbard was in Cyprus, with the army for Christ's sake, and my mates at the bar, who wouldn't have believed me if I'd told them. But I didn't. Didn't dare.

'Got somethin' special Arthur? Our Carl's home for

Christmas. Thought I'd treat him, you know,' she says, with that lick of the lips and a smile – in anticipation of someone else's benefit.

Even now, I can't look her in the eye. Especially now. Sometimes when it was slack I'd imagine she'd come in, wearing a short skirt, like her New Year's Eve one, and the things underneath she'd worn that night – not much, but silky and complicated with straps and elastic all tangled, like it was in the car park, when I'd made a fool of myself. She would come in and shut the door behind her, pulling the light blue blind down, the colour of sea in the sun. She'd lean back against the door and show me her secrets that weren't secret any more, and I'd do it properly this time, on the floor behind the door. But when I thought about it, it would smell, of fish, and it would be cold, and Madelaine was here now, at home, and it never got beyond a quick think.

But here she is and I have to speak to her, with no-one else in the shop.

'Monkfish. Monkfish is nice, you know, for a special occasion.'

'Monkfish?'

'Or plaice. The plaice is good.'

'All right. Plaice. He won't notice anyway. He's been gone six weeks,' she's laughing, dirty and deep, and tucking her hair behind her ears with a sucking in of her cheeks, 'know what I mean.'

And I look away, filleting the plaice for her with my magic swipes. It would be easy to ruin its thin web of white flesh. It could flake to nothing under a harsh touch. But my fingers twirl and dance it round the slab. In three caresses it's off the bone. No skin. Perfect and ready for her to ruin.

'Clever that. The way you cut 'em.'

'Thanks.'

'D'you ever cut yourself?'

'Never.'

'Not once?'

'Never.'

I keep looking down, at the two flat white fans, flesh that could burst with juice if you didn't go too far in the cooking of it. I'm proud that she's passed comment but I can't let her see a smile. I'm not a sad case. I know that cutting up fish, fast and properly, isn't really anything to be proud of. But someone has to do it, and if it's going to be me I may as well do it right. It doesn't stop it being nice when someone mentions it. Everyone likes a little praise. There are certificates on the wall to say I can do it right, that I was best in Year, best in County. Awards gained while Madelaine was away. She went away and I perfected myself – in that regard.

She flicks a note over the glass shelf and I feel a resistance as I take it from between her painted fingers. Like talons. Nothing fishy about this Karen Dugg. What you see is what you get. I had, and I wouldn't again.

I sell more fish on Friday than the rest of the week put together. I suppose that faith still counts for something, even in Slipp. I used to have Andrea on Fridays. She was Madelaine's idea. She couldn't cut fish, and only knew the popular varieties. She didn't know that moules were the beardy things in the black shells. 'Oh, the beardy things in the black shells.' This was what I was up against on Fridays, so I got rid of her, but I've not told Madelaine. It's not much of a secret to keep from your wife, and in any case, she never mentions her work or the people she meets there. The boys reckon Madelaine got her in as a spy, to keep me on my toes. That's why Andrea looked the way she did, with her facial hair, like a moule in places. They were only joking.

They know I'd never cheat on Madelaine. She's everything I've ever wanted, in that department. And I never have, apart from that one time, in the car park of the Masons, and they don't know about that. It's good that your mates might think that a wife like Madelaine would care that much, good that I can let on she might have a cause for concern. But it's only letting on. They know the real score. No, it's me that needs the spy.

I can see the envelope again, with time to ponder its insides again, now Mrs Hubbard's gone. I want to read it, but I'm resisting. It's like at school, when we'd sit in the gym for assembly, on mats in short grey trousers that rode up and went tight on your inside legs. The matting would go sticking and clammy. There'd be nothing to do for twenty minutes. We got told off for picking the matting, for making perfect balls from its airy foam insides. They were looking out for it. So I'd pick my legs instead, my dried blood knees that I wanted to heal but couldn't leave alone. I'd get my nail underneath and my toes would curl, expecting pain that didn't come. I'd get the scab panel to come away, looking worse than it was. It wouldn't hurt until you stood up, when the skin flexed.

I've got the envelope out – in the back with the 'closed' sign up. You shouldn't let anyone open your post. Not if you've got something to hide. Madelaine plays hell with me if I open her post. It was a genuine error, this opening of her mail, on the occasion which triggered the monitoring of all communications. I saw the insurance company's logo on the envelope. She was away. I knew she wanted it sorted out for Christmas. So I opened it. In good faith. Good faith, bad faith, is there a difference? I can see that by not opening it, you're denying yourself knowledge, the special knowledge of the parts of a person's life that they want kept secret. And since I've been policing her mail, which they do in some countries as a matter of law, for the general good, I have seen what a fool I was not to start earlier. 'There's nothing wrong with a bit of mystery in a relationship.' People say it – on telly and in the problem pages. It's easy to say. I might have said it myself a week ago, when I never used to open Madelaine's mail.

There were eight pages of it, the medical report from Dr Hart, the insurers' consultant psychiatrist. Madelaine had an accident in the summer. Nothing serious and not her fault. Just a bit of whiplash. I said to go for more, to claim for anxiety. It was my idea, I'm good with money.

If a total stranger read the report, they'd think they might know Madelaine. I've read it and it's made me wonder if I know her at all.

Mrs Gill is a twenty-seven-year-old married woman who works as a theatre producer. She lives with her husband and has no children.
Physical Sequelae:- Mrs Gill experienced pain and stiffness in her neck for a few weeks following the accident.
Psychiatric Sequelae:- For the weeks following the accident, Mrs Gill felt low in mood . . . felt tense and irritable . . . She has now recovered her normal level of confidence whilst driving.
Past Psychiatric and Pre-Morbid Adjustment:- . . . pre-morbid personality does not suggest any problem with inter-personal functioning.
Past Medical and Surgical History:- Nil.
Personal History:- No perinatal problems. She has one sibling. She has not seen her father for six years, since he deserted the family home.

Her late schooling was disrupted by her parents'
divorce. There were otherwise no problems at
secondary school and she left at the age of
eighteen, to go to university where she obtained
a BA. Mrs Gill married at the age of twenty-one.
She had known her husband for four years. Mrs
Gill's husband is not her sole significant
relationship.
 Mental State Examination:- No evidence of
abnormality, of any sort, was demonstrated.
 Diagnosis:- Phobic anxiety - now resolved.

And there you have it, buried in all the jargon, is the sig-
nificance of my wife's relationships. Not 'sole'. 'Significant' in
type. How significant? Who with? Where and when? How
many? On and on the questions come.

I don't just wait for the questions though. Long minutes
between the jangles, sometimes an hour, with everything
spotless and ordered. What to do but backtrack. Log her in
retrospect. Focus my eye for detail, throw light on those
thousand images. Looks she'd give: tired, happy, drunk, sad,
irritated. Looks she'd give at certain times, which I'd pin
down in the diary that went backwards, until I'd coloured
in the year. The diary doesn't tell it all. Not the preenings in
the mirror, the cast off clothes. Not the phone calls.
'Late home, sorry.' 'Late home', no 'sorry'. Then no
phone calls. Six thirty not six. Then seven. Through the
thirties to nine, sometimes ten. Once a week. Twice. Sometimes more, not getting less. Creeping. Almost imperceptible
over a year.

Closing-time. I've phoned home, to see if she's there.
She's not, which I knew before I tried, but I've got to try to
prove myself wrong. I've got to unearth some evidence for

the defence. The phone I had put in the car isn't answering. So, with my shirt off, I scrub down again, up to my shoulders with a thick block of soap and a brush. My face is mottled where the metal base shows through in the mirror. I can't see any change in me, from the eight years I've been doing this. I'm not doing anything different. I can't see a change in myself. But I am not the same, don't feel the way I used to. It's not just the tiredness with Slipp. I've lost something, slowly. Let some other thing creep into its place. I feel less secure. Exposed. I don't smile as much at myself, but there aren't any wrinkles or grey hairs or black bags under my eyes. I look young, younger than I am, and anyone would think I had my best years still ahead of me.

I think it might be fear. Small bits of it. Getting everywhere.

Here I am. Me who asked her out. Me who went breathless when she said 'yes', when she flashed me a look that said she wanted me, with a mouth shaped like a smile, but serious eyes: a deep look that wouldn't let me go. Not a look she'd let slip in the flirting. It felt reserved, for me. I'm trying to picture it now, but I can't. I can see what she was wearing, the way her hair was, but not the look. I can see the younger me. I can feel what it was like to be that me who used to go downstairs when my Nana called up, 'Where's my Artie, such a lovely looking lad, like his father.' She'd stroke my face and part my hair with spit on her fingers and say, 'Such lashes. There's many a girl that'd kill for them lashes.' Before she lost her marbles.

I've got as much of the smell off as I can, so I lock up and go to the Dog. It's the Dog and Partridge, but we've always called it the Dog. We got it off our fathers. It's at the bottom of the High Street, on the corner with the Railing Road that takes you into the city, and to the supermarkets – on its three lane carriageway, flanked all the way by low, tin-roofed buildings and car parks and scrub.

There's not much left on the High Street now, and as I walk down the hill, angling myself backwards to stop its steep slope running away with me, I see they've shut another one down. The launderette. There's hardly any left on our side of the street. Shops rely on passing trade, pedestrian counts, to get their business. I know this, from geography, and my dad – except he didn't know it was called a pedestrian count. You need people passing, on their way to other shops. You need to be somewhere with life. They told me times were bad last month, the agents. They put the rent up expecting me to go, to finally throw the towel in and move to The Phoenix in the city like the rest of them. But they're wrong. Business isn't bad at all, not if you take care of folk. People will make an effort if you look after them. There is such a thing as loyalty.

2

It's raining and going dark, but it's as busy as it gets on the High Street. The money's doing its rounds. There's a crowd outside the betting shop. Tommy Jack, the bookie, wants to get home and they're shouting at him through the doorway. They want one last bet. On the dogs, at Crayford.

They aren't queuing in the Spar or at the baker's. They used to, at this time. They'd go late to get stuff cheap, before it perished. But they've closed them down. Moved to where they want the money to go. I used to enjoy these Christmas walks home. A good day's work behind and going dark early. Christmas lights and tinsel in the windows, and people who don't normally say 'hello', saying 'hello'. It's still all right, but not the same. Not as many lights, and less people. Not so happy.

The Dog is a Great Dane of a pub, large and rambling.

Red bricks gone brown from age, tiles missing from the roof and windows not matching. They're doing three courses in the lounge for £3.95, but we won't be in there. It's crap in the lounge with its cheap brass and cheap prints and cigarette-burned, new red velvet. The boys will be in the vault, with its dark wood and lino and calendars – some with naked women, some with football fixtures or race meetings. And the beer's 2p cheaper. It's got a pool table too. It's got it all.

Some of the boys have been in since dinner. They're singing along to the juke box with a table full of glasses and a piled high ashtray. I know the song but I have to wait for the chorus before I can put a name to it. It's 'Shipbuilding', not the original, but I should have known it straight away. They all join in with 'It's just a rumour that's going round town.'

'Artie lad. Wanna game of doubles?' I hear him behind me.

'Denny!' He's been gone for months, diving. Jesus. When he comes back from diving he drinks for a week. Non stop, especially when he's been to the Gulf. He's got me from behind, lifting me in the air with a squeeze that caves my lungs in and makes my legs kick. He's kissing me on the cheek. His long hair's on my face, oily, and the stubble on his chin is grating my neck. He's drenched in the sweet fumes of drink, enough to make you wonder how girls can let us kiss them when we're all pissed up and smoked out, with our fat tongues and stiff dicks. They'd have to be drunk.

'Get off me y'puff!' says Denny, throwing me down. He's beaming, cutting through the laughs all around.

'You're the fuckin' queer, Lane. Two months with those Arabs in their frocks and no women to go at. Bet you give a camel one.' I grin as I say it, and our eyes lock together. I feel light. Happy he's back. Kind of giddy.

'Get us a drink and we'll take some money off these bastards.'

'Right,' I say, and they all start up, all the lads.

'Artie's gettin'em in.'

'Get us one Artie.'

'Get your wad out lad. Jesus see that? Never seen so much brass.'

They kid on that I'm rich, because of the shop. They don't really think that, just taking the piss, but I'm doing all right. I never take holidays. Sundays, Bank Holidays and two weeks for Wakes, like my dad. I watch the cash, not like my dad. I'm careful and Madelaine earns good money. She says she doesn't, not as much as she could get in London. But it goes a long way up here. It's good for a second wage, which it's not. I've stopped saying that. She's even got me to stop thinking it. But it's let me get ahead, allowed me to accumulate. It's doing all right, the shop. Madelaine underestimates me, in that respect. She's allowed the look of things to deceive her, which is good – it gives me more options. It'll be there to comfort and distract me, when I'm on my own.

'Fuckin'ell, Artie,' shouts Denny, 'What're you like, lad? Dreamin' away when us beers is empty.' I catch myself turning to smile, in the mirror beneath the optics. Denny is my best mate. Denny Lane, like the third man in Wings with the McCartneys. Nobody else knew who Denny Laine was, but I did. I've got three hundred LPs – in boxes in the spare room. Ready to go, if needs be. So when he turned up for his first day at school in a leather jacket – not a fashion one, but a proper biker's one with zips on the sleeves and heavy lapels – I could see the rock and roll in him. We were supposed to wear blazers. He told Mr Marsh to 'fuck off' when Marshy told him to take off the biker's jacket. He was sent down to see Thundercliffe after that, and he came back with red eyes and the next day he wore a blazer. It was a second-hand one, and a different shade to the rest of us. But at least he'd told Marshy to 'fuck off', and I got to be his friend because I knew who Denny Laine was. It gave me an advantage, changed my friends forever. I became hard overnight, by association. For someone like Madelaine I was dangerous to be with, at least to be seen with, even though she had all the benefits of me being the way I really am.

She tried to reform me and largely succeeded. Denny said she was a 'poor little rich girl' which I didn't understand to start with. I liked the sound of it, something to protect, and something Denny didn't like. It came between us and got them fighting for me, even though I didn't have to do anything to get them going. It made me important, them being strong like that, not wanting to share.

'Come on, Artie lad. Fuckin' dyin' of thirst, lad.' His voice, the resonance of it links me to what I remember I used to be. I don't know whether that's for better or worse.

'All right, Denny, all right. Hey, it's good to see you, mate,' I say, handing him his pint.

'Shut your noise, lad, and get yourself a fuckin' cue.'

*　　　*　　　*

It's eight o'clock and we've beaten everyone in the vaults at least once. I've had too much to drink, for me, and I'm struggling on my shots, but Denny's good enough for both of us. I can't drink like the rest of them, like I used to be able to. I got out of the habit after we got married, so I'm taking time out, to phone the house and the car again, with my expectations kept in check. I know she's not going to be there.

Billy McCafferey's coming in the back way, from the car park. He's with a couple of shavenheads.

'All right Billy,' I say. 'How's uni?'

'Great Artie. Really good.' His eyes light up when I mention it. There's life in his head, dancing behind his eyes, you see a spark. One of the shavenheads is calling him, and the life goes out like a light. He follows them into the vaults with his shoulders hunched and his hands going in his pockets. 'See you,' he says, not even looking, but I've seen the dread come down, before he turned his back on me.

I collect my disappointment from the phone that won't answer and follow them in. Denny is at the bar, calling across for me to rack them up, ready for another game. This is his turf – his time, his place. Now he's back I feel like I belong, even though I live here and he doesn't any more. The room is full of music and smoke and laughter and it's easy to see why they come here until the money runs out. It's not as easy as that for me. I went a different way. It started with a tiny difference, with a long kiss on a short summer night. But the gap's been widening ever since. Still, I'm better off here just now, for a while, dipping into and faking it with my past. An empty house would be bad for me. Very bad for me, although there are things for me to do there, things to check.

Denny's coming back from the bar, with a grin and a whisky. There's someone behind him who I recognize. I think I do and I'm sure he's been talking to Denny, the way he watches him walk back. I can't put a name to him. He's dressed for somewhere smarter than here. He's small and thin, with slanting eyes and bad skin. Even from here I can see the shadows of the pock marks on his face.

'Who's the guy at the bar?' I say.

'What guy?'

'That guy,' I say, turning and knowing that he's up to something, something not good. 'He's gone, he . . .'

'You're losing it, mate. C'mon lad we're up again. More sad fuckers come to see how it's done.' He looks at the two men at the other end of the table, the two who came in with Billy. 'Let's get it done with.'

From the way they're dressed and look they've got to be from the Nelson Estate. They don't normally cross the Railing Road, aren't welcome on this side of town, Top Side. They're supposed to stay down the hill. One is stood with a cue in his hand, blowing blue chalk dust from its tip and looking straight at me from piggy puffed eyes. The other is crouched down, collecting the balls from their tray and looking at Denny as he does it. He's got a V-shaped scar on his neck, a fresh one jagged pink, fresh from a glassing. They are wearing T-shirts and jeans, T-shirts that stretch over muscles that are worked in gyms and on building sites. Denny struts round the table, chatting away to himself and tapping the cue on the floor. The one who hasn't got a scar, no scar you can see, has a tattoo chain on his neck. He fires the cue ball into the triangle of balls and Denny sniggers when none of them sink. 'Soz, Scar.' He's actually called Scar. That might amuse me in different circumstances. Scar takes the cue from his mate, nodding as he grips it. He gets a nod back.

'Fancy yourself, eh? Fuck face,' he says. It comes out higher pitched than I expect.

'Yeah,' says Denny, crouching down with his snakeskin boots pointing east and west from Cuban heels as he lines up his shot. He shakes his hair from his face and the white ball screws back to within an inch of the tip of his cue. The table rattles and swallows a striped ball. 'Fuckin' gorgeous, ain't it.' He's standing up straight, holding the cue like a staff and staring straight at the one with the high pitched voice. He smiles and says, 'Don't worry pal. You're not my type,' and he crouches back down for the next shot which he hits casually and misses. 'Money on it?'

'Sure,' and a fiver lands on the table.

'That all? You're not so fuckin' sure,' Denny throws a tenner on and smirks, 'or maybe all you're sure of is you're goin' to get fucked.'

'Fuck you,' says the squeaky one and throws down a twenty, takes back the five. They all look at me. I delve for a tenner and put it on the other notes, not wanting this, missing the point and not caring if I lose.

The boys have stopped milling round the room and everyone's watching the game. I'm looking at Billy McCafferey. I can see my fear in him. If I can see it in him, he'll be seeing it in me. All I can think of is the cues and the bottles and glasses, and that if we win and Denny takes the piss, there's going to be a fight, and I'll be the first to get hit and I can't believe, looking at these two shavenheads, that I'll be able to do anything that could possibly hurt them. My knees go soft and I hear a voice say my name, and it's Denny smiling and handing me the cue and saying 'Stick it up the fuckers, Artie lad.'

My hands are trembling. I get down for my shot. I'm weighing it up, not wanting to win or lose, not wanting either consequence, which will be the same. Beyond the top pocket is the smart tailored suit of Denny's pal, the one from the bar. He's stood in the hallway that goes to the toilets and the car park out back, smiling at me like I'm supposed to know who he is. He's talking to Bruce, the landlord, and looking at me. Even as I make to play the shot I can feel him watching me. I can't concentrate, can't focus on the part of the ball I need to hit, so I stab at the cue ball, just to let it be over. When I look up he's gone.

'Two shots.'

'OK, shithead. We know the rules. Fuckin'ell Artie lad, shape up.'

'Sorry Denny,' and I can't look him in the eye because he'll know that I'm scared, even though there's more of us than them.

They crouch and pot and the balls rattle the holes: first them, then Denny, then them again, then me, with Denny's voice through the mist and everything else gone quiet. But the door opens and there's three more come in, with the shaven heads and tattoos, and I see a flicker behind Denny's eyes, but I can't tell if it's fear or relish.

'Come on Artie, top pocket and we'll have these cunts,' saying 'cunts' with an upward sweep of his head at the door and a look at the three who've walked in. I pot the ball, and another, and I can barely bend down now because the muscles in my arm spasm when I crouch. 'Played Artie lad,' and he takes the cue from me, 'we'll have 'em,' and I know exactly what he means.

The one with the tattoo chain pots their last two balls and lines up the black. It's a tough shot and he'll probably miss. Denny's go next and we've only got two left. Denny will pot them, and probably get the black and we'll win. Then it'll go off and I'm working out where I should stand to miss the first wave of strikes.

'Yyyeeesss!' The shavenheads are shouting and the one with the tattoo reaches for the forty quid on the edge of the table. The black ball has gone and they've won. As he picks up the money, a cue swings round into his throat, curving the ink links in his blueskin chain that's bending in slow motion. His eyes bulge red, then his head jack-knifes down from a kick to his balls. I hear a smashing sound, then a dull thud when the slate-bedded table

hits the side of my head. Everything is quiet and I reel to
the lino.

Next thing I know there's sirens getting closer and car doors
are slamming. I'm not in the vaults any more and I can hear
a scuffle outside. I blink up into the dim red shade. The
shadows unblur into Denny and Bruce.

'Come on, Artie,' says Denny.

'Go, Denny. Leave him.'

'No.'

'You'll get done.'

'I'm not leaving him.'

There's a stinging on my cheek, then the other, and I can
hear the scuffle getting clearer, with shoutings and the slaps
of bodies on the pavement outside. My body's bending up
with a weight on my legs that buckle and then straighten.
Denny's got me, slapping my face again, up close with beery
breaths on my face.

'Artie. Artie. C'mon lad, come on. S'all right.'

There's blood on his face, in splatters, like fat on a stove.
Blobs of red fat.

'Come on, lad. Let's get a drink,' he says, laughing but
looking sad, 'The boys have gone to the Masons.' He's
laughing for the benefit of others, but if you ask me he's
scared as we run out the back, and up the High Street, past
my shop.

'Very funny. Very fucking funny,' I say.

'You didn't know?'

'No,' I say. If I had known, I wouldn't have gone in the
first place, but I couldn't let them know that. Maybe that's
why they didn't let on, because they thought I'd have left if
I'd known. Known that Denny had got the boys all lined up

for the shavenheads, from the Rainbow on the Nelson Estate. The shavenheads had been asking a grand a week for not trashing the Dog. Once the boys have told me though, I know I've got to get out of here, away from them. Even though we're in the Masons, up the hill and safely distanced from the Nelson. I'm not part of it. Not strong enough in the right ways for this. If it hadn't been for Madelaine, I might be more like them. If it wasn't for Dad, and his dying, I'd be more like Madelaine and less like the same boy she left behind in Slipp. If it wasn't for the taking care, the staying put.

Madelaine used to tell me I'm strong, 'so aahh, powerful, so powerful, Artie'. She'd come close so I could smell her, wafting up as she closed the gap between our bellies, and kissing me, the way she used to, like she doesn't seem to do so often now. Afterwards she'd tell me she loved me, 'You're so kind Artie, so gentle', and this time not 'aahh', but a 'hhmmm', that purred as she made the first noises of sleep.

But I'm here, in the Masons with the boys, feeling my strong face slipping and the softness about to show. My head hurts, pain thinly spread around my skull. It pulses, this pain, and ends up in my temples, clogging. Not a bad pain, it will ease, just a bit of bruising. But I want to be with her, knowing the time has nearly come when I won't hear the first sounds of sleep again. I want to be with her in ways, and for reasons, that are new. She's brought out the insecurities in me. But without her I know I'll slide into freefall. I'm not ready for that yet. I don't want to be alone. So I'm doing the simple thing, going into the night.

I can see the shop. Its sign reminding me, in fresh blue paint: 'Gill and Son.' It wasn't my choice, to spend my life amongst wet fish and old women. I had plans like any teenager should. But they were shelved when Frankie left home. Left me to it. Left me to be the one to promise Dad I'd take care of things, when he got the cancer. Even though I was the one who'd tried at school, who'd surprised all the teachers, who could have got to college: 'Not one of the more prestigious ones, you understand,' they had said to my mother in front of me, 'but quite frankly he'll have done well to get into a polytechnic, considering (and this is where they give me a look of contempt, undermining all my efforts, which seem to count for nothing) the bad lot he's fallen in with.' And it felt like I was getting what I deserved when I couldn't take up my college place.

You'd have done the same if you'd seen your dad lie there with the skin hanging off him. If it made him smile, you'd have said anything to give him a happy moment, and kept your word. Even if you didn't really like him, and probably, almost certainly, hadn't been loved by him.

'Take care your mum.' A demand, the way he said it. Making my face crumple on the inside, to see he cared for her. He leaked it to me. I knew he'd never show it to her. And the bastard turned his selfishness on me – with his last words. Because the tears I didn't shed were for me. In the care he showed for her, he showed he didn't care for me. That didn't slip. 'Take care your mum.' Cruel words in disguise.

After he died, that spring, I waited for the next thing. I was ready for it, saw ways to get over it. Prepared my distractions. All summer after the exams when Madelaine came to our house because I wasn't welcome round at theirs, I'd wait for this to be the day when she'd tell me she'd outgrown me. Tell me it was time to move on, in every way. I had a hundred different preparations, early warning signals to shore me up to however she'd begin it. I could have coped, then, if she'd ditched me for her ambition, for a fleshless something else.

I could see it coming:

'Artie, it's time we discussed our future . . .'

'Artie, things are going to change . . .'

'Artie, it's not going to be easy . . .'

And in the imagined conversation, I would wade in, save her the embarrassment, spare myself the shame. I'd pre-empt, I'd get my retaliations in first.

Her excitements grew over that summer as she prepared for her future. She excluded me. Shut me out with the packing and the shopping and the reading lists. But the conversation never happened. Not then when I was ready for it, had my own new beginning. A future without her – nothing to be scared of. No dependencies then, just opportunities. That's how I had seen it.

In the end she just went. The phone calls and letters happened as though nothing had changed. And I accomplished the task of establishing pride in my shop, the goals I set myself – regardless. I made it more special than it was. Created a heritage for myself. I did all right. Taking care of Mum and making things better, where I could.

'Gill and Son.' I've stopped outside the shop. The sign is wrong in any case because I haven't got a son. If I did have, I wouldn't want him to run the shop, to be the one to feel guilty when the sign needs painting, when the reminders come down from above. I'm not the son either. The son is my dad. My grandad's son. I just get the sign painted every year. I don't often see the shop when it's closed, and I can't help feeling proud. It's the cleanest on the row, between the boards and grilles of the bankrupt shells, three on either side. I've looked after it, kept it well and restored it bit by bit to its former glory – or at least to what it looked like before my dad let things slip.

They came round last week, to try to get me out. They want me to make it seven in a row, so it's big enough to build something new on. They've put the rent up and offered me money, telling me I'd be better off in a sealed unit in Town, in the new centre they've built. They don't know about all the fathers above, that I'm only the son left. What they do know, what they must be able to see, is all the work I've put into it, to make it like it used to be. But all they said when they left was that next time it wouldn't be money they were offering.

Inside, the four walls of tiles face each other, in the weak light from the street lamp, and they bounce a yellow glow. It looks warm, even though it can't be. I know it's cold in there, with its tiled walls and tiled floor and the marble slabs and glass panels. Even the fridges and the freezer are steel, stainless. Inside them is the planished, scaled flesh that looks and feels like metal when I take it out. As I slowly pass, I can see my reflection in the glass. It's faint and floating across the yellow tiles, but I can see that I'm smiling at myself. It doesn't feel like I am, but I am. I can see it and I look strong. I am tall, and broad and with the blood coming slowly from the gash above my eye, you wouldn't want to mess with me. I was in the fight. I did stay, and I have got mates, and I'm still married. That's what it looks like.

I carry on, down the hill, with home behind me. The empty house. I let the High Street speed me away above its wet light shadows with the Christmas jingles coming and going as I pass the pubs, which are spilling over onto the streets. Towards the main road the traffic hums and blasts. A chain of police cars snakes towards me, and then an ambulance. There's more than you'd think they'd need for a pub fight. I should be going up the hill, to my house on Top

Side's new estate, but I want to go down, to check on my mum, from the outside.

The underpass is taking me further away from home, towards the crescent on the Nelson Estate. They let you know what it's going to be like now, where I was born. They're announcing it with urine in my nostrils and graffiti I have to squint for, because they've broken all the lights. At the lowest point of the underpass, under the middle of the road, the urine has gone and it's sour, sweet tang is taken up by a deeper smell of bowels. It's hard not to sniff, and I can't resist, so I run towards the orange light from the lamps around the green. There's glass underfoot. Sounds of dogs getting closer.

The ramp takes me up, to the wrong side of the Railing Road and I can hear more sirens in the distance. On the far side of the green there's a gang, mainly girls. They skip around, sharing cigarettes, performing early flirting rites of swearing at each other. They laugh. It sounds older than it should. I can't believe how short the skirts are getting. They can't be more than twelve, maybe thirteen. I'm feeling glad that at least Madelaine grew up in time, before this tainting process came to Slipp. Glad for the untarnished time we had together.

There's another group coming to the front of the crescent. All men, and wearing balaclavas and T-shirts and tattoos. Another siren starts up in the nearer distance and the gang runs away, round the back of the houses. A flashing light goes along the road and its siren sound bends away, then towards. I move away, to the far row of houses that curve round the green, away from the road.

A group of police walk towards me, nearly marching, with ribbed protectors on their chests, and helmets with visors. They're coming from where the balaclavas had been and an ambulance pulls up. The back doors open and a light comes out, showing up a policeman. They're sitting him on the tailgate and there's blood matted in his hair, dripping off his face onto the road. In the light from the ambulance it looks luscious, unreal. Like ketchup. There seems too much for it to be real. The rest of the police are pulling sticks from their belts, and forming into two ranks that move off slowly. They're coming nearer, going where the balaclavas had headed. I can hear the crackle and belch of their radios.

From the shadow, I watch them skirt away from me. I pick out the house, not needing to count in from the sides of the terrace or look for the colour of its peeling frame. I lived here too long to need to do that. A light turns off in an upstairs room, and another one comes on. It's as though my past is winking at me over its shoulder and I move into nearer shadows beneath a tree so the woman in the window can't see me. Her head buds between the curtains, just above the sill. Too low.

The ambulance moves off and the house lights all around go dim behind curtains that close. Apart from one. If she's still looking, all she'll see now is the low-angled slant of my childhood, but dirtier, and smaller than it used to be. It used to be new, this modern crescent around its freshly turfed green. It used to be the future. But the future has come, with its flaking concrete and aerosol messages and its bins that don't empty, and the green is just a patch of grass with rusty cans and drifting paper and crap from dogs and cats. The future's here, gone old. A sick paradox. Another one: this is what keeps me here and what makes me crave for anywhere else. The budding head between the curtains on this dog turd estate. Cause and effect. Get away for getting away's sake. An end in itself – for my sake, for Madelaine's sake.

I can't leave, for all the good it would do me. It's crazy. This place is bringing me down. I'm living up on the hill now, away from the worst, but it's still bad. Not too bad to bear when everything else is going fine. But it's got me thinking. These changes around me. There are dangers with change. They could multiply. If the shop went, or the house, or both, it would provide opportunities. Wholesale change. No, I need the ties. Until I know. The ties to our youths, to this filth, to each other.

The Estate is different. Different from when I used to run in for tea when she'd call me. There are more cars now, but they're jacked up on bricks and tomorrow's Saturday so they'll be not quite mended by men who've not quite made it. Not nearly. But come tomorrow evening, around eight or nine, the men and women will still leave the crescent in ones and twos and the kids will play on the green, not knowing what it's like to have grass without metal and smells. After midnight they'll all come back, the adults in groups of four or more, and they'll switch on each other's lights and wake the kids with old music.

I've made my future different though. As different as I can, where the cars are in the garages and we don't speak to each other. It's where I've got to go now. 'Go now', as Denny Laine sang before he was with the McCartneys. The woman has gone from the window and the house is winking at me again as she passes through it, wheeling away for tea and more telly. Then the bottles of barley wine that get her to sleep, the way they always did. I've seen enough.

'Artie. Aartieee!'

Shit.

The door is yawning at me, around the low cast shade of her dressing gown, that she wears in public, with the buttons undone even though her slip is not clean on. Monty is winding himself around her chair. She bends to pick him up, unbalancing with a grimace. She kisses him behind his dog-eared ear, except he's a cat. She's stroking his fur. Poor Monty, the only one left to soak up her drunk love.

'Come on in you soft lummox. What're you doing skulking around like that?'

I've got to do as she says, or the whole crescent will see me, and hear her. See me not appearing to mind that her buttons are undone with her breasts looking all heavy. So I'm going in, and I feel as though the smile is there, getting there from the inside out. She doesn't wait to greet me. She spins herself round with a bang and a curse. I walk into the shadow of her drink and as I pass the mirror I can see that the smile's come through.

'Cuppa tea, Artie?' She's calling through from the kitchen.

'No thanks. I've got to get back for Madelaine. Can't really stop.'

The trophies are down off the shelf. She's been cleaning them, thinking they're more precious than they are. I can see my name on the plinths, under the lunging plastic swordsmen. The men are supposed to look bronze, the epee silver. They're only here because they gathered dust at my house. Madelaine didn't care for them or my fencing. She did to start with. It was her idea to do something together, invent something we could have in common, something with romantic connotations. But she got bored with it and I didn't. I got good at it, before I gave it up – to have more in common with her, more time together when time was running out. She now tells me it was a stupid thing to do – giving it up.

'Why are you standing up? Sit yourself down. Let her wait. Is that a cut you've got?' She puffs and wheezes as she wheels herself around. Like she's an old woman. But she's not, she's not even fifty.

'No, it's nothing.'

I sit down, and she stops next to me. A tray on her lap and her smell that's ingrained stale. She leans across, kisses me, with a hand on the back of my neck. She flops back with a sigh, muscles in her face untensing from the pain her act of love has brought on.

'Did the nurse come today?'

'No.'

'Jesus, Mum. I'll call them.'

'No. Don't make a fuss.'

'Have you bathed?'

'Do I smell?'

'No.'

'I do. I must.'

'You don't. What about your tablets.'

'Don't myther. You've got your own problems.'

'What?'

'You know. The shop and everything. There's been trouble tonight.'

'What do you mean?'

She tips the bottle into the mug quickly and a brown froth bubbles above the rim and subsides without spilling. She watches it happen, knowing it won't spill because the physics of the thing is known to her from years of practice.

'Frigging thugs been at it again. Dog and Duck so they say.' I don't know where she's got 'frigging' from. The way she says it you can tell she doesn't know what it means, doesn't know she wouldn't have said it before she lost her religion. I know her well enough to know she likes its sound. 'Mary's lad's been taken to the General. Lost an eye they reckon. I'm glad you're up the hill now, out of harm's way.'

This couldn't be true. She'll have got it wrong. 'You'll have your eye out with that,' she said when we were kids. 'Put it down, you'll have your eye out. Careful with that knife,' and now it was my trade, and her language had got stuck. It was a figure of speech.

'Come right out of its socket, hooked out with a bottle. Frigging bastards.'

'Are you sure, Mum?'

'They reckon he put it in a pint pot, so as they could stitch it back in for him. Amazing what they can do these days.' She pulls a cigarette from the packet and puckers her lips like a girner as she lights it. The smoke comes out thin in a trail to the ceiling and there's still smoke coming out as she carries on. 'Shame they couldn't, you know, with your dad. They could do better now.'

She takes another drag. I could tell her to put it out. That she ought to stop. No point. I could get her into a home. This is all she's got, though – this, that I see now, on a Friday night. It doesn't get any better for her. The pain is under the drink and she's happy as can be. Would you take it away? Take her away. For her own good.

I have to go, for too many reasons. It's time Madelaine was back. Midnight is late. Midnight is a watershed. You can go one way or the other from a watershed. There's one in Brazil where a single drop of water can land and split in two. One half goes into the Pacific Ocean and the other into the Atlantic Ocean. With the processes of convection, one will rain on some bather in Hawaii, and another will fall onto an umbrella in England. They tell you in geography that Hawaii is a hell of a long way from England.

3

It's one o'clock and the key turns in the door. All the conversations I've been rehearsing slide onto my lap. I have to run to the loo because it feels as though I might croak if I try to speak to her. I've had too much time to think. Dwelling is bad for me. Since I started to unearth the evidence, empty time swells with brooding.

'Artie. Aartiee.'

The voice is deep and distracted. It sounds as though it might get annoyed if I don't say anything, but I wait. I'm listening to hear if she's on her own. I'm praying for there to be another voice, a friend who's come home with her, for a coffee, to show me it's all in my mind – this ebb and flow of who and where and when and how often. I'm actually praying, stood over the toilet with the seat down and my hands clasped together. I'm asking God for this stupid favour: to hear a female voice that isn't my wife's, to serve as evidence that she's been out with a friend and nothing worse. But there are no other noises, no pleasant chatter. Just another 'Aartiee!', louder and annoyed, so I turn to the door. I'm unlocking my way out with a reach back to flush and a raising of the eyebrows to the mirror, to say 'Don't blow it. You're not ready yet. Stay with it.'

She smells of drink when she kisses me. But she would kiss me, wouldn't she. Wouldn't you if you'd been with your lover? She's telling me where she's been and who she's been with. The way you would. She's not expecting me to remember it. To mentally note every detail, or to check it out later. She can't tell I'm doing these things. That's what gives me the upper hand. She can't tell that I'm not going to just let it go and one day receive a card from Hawaii, or somewhere else not here, and let her get away with it. She doesn't know how much I'm going to do to find out, then get her to stay. Even if it's against her will. There'll be a way. She probably doesn't even know I couldn't bear for her not to stay. It's not the sort of thing you talk about – not until you're fully prepared.

'And what have *you* been up to? Is that a cut?'

'Oh, nothing. That? That's just . . . Hey, Denny's back.'

She smiles while I'm saying his name. She never used to smile when I said his name. She used to complain when I went out with him. There was a time when she complained if I went out on my own, with anyone. I don't know when that stopped being the case. Not overnight. Another slow ambush.

She thinks he's a bastard, Denny. That's what she says. Women go for men like their fathers. That's what they say. Her father was a bastard, is. I'm not, never have been. Imagine that: with your best mate. I can see her wearing Karen

Dugg's pants, ivory silk and pulled to one side, jutting towards me as she arches back and her palms spread on the red bonnet. I'm wearing a biker's jacket. I go into her and she's saying 'Denny'. She closes her eyes and smiles with dirty pleasure. Filthy, pucker mouth. She says it again, slower, hot breath misting on my bruising skull. Scratches at the bonnet and pumping the ivory silk at his jeans.

'I hope he's not been getting you into trouble. How did you get that cut?'

'Do you want coffee?'

'Please.'

I go into the kitchen and I can hear her pouring a drink from one of her decanters into one of her crystal glasses. She's talking to me through the open door.

'There's a hell of a commotion down near the main road. Looks like it's the Nelson Estate. Do you think we should call your mother? There's police cars and ambulances all over the place. What did happen to your eye?'

She's in the bathroom now and there's plenty to do. More catching up. I've got five minutes or so, while she's taking off the make-up; cleaning her teeth, peeling away layers that she wants everyone to see, except me.

Her pants are rolled into her tights at the top of the laundry basket, like a strudel, secrets to savour. She'll only have to unravel them in the morning. They're different colour washes, and it makes life more difficult for me. I've pulled them away and they snap from the nylon. They're a bad pair. Small, with a lace inset triangle that would show the hair underneath. She bought them herself, which was bad – not that I knew it then. They are the sort that wives should have bought for them, by husbands. I put the tights back with the laundry and I'm running to the bedroom, with the pants. I sit on the edge of the bed with my back to the door, in case I'm disturbed. I've got them under the lamp. Nothing. Up to my nose. Whispers of faint tang. Not sex. Under my fingers, rubbing for crusts that aren't there. No changes of texture. Not the slightest. Too clean. I'll have to check her bag for an old pair. Wouldn't you do that? Change them, I mean.

They'll have to go. I've pulled out my drawer and got the lumpy, stuffed football sock from the back and I'm putting the pants in the sock with the rest of the bad ones: the ones that would make him like her more. It's surprising what you can gather in a few weeks.

'What are you up to, Artie?'

'What?'

'You're skulking around. Are you up to mischief?'

Me? Am I up to mischief? That's rich. And what's with this skulking around. Do I skulk? My mum said it too. 'Skulking around,' she said.

'Don't be silly, I was just, just waiting. For you, to come to . . . you know.'

'No, I don't,' she says, looking mischievous now. I don't like it. She's crawling onto the bed towards me with a look on her face that she gets when she's drunk. A bawdy look that tells me she's going to do what I'd be doing – if I'd been with someone – in a car. Or somewhere quick. If I didn't want my partner to know. I'd do it with them, to show I'm still hungry. But that's as far as I get because she's kissing me now, with boozy lips and a boozy tongue that's wetter and warmer than it normally is, and she's fumbling with my buttons and pressing her breasts into my belly and I'm falling off the bed.

She's looking down at me, giggling. Unbridled, she is. It's going to be difficult for me to cope with her like this. Diffi-cult to resist her hands and noises and shapes. Her giggle stops and the lids of her eyes are dropping, and she breathes out noisily. Serious and intent.

'Aartie. Come on.'

I climb up and she's at my buttons again, and my flies, with fast moving fingers and nails that know what they're doing. My clothes are off, knotting at the ends of my arms and legs so I can't move properly. I'm being put on my back. She's sitting on my belly, rocking to and fro with her eyes almost shut. Her noises are getting deeper. I can feel a sticking on my belly, getting higher as she rocks and she leans back. I can't see her face any more, just the crease under her breasts disappear. She slides herself towards me and she's coming closer to my face. I can't move. She's not done this before, not like this. Not remotely like this for years and years. This is new. Before I've worked out the moves, she's on me, on my mouth. It's hard to describe what she tastes of, but there's warm flesh and caramel and salt on its edge. I'm struggling to breathe with her hairs pushing on my nose, with soft bone underneath. I can hear, dull through my own inside noises. Her groans are gasping, getting shorter and quicker and louder and she's pounding my nose with her bone and the caramel melts and it pokes my tongue and the rocking stops dead. Her head comes back up, with a flat smile and her mouth barely moves.

'Keep it there.'

She's leaning back and taking a hold of me and pressing her thumb on the top of my cock, then lightening the pressure, then she presses then lightens, and the hold tightens. The hair and the flesh and the taste goes away and she rolls off me and slides down the bed, making animal shapes that make her look like a stranger, smiling at me before she disappears below my belly. She takes her thumb off my cock and I hear her breathe out, with a blow and it's soothing cold on my cock and I gush, then pulse and when her face comes back up, it drips and she's smiling, not dirty but kind and I can't believe she's not done this before.

She's thanked me and kissed me on the mouth and given the first sounds of sleep. Left me to the night, on my own. I can smell her. A film of her smell around my mouth. I'm on my own with the lamps outside, waiting for their orange to go pale and spread. For the birds to make their sounds so I can get up. Start a new day.

She's curled away from me, with her bottom on my thigh. Her hair has fallen over her face hiding the soft noises of sleep. I can smell myself on the sheets and under her hair. It's a cleaner smell than hers, a smell you might get in a hospital, a chemist shop. A place where Mary's boy would be. Young Billy Mac with his eyeball in a pint pot. The distant wail of an ambulance comes and goes, then another. The night is passing slowly over me. I want it to go the other way, for yesterday not to have happened.

I pull back her hair. My smell gets stronger, from where I've stained her with flakes on the tiny hairs on her cheek. I wish she'd washed it away, like the Madelaine who had come back from university would have done – even though she wouldn't have needed to. She looks content, more than she ever used to. Is there a pool of it, this contentment. She's using mine. And control too. She's taking that away from me, with her late nights and smells of drink and the secret things she does. Places and times I know nothing about.

I'm trying to get to sleep, but there's the key in the door gone midnight. There's pool cues, and ivory pants, and three plaice not four. The familiar face in the smart suit I can't recognize, and new tastes. So I get out of bed. I'm going downstairs, writing my silent shopping list of things to do before morning.

First, I'm doing the usual in her bag. Staring into it to see what's on top, and where, so I can make it look as though I've never been into it. I've taken it behind the sofa in the sitting room. I can crouch down if she catches me at it. I'll shove it all underneath if she comes downstairs without me hearing her. I've got my wallet which I'll produce as though I've been looking for it and I'll take her away, to the kitchen for a cup of the tea she drinks. It's camomile. It never used to be. It's one of the changes, like the shorter hair and the clumsy heeled shoes she wears and the new hole in her ear at the top. New names she brings into the house. Names of people I never see and names you don't often hear, like Genevieve and Cinnamon and Maurice, but names that I suppose go with her job. They say that if a man eats cinnamon it gets into his semen in twenty minutes. A woman would be able to taste it.

There's no change of pants in the bag. Weird disappointment. I'm getting the contents into two piles. Secrets and Boring. You find the most unusual things in the Secrets pile, things you probably wouldn't guess.

Tonight's Secrets pile is:

Address Book: I'm checking for new entries: men, and women with men names that could be code, e.g. Patricia, Danielle, Charlotte, all of which have been genuine, so far. There's nothing tonight and it doesn't take me long because I know all the old ones. Just Brenda, who could be Brendan, but I know she's not because Madelaine's been round there. I've checked it out.

Telephone Bill: Which she attends to, unlike the rest of the bills. There are four new numbers, but only one is local. I note them all down anyway.

Lipstick: This is bad news. It's the pale one she knows makes her look good, and it's been worn down since I last checked. Someone's been getting its benefits.

Credit card receipts: One from a department store, with no verifying receipt, for £25, which could be a present. I check the Boring pile again, but there's no receipt. One from a bistro for fifteen quid, which is a small enough amount for her to be going Dutch. 'Chez Maurice'. A link, so I'm taking a note and I re-check the address book for first initials. 'Gray, Melanie'. She's talked about Melanie but I've never met her, so I'm adding it to the list.

Car park stickers: There's a new one here, from the far side of town. It could be near Chez Maurice. But would she pay for a meal in a place owned by her lover? It's possible.

And now the worst. I've left it until last.

Femi pads: Eight left. There were ten this morning. I remember the clean lace triangle that I stuffed into the sock. Too clean. No spare pants. No surprise.

Am I wrong to be doing this? Is it strange? Given the threat I'm under. Given what's at stake – what I'll be left with if I don't catch up with what she's doing. It's not crazy. I'm not being paranoid. I've got it here. 'Paranoid': abnormal tendency to suspect and mistrust others. I'm not abnormal. There wasn't a tendency, not until I saw the letter. If I was mad, or at least paranoid, I'd be looking for things that weren't there, not missing the obvious. Under my nose. She's clever, you see, they both are. Take the postcard. Innocent enough, you might think. 'You'd love it here – wish you'd come . . . See you soon, love D.' No problem with that, if she'd told me Dorothy or Danielle had been going to the Caribbean. Or if it hadn't been sent to work, not home, leaving me to trawl it from her briefcase.

The toilet is flushing, upstairs, so I pile everything back

into the bag, with the last things going in on top, just as I remembered them, just as she calls me.

'Artie? Are you downstairs?'

'Yes. Yes, love. I can't sleep.'

'Again? You should see the doctor.'

I should see the doctor? After this find, I should be seeing a private investigator. I'm putting the bag on the sofa as she opens the door, holding my wallet like a trophy.

'Thought I'd lost it. You want a cup of tea?'

'Don't be ridiculous, Artie. It's three o'clock. Don't wake me when you come up. I've had a hell of a week.'

'Good night.'

But she's gone.

She's left me alone, to move, unwatched, through the house. Uninhibited, not having to skulk. She'll be in a deep sleep now, which I'll test from time to time, with a prod and a slam of the door, before I do anything too dangerous.

Going from room to room, a stranger would be able to plot her progress from the photographs: her changing hair; the different clothes; the more confident postures; her passage from girl to woman which has no single cusp. Recent ones have been censored – she's worrying about the lines on her face, which you've got to really look for to see. There aren't many pictures of me. You couldn't spot my changes anyway. Not by looking at me. Not without being able to feel my weaknesses, being touched by the small things that scare me. These recent changes.

I look the same now as I did when I didn't go to college: same hair, more or less; same young skin; same smile – always the same fucking smile which leaves people clueless to what's really going on.

Where will her changes end? What will she be like in ten years, if she's still on my walls by then. This little thought triggers me. A man knocking nails in a wall. Her holding the ladder. Her new face going up on their new wall. What practical steps would I take to prevent such a thing? I'm here, in the noiseless house with the evidence mounting, and I don't know.

I have many options. Letting her go isn't one of them. I couldn't have her being with someone else. I don't mind being on my own. I could handle that, I think, given time. But I couldn't have it filled with the riddles of who she's with and what they're doing. I couldn't have her photographs on someone else's walls.

That sounds like a pride thing. It's not. It's just something that would weaken me, every time I saw it. It's not a pride thing. It doesn't make me a nutter, or paranoid. It feels natural, what I ought to be feeling. I'm doing the things I ought to be doing. I'm going to do them well, and I'm going to find out – even if I'm not sure I want to, or whether it's in my best interests. It feels right. I couldn't actually do anything else.

I have no options.

4

Police have been unable to identify the ringleaders in last night's pitched battle on the Nelson Estate. Violence escalated after a fracas in a pub in the town centre and police moved into the Estate shortly before midnight to interview suspects. They met with disorganized resistance, but by the time the riot squad arrived at one a.m., barricades had been set up at the entrances to the estate, using two buses which were highjacked then set alight. Drugs and protection gangs are thought to be at the root of the problem. Certainly, we've never seen anything like this in Slipp before.

'Bloody hell.' Words that don't go with her body, or with the girl I fell in love with, then married.

'You having some breakfast?' I ask.

'Did you hear that? That's what I told you about last night. Jesus, it sounds bad. Thank God we're up here.'

'You used to be religious. You used to go to church.'

'What?'

'Every week. You don't any more. You blaspheme. You never used to. You swear.'

'Artie, what are you talking about? Anyway, what happened to your eye?'

'You're different.'

I don't know why I'm saying this. I'm saying things I promised myself not to say. But here, in the kitchen on the morning after the riots and the missing femi-pads, it's slipped out.

'I'm no different. I'm the same girl, we just develop. I'm growing.'

And she's starting with this jargon babble. Sounds to impress. Impressing in the company of people who talk like this. These words mean nothing. I skulk. I checked it out last night. I do, the dictionary says so. It feels as though I skulk around, in an animal shape on four legs with my neck bent, keeping myself concealed in cowardice or intending mischief. The dictionary describes the way I skulk and it's true. It means something. It's a shape I make when people around me change. Madelaine has friends who worry about 'growing'. They're pretentious twats if you ask me. A twat is female genitalia or a stupid person. I know all about both of those. We found 'twat' in English when we should have been doing something else. It was good back then to find something so bad where it shouldn't have been.

I turn away from her and check the eggs. It's still dark outside. The light inside shows my face on the window, moving across the trees and houses. I look strong. I like the way my hair is now, wet from the shower and slicked back. I am handsome and tall and broad and strong. I like this morning darkness of winter, when it's warm in the kitchen with breakfast smells. I feel a waft of pleasures from Christmases past, a tingle at the thought of the thrill she'll get from my present. It's proof how much I care.

'You never used to stay out that late,' I say, 'we never go out together.'

'That's not true.'

'It is.'

'We've been together eight years, Artie.'

'Nine. Nearly ten.'

'OK. OK.'

'You'd forgotten.'

'We can't live each other's lives. We were very young, you know. We've grown up together, we're still together, but you can't expect us not to change. We're different people.'

'I'm not.'

'Different from each other. And you are, anyway.'

'What?'

'Different. Never mind.'

'What are you doing today?' I ask, not ready to follow through on my line of inquiry. I'm not sufficiently prepared.

'I don't know. I've got to go shopping. There's only five days to go and I've done practically nothing.'

'Are you shopping in Slipp? We could . . .'

'There's nothing here, Artie.'

'That's because nobody shops here. You should buy what you can here.'

'I'm going into Town.'

'We always used to.'

'What?'

'Shop, at Christmas. Together.'

'You're working, Artie. I'll be done quicker without you, you know how you faff.'

No I don't. I'm deliberate. They said so at school. They

didn't say 'Artie makes the most of his ability. He is hard working and he faffs'.

'When will you be back?' I ask.

'I don't know. You've got to see your mum anyway.'

'You could come with me.'

'I've got things to do.'

'When will you be back?'

'Late.'

'What's late?'

'You tell me. What did happen to your eye?'

'You've changed more than me.'

'Is that supposed to be a bad thing?'

I've got a horrible feeling where this will end up if I carry on, so I stop. Like I always do, like I know will annoy her but not doing it for that reason.

'Oh fine. You have your sulk then, and let me know when you've finished. You're the one with the fucking problem, Artie.'

Too right. The door slams. I know I won't see her again until two, when I've finished at the shop, taken my mum her lunch. Even then she might still be out. I'm checking the clock, logging her time of departure, which is too early for the weekend. It's not a spontaneous storming out either. Not at this hour. She's going somewhere definite, to do something she's arranged, something she's not telling me about.

She shouts. 'And see a doctor about that eye.' Another door slams, and I hear a fainter shout which sounds as though she's saying 'fucking jerk'.

Anyone would think she cared.

Changes in people. They're difficult to spot. The closer you get, the harder it is.

'Hasn't he grown,' they'd say. 'Shot up,' pinching my

cheeks. Bending down with their water balloon tits coming to drown me. Coming at me in rafts of sickly sweet perfume. Old ladies' tangs that burn poor young nostrils.

And my dad. Hospital visits just a week apart. I could spot his changes. I can plot them now, against memories, against images set in stone. Memories that are calibrated, hardened in time.

Try spotting the changes in a constant stream. Seemingly constant.

A river in its lower reaches. Give it a hundred years and it can go from a U-shaped bend into an ox-bow lake. It cuts off its own life supply, makes part of itself a lake. A real change. Sit by the river, with flasks and foil and a rod. Stay for a year. Ten years, a lifetime. The river would change and you wouldn't notice a thing. Unless you lived to a hundred and fell in with its caving banks. You're too close.

Mother. She changed. She knew it was coming. The doctors told her. But she didn't want to worry me, didn't tell me. Let me believe it was her drink – making her shake and stagger. I didn't know what was happening till she came back in an ambulance one day. They wheeled her out. I hadn't known. Couldn't see it under my own nose. I wasn't looking for it.

Madelaine. She's changed, most people who know her would say so. I can see it myself, looking back. Knowing what I'm looking for. Delving into time, measuring it.

I can see some of her changes: hair (length, colour, style); clothes (shapes, fabrics, colours); holes in her body (four instead of two – excluding orifices); behaviour (the times she gets in; the names she mentions). These can be identified, measured. Even looking back, they can be spotted – once you know what you're looking for. Less easy is attitude (to me, to things I value). Impossible is love, fondness, happiness – which don't necessarily show in behaviour. The change in behaviour comes afterwards. The real changes could have been going on for years.

Me. If I can't spot the changes in others, what chance have I got with me? I know I'm different. How could I not notice, even if my changes aren't conscious. They're not by design. I don't want to be scared, but I am. I didn't used to be. Something's made me this way. It scares me. Scares the shit out of me to change and not know about it, until it's happened. One day, it's staring at you. You can see the fear in your own eyes. By chance, stopping yourself in reflection. With your own scared eyes you see your own scared eyes. It's proof, but it doesn't explain why.

Does this make sense? Does it make me mad? If you know you're mad, does that mean you can't be? Mad. An everyday word. I'm too close to know. I'm too close to know if I'm not.

I'm unlocking the door and the bell jangles to say I've come in. The cold hits me. Prickles me cold where my jumper touches skin. I'm late, but still too early for my first customers. People come here last when they're shopping, so they don't have to walk round with the smells they get from me. I used to be last on the High Street rounds. Now they come here on their way home from the mall. It's a long wait, on your own, so I've put the radio on. They're telling me more about what I already know, about why the riot started, and why it isn't stopping even though they've all had time to sleep it off. You had to be in the Dog last night to know why it started, and you have to have lived on the Nelson, and still know people who live there, to know why it isn't stopping.

The people there are getting poorer, it's distilling. What

money there is gets more concentrated, in the hands of fewer and fewer people, the people who sell. They'll sell videos back to people who've had them stolen by the people they sell the other stuff to. They're going round in circles on the Nelson. You can't blame them if some want to get off.

I'm in the back and putting on my apron. It's clean and starched and doesn't yet smell of the things I sell. I wash my hands and catch myself with the mottled face. I do look young. Younger than Denny and the rest of them, young enough for Madelaine to comment on it, because she's getting the crow's feet.

Time warps when you look back. I can see it clearly though, as clear as the skin on bones, and their shadows, that make me look the way I am in front of myself. I've been looking back a lot, lately. Too much for my own good. It was another New Year's party. Not the one with Karen Dugg when I shouldn't have. It was ten years before, eighteen years ago, in ten days.

One minute I'm in bed with my dad smiling in the doorway. My mum's bending over to kiss me, showing me the bulging crease between her breasts. The next minute I'm waking up, with Frankie still asleep in the other bed and the house silent. I get up and wander round, turning on the lights as I move through the house getting myself scared. I can't wake Frankie. I'll get hit, even though I'm bigger, so I look through the curtains. The lights are on at Kev's house. When I open the window the cold brings in music and singing with it. I can still hear it now, the sound of people having bad fun. I trace the sounds to the lights at the Sellars' and make my way into the adult night.

My dad opened the front door. He had a bottle in one hand. His other arm was wrapped around Mrs Sellars, who pulled her face away from his cheek with a kiss and said,

'Artie. Ooh Artie, such a love,' and she picked me up, even though I was eight and big for my age. She kissed my eyes. 'Such lovely lashes, who's a lovely lad. Handsome fella just like his dad,' and she stroked my dad under his chin with her finger and he grinned. It seems so real. I can hear their words and see and smell them.

He wasn't annoyed, my dad, and they let me into the front room where the food was. Mrs Sellars brought me a plate and told me to help myself. She kissed me again and pressed my cheeks with the palms of her hands, and went out. I saw a lump of white leg fold down over the tops of her stockings inside the skirt that was too short for her. My dad was stood by the door, catching me looking. He winked at me, with a smile.

'You stay there lad, else you go home. Understand? Good.'

I can remember, 'good' sounded like a threat. He was like that.

The noises from the room next door got louder. Men and women came in to get food, then left; or they came in and saw me, then left without getting food. I finished my food and wanted my mum. The noise was dangerous. There was singing and banging and clapping. Occasionally a female scream and a male laugh would come through the rhythms. Then the music went quiet. The shouting stopped.

I went into the hall and saw people dancing in the back room. It didn't look the way it had sounded before. They were hugging each other and swaying to the music, not fast like it had been before. I got closer to the doorway. One of the couples who'd come for food, and gone away without getting any, were kissing. They were doing it fast, out of time with the music, with their hands in each other's hair and lipstick around both their mouths. I went right into the doorway. Everyone was doing it, even my mum and dad in the corner. Except it wasn't my mum and dad. Mrs Sellars was stood where my mum should have been, with her skirt riding up under my dad's hands. My mum wasn't there. Not with dad, or anyone else.

The bell jangles. It shouldn't because we're not open and I thought I'd locked the door. I'm trying to put my smile back on, but it's slipped. Before I can do it, I see a mottled shape, through the mirror, standing in the doorway. A biker's jacket, long hair in thick, greasy strands.

'Artie lad, what's up?' says Denny. I don't turn round but he can see me anyway. 'You look like shit.'

I check in the mirror. I do. 'I'm all right.' My eyes have gone red and the sides of my mouth point downwards.

I'm looking at his image and I'm glad he's here. But it's bad news – you can see it. His face is swollen red on one side, going blue at the edges and his lip is split, but that's not the bad part. It's his eyes. They're fixed and wide and focusing through me, through the mirror, but he's talking to me, and his breaths are short and loud and quivering.

'What's up?' I say, turning round, going towards him. I can see he's trembling, still looking through me, with pupils like pin heads. His chest is shaking under his T-shirt, making tiny ripples.

'It's bad Artie. Too fucking bad. It's gone too far, too fucking far.'

'What happened to Billy? My mum said he was hurt.'

'Yeah.'

'Is it as bad as I heard. His eye?'

He's nodding, but I can see he doesn't care. He doesn't care that a lad we went to school with, a younger lad below us, but with a brother we walked in fear of, had an eye ripped out for drinking in the wrong pub, for having the wrong mates.

'Was it you? Denny, for fuck's sake, did you do it?'

He's still nodding and I want him to stop. I want to be able to still like him. I need him to be my friend.

'They've got our kid.'

'Stevie?'

'Yeah. They're going to kill him.'

'Come on Denny. Sit down. Calm down.'

He's shaking his head and he puts something small in his mouth. Whatever it is, he pops it between his teeth and tilts his head back. The lump in his throat goes up and down and he shivers. He's tilting his head back down and a smile comes slow across his face. The eyes focus into me. His pupils bigger.

He's got a bag in his hand. It's paper and brown and he hands it to me.

'Fucking blue. Just like mine.'

Tears come from both of his.

5

Denny's taken his brother's eye – in the brown paper bag that's gone purple and wet, so he has to support it with the palm of his hand. I'm left to my serving, until one o'clock – the way it's always been on Saturdays.

I'm filleting plaice for Mary McCafferey, who anyone could see has been up all night and crying. She still came in, because that's what she's always done, at quarter past ten on a Saturday morning. Even when her lad is lying in the General, without the eye that my mate Denny Lane had out with a bottle in the Dog.

The blade is sharp and I swipe and jag and flip it over. The eyes only show on one side. They're looking at me now, wide and accusing. I didn't kill it. Just making sure it's not a death in vain. Despite what I do for a living, I could never kill a fish. Is that crazy?

Flatfish are all the same, blind on the top or the bottom. When they're born, they swim upright, but early in life they turn sideways, so one eye has to move over, with a startled look that's lopsided. They can go one way or the other, it's up to the fish. It's their first self-determining act. It dictates what they look like when they're pulled out of the water and given to me to run through with my knife. 'Careful with that knife, you'll have your eye out with it.' Lopsided. Lop – when you cut off a person's limb or head.

And there's Billy – Mary McCafferey's lad, not so tough as his brother Johnny. Johnny, the other son who signed up for Ulster, earning enough for two so Billy could get out. Billy, home from college in his final year, for his last Christmas before he's the first off the Nelson to graduate from university, lying in another institution and on death's door. And young Stevie Lane, the youngest of all the Lanes and still at school with his eye in a brown paper bag that's been in my back room, next to the bins that are filling with heads and bones.

So, Mary McCafferey has come for her plaice, on Saturday and cocking a snook as my dad used to say. Mr Fagan told us in History what that means: how the proddies would come in on a Saturday for their fish, 'no respect', and 'their idea of a joke'. My dad said Mr Fagan was a Fenian cunt, which lost me completely at the time. My dad said he was going to go down the school, until my mum stopped him. She could make him do as she wanted, when he was sober. 'At least he knows how to cock a snook now,' she'd said. I couldn't have known at the time, but it was proof that the faith had been knocked out of her, the faith of Delores O'Brien, her mother. Knocked out of her by my father.

I can still swipe and jag with my fearsome blade with a rock-steady hand. I don't feel good about being able to do this, as though nothing has happened. This magic of mine appalls me and I want to slow down, as a kind of penance, to let her know that I'm sorry, but she can't know that I've something to be sorry about. I've promised Denny. I've got to keep my mouth shut, but it doesn't stop me wanting to be forgiven. To confess. Even though I'm not to blame. I haven't got what it takes anyway – the words and motions.

It's a mystery to me, the way these things work. The mystery of the faith that Madelaine left behind. The mystery of her biggest change. The faith that hid in scars, from the old school. From before her dad left her and her sister, to her mum. It destroyed all their faiths. They must have lacked fortitude. This mystery has labels: communion and contrition; penance and benediction, which you could look up. The difficulty lies in everyday words with different meanings. Faith and forgiveness.

Mary McCafferey goes with a jangle of the door and I go out the back, to get the mullet I'm going to cook for Madelaine's lunch. It's a surprise, and something light because we're eating out tonight. Whoever it is who has got her attention won't be able to prepare a dish like this. Choosing the best fish, and getting a sauce that lifts its earthy flesh in the mouth. If you cook it right, it doesn't taste like fish any more. Like a trick, you can make it taste like meat. These are my advantages, and the time alone to do it properly, which I may as well start now while there's no-one in the shop. There'll be plenty to do when I get home, before she comes in. After I've been to my mum's.

We're having dinner, at Brenda's new place in Town. I tried to get out of it but Madelaine wouldn't give in, which is good. It probably means that Brenda doesn't know. One of the things I'm scared of: the discovery of all the parts of my life that got there before me. Friends. People I know who aren't even friends. People who'll feel guilty about not telling me. People who've got to stop laughing at me, because now I know and it's not funny any more.

*   *   *

I take care of my mum. It's official. The government says so. I'm here and available, so they don't do her laundry or lunches at the weekend. A paradox. Because I'm here and available, I can't be not here and unavailable. Even though I work on Saturdays, I don't. Not according to them. It does not compute. They can't understand that I work six days a week, fifty weeks a year. It doesn't fit. So I close at lunchtime on Saturdays.

She was bad today. 'Good days and bad days,' she says. That's shit, with respect. The days are all the same. It's the moods that change. Her illness amplifies them, changes her resistances. The pain's always there. The doctors told me. You can see it through the smiles that go thin and wilt in front of me. A change I can see. A change that means something and is real.

There's nothing I can say or do. Just take the lunch, not much but what she wants. Ham sandwich, with mustard. It's easy to eat, get to the mouth.

Once, I came back home not upset. It upset me. Not today.

*   *   *

Mullet is a joy to handle. I'm patting its small and ruby skin, silvery when it catches the light and firmer to the touch than you think it's going to be, which will carry into the tasting of it. I've got the peppers roasting in the oven. It's the best way to blister the skins, to ease peeling, and it fills the house with a sweet smell that will distract her from my mischief if she gets back early. The fillets are laid out, lightly dusted with flour that takes away their sheen and sends them pink.

I've made it seem as though I'm in the middle of cooking – for anyone coming early or unannounced. So I'm free to go upstairs, locking myself in the bathroom, removing the panel from the bath, getting the parcel of brown paper and string, and my database. I can't allow her to suspect my suspicions, alert her before I've gathered my proof. Not that I want there to be anything to prove. I want that report to be innocent: an administrative error or a misunderstanding. I'd rather not have known, which is stupid, because what appals me as much as anything now is the thought of not knowing, despite the way it's affecting me. If you'd given me that envelope and said, 'You're not going to like this. But you don't have to know. I can give it to you or I can turn back time, so you don't even know it exists, I'll even remove that mystery,' I wouldn't have. I'd have still opened the envelope, still picked the bones from her briefcase, knowing it could destroy me.

Madelaine doesn't even know I've got the parcel, and her mother doesn't know it's not in her loft. If she'd wanted it to stay in the loft she should have trusted her daughter, not me, with the key, when she went to stay with her sister last month. And she should have made her daughter the faithful type.

On top of the pile is the photograph album. Closed. Every image stacked up inside me, flicking up in sequence. Madelaine in her first term with the other five: two girls and three lads. Odd, isn't it? A cosy sextet, when one of them's your girlfriend, the sweetheart of the boy who stayed at home. Nick and Phoebe are married now. Caroline stopped going out with Alex in the second year, and Bill, well, Bill's dead. Shame that. He was a nice bloke. 'A really nice bloke,' Madelaine told me on the telephone that Christmas, through tears I couldn't see. Even though we'd split up, she phoned me. And seeing the image of him now, this dead youth, I can feel only relief. It's a bad feeling, I know, but I like being able to look at him knowing he's out of contention. Not a suspect.

'I'm sorry,' I'd said when she'd phoned. I'd met him once, on my first and only trip down. He was all right. More down to earth than most of them. He was a decent bloke.

'Can I see you?' she asked.

'You finished with *me*, remember?'

'Oh, Artie, please. I'd really appreciate it.'

She came round and we talked. I listened. She had a new pair of jeans on, and a soft cardigan, buttoned up and short so you could see her tummy, even in winter. I could see the mole under her navel. She was fatter than when she'd left. I sat there, in the front room at my mum's, trying to work out if her breasts had got bigger – what they'd be like. Even though it was only a month since we'd split up I couldn't picture what she'd look like, not just sat there, in an ordinary posture. I could see a life beyond her. A future that excluded her. I was getting on with it. I could see why she'd wanted us to split up. I hadn't liked it, and I wouldn't have been the one to break it up. But I could see why, I understood. Then.

'There's a service next week,' she'd said.

'Are you going?'

'It's in Wales. I don't think so.'

'How did he die?'

She looked vacant, not upset. Just tired.

'On a motorbike. It wasn't his.'

'Are the rest of them going? Your friends.'

'I don't know.'

'Best stay at home then, eh?'

'Can we try again?'

And that was it.

'No. I don't think so,' I said. Knowing her well enough.

'Why not? You said . . .'

'You're down there and I'm . . . well, it didn't work out, did it?'

'I'll come up. Every week. It won't matter.'

There it was. Within a year we'd bought a place in Slipp and we were married. I knew she'd be coming back to me, and she did. Ever since then, I've felt as though we'd always be together. I've never questioned that. If she was ever going to leave me, she'd have done it then, the easy way. Not waited, and made it impossible for me to cope with. I've based my life on that assumption. Until recently. I've never thought she could be that cruel. To wait for me to entrench myself, so she could go without resistance. But you wouldn't think that, would you? Not if you liked yourself, had pride in the small things you'd done right.

They've had a service, a kind of party for him, this Bill, every year since. His mother does it. Her husband died the following spring. A broken heart for the only son, according to Madelaine, who's never been. Not until now.

I've got names to go with all the faces that would look out of the album, if I was to open it, but I'm going straight to the database. The index cards are alphabetical, and I find Gilmore, Alex, no problem. I've been thinking he might need to be reclassified. Simple information, like on all the rest. Thirty-one in all. Thirty-one is a hell of a lot of men for a married woman to know, to have their telephone numbers in her book, or to have their faces in a photo album, or to have their name in her diary. I know you shouldn't read other people's diaries, not if you don't want to find trouble. Unless you're looking for trouble.

Gilmore, Alex	
D.O.B.	16.3.69
Girlfriends	None known
Contact	University
Things in common	Drama, middle class, friends
Photo count	Six
Appearance	A/B
Diary entries	31.12.88, 30.1.89, 15.2.89, 20.2.89, 21.2.89, 25.2.89
Last known contact	June 1991
Address	see book
Phone check	Clear
Priority	2

His Priority 2 status is a miscalculation. There's a suspicious diary entry – the day after Valentine's. *'Feel terrible. Overdid last night at the Haverton Ball, but Alex came round and got me some paracetamol. Caroline's finished with him. I'm never going to drink again. Thinking of switching to stage management. Aaargghhh.'* There are three more mentions in the next ten days, then nothing. Nothing, even though there are photos on record after then, she still keeps his number, there's no trace of a new girlfriend or marriage. There's an asterisk going next to his name on my master list, and I put him with the Priority 1's. Of the thirty-one names on the master list, eight are Priority 1, six are 2, nine are 3, and eight are Remote.

Now the worst part. I've got to choose my number one.

It's supposed to be scientific, but I know who I want it to be. He's only a Remote, but it's important that I eliminate him. This is the one which will hurt me most. I should really go for a Priority 1, but I don't. Alex Gilmore goes back in his place and I've got hold of Lane, Denny.

D.O.B.	24.9.69
Girlfriends	Numerous
Contact	School. Me
Things in common	Me, living in Slipp (part-time)
Photo count	N/A
Appearance	A*
Diary entries	None
Last known contact	Ongoing
Address	N/A
Phone check	Clear
Priority	Remote

I'm making up an action list for Denny. It's not appropriate, but if I don't stick to the system, well, that's how mistakes get made. Most of the action points are not applicable, and I'm left with four things to do.

Raise in Conversation (nb also with DL re Madelaine)
Set up and tail (evening)
Cross ref. places file
Cross ref. dates file.

*   *   *

Scarlet ribbons trail behind the spoon as I stir my coulis and she answers her car phone. It's like blood curdling, when I hear her voice.

'Oh, Artie, it's you,' and I could swear I hear a giggle, then a 'sshh.'

'I thought you'd be home by now.'

'I didn't say a time. What does it matter?'

'I've done you some mullet.'

'But we're going out tonight.'

'It's only something light.'

'I don't want it.'

I think of my mum's ham sandwich, and her appreciation of what I'd thrown together and delivered in a rush, so I could do this. She hadn't stopped thanking me, telling me 'there's no need'.

'But I've done it now . . . I did it for you.'

'I don't want it.'

'If you'd been on time . . .'

'On time?'

'It's three o'clock.'

'Look Artie. I've been shopping, OK? It's Christmas, it's what people do at . . .'

'Who's there?'

'Where?'

'Now, with you, in the car. I can hear someone.'

'It's the radio.'

'Turn it up then.'

'What?'

'Turn it up.'

I've let my defences drop again, gone too far. She mustn't know that I know. I'll never catch her.

'Artie? have you gone mad?'

'Mad?'

'Yes, mad.'

Mad. I'm not foaming, or twitching. I don't rant or mumble to myself. I don't match up with those labels. I'm not a danger to anyone. Could I be mad, without seeing it myself? Mad. What does it mean? Does it make me mad, to lose its meaning? Words can do that, if you say them over and over again.

'No. No I'm not. I don't think so. I was just wondering if you were listening to the same as me.'

'About the riots?'

'That's right. Hurry home. Come the back way. They've got the main road blocked. I'll try to stop it going dry.'

'What?'

'The fish.'

'Goodbye Artie.'

We used to play a game when she first went to college. I'd phone her, or she'd phone me, and we'd both try to be the last to hang up. It meant you cared the most. But the phone is purring and I'm left with my curdling ribbons and the table set for two as though there was something to celebrate. It will be four by the time she gets home, so I take the mullet off the heat and put the coulis in a bain-marie.

I've got the radio, tuning it to her favourite station, to check her out. Not catching her out – she's canny. You've got to give her that. They are reporting the riots.

Police have been unable to enter The Nelson Estate in Slipp after a sixteen-hour siege. The mood of the rioters has deteriorated since this morning, when William McCafferey was placed on the critical list. McCafferey lost an eye in a fight in the Dog and Partridge public house last night in an incident which triggered the violence.

In the early hours of this morning another youth, Steven Lane, is believed to have suffered the loss of an eye in a revenge attack. It is becoming clear that what we have here is a case of gang warfare, with the usual hallmarks of drugs and protection money. Police wish to speak to anyone who knows the whereabouts, or has seen, Lane's brother, Denis. Denis Lane has been identified as having been in the Dog and Partridge public house last night.

I may as well put the card back. By the sound of things, Denny's not going to be around for a while. Unless he's with Madelaine now. Unless she's sheltering him. But if she is, he'll have to move on soon. It's only ten days before she goes to Pembrokeshire, to the house where Bill's mum hasn't got over him, for eight years.

6

Madelaine changed her car about three months ago, after the crash. We didn't discuss it. I didn't discuss it because I didn't know it was on an agenda. She didn't discuss it either: because she didn't value my opinion; or because she thought she might not get her own way. It's not in my nature to win an argument, she knows that. It would be against my religion, if I had one.

She drags the car back into second and puts her foot down and we're going towards the city on the wrong side of the road, alongside the line of traffic, with headlights getting closer and still two sets of tail lights to overtake. She drums on the steering wheel and reaches down to turn the music up. Guitar sounds that are tuneless, from an Indie band she didn't used to like, fill the car. The lights are getting closer. We're alongside the last car now, and I look across to see if she's scared. She must know we're not going to make it. I'm not scared, but she's got more to lose than me. She's smiling and her arms go into a stiff lock at the elbow as I shoot forward in my seat. The seat belt rips into my chest and the headlights are on us, then past us, with a blare of horns that enters the music then warps away, with another blare, then another and the beam and dip of flashing lights.

'Wow. We'd never have got away with that in the old car. Aren't you glad we changed it?'

'You don't have to drive like that,' I'm saying. There are no traces of phobic anxiety here. There was a time when she didn't drive like this.

'Oh Artie, come on. What's wrong with you. It's just a bit of fun.'

'It's dangerous. There could be children in those cars, and . . .'

'Hey, Artie. Chill out. I'm in control.'

'Sure. Have you got the address?'

'I know where I'm going.'

'You been there before?'

'Yes.'

'When?'

'I went yesterday. Brenda's a friend, OK?' She says it like a threat.

'You didn't say you were at her house.'

'So what?'

'And you drove home?'

'Of course I did. You know I did.'

'You'd been drinking.'

'We went back for a coffee. I waited till I was OK to drive.'

'And that's why you were late?'

'Yes.'

'You were out of it.'

'What?'

'When you got home.'

'Artie.'

'You were . . . you were different. Were you smoking dope, or something.'

And she's laughing. It's an unprotected, dangerous laugh. The kind of laugh you could catch, but not off your wife.

'Oh Artie, you're such an old fart,' and she's still laughing, out of control. I've got to forget her driving, distract myself.

There's going to be five others at the dinner party, which strikes me as an odd number, strange. It's the same number as the faces in all the images of Madelaine that flick up, in sequence: spilling out of an open top sports car, sprawling on a lawn, gathered round stocks on a village green, on steps outside a hall dressed in gowns and dinner jackets, on a cliff in Pembrokeshire with a hamper at their feet and bottles of champagne.

1. Brenda. It's her flat, which is odd. People in Slipp don't live in flats. There aren't any flats, apart from corporation, because the houses are all so cheap. I won't tell you what Madelaine says Brenda paid for her flat. It's ridiculous. But Brenda is 'terrific', and Madelaine's job 'would be so dull if it wasn't for Brenda, she's so kookie, 'Kookie?' She's also 'a genius' at stage design.

2. Cinnamon is black. I'm hoping I don't put my foot in it. 'Don't put your foot in it, Artie. Give her a chance.' I wonder if you could taste her in your semen; if one could taste her in one's semen. Maybe her juices would taste of it, if there's anything in a name.

3. Spike is a male friend of Brenda's. Madelaine's met him a couple of times and 'he's ace. Great fun.' I've been told not to stare. Because his hair is blue, or at least it was the last

time she saw him – she didn't say when that was. 'Just ignore it, Artie. Look at something else.' 'What?' 'Don't be a wanker, Artie.'

4. Des is sponsoring the theatre's latest production. 'We'd be lost without his money, so be careful.' He owns a car dealership and two restaurants in Town. Madelaine says most of his money's come from property development and that he's 'probably a millionaire'. Jesus.

5. Bianca is Des's girlfriend. The latest model, even though he's still married, to someone from school who's proven unsuitable for later purposes. Madelaine didn't seem to think there was anything wrong with him having a girl-friend. 'It is the nineties for Christ's sake.' Not that she approves of Bianca, who is 'obvious. You know the sort, an ornament.'

There's another blare of angry drivers and we cut across two lanes of traffic without slowing down, onto the ring road, going towards the docks. Apart from the water, you'd never know. There are blocks of flats flanking us along a new road – wide and not cobbled any more. Everything is 'for sale', and the bigger, glass buildings behind are 'to let'. There's no boats or cranes or dirt. I used to come down here with my dad, just before they closed it down.

I don't want to go now, now I can see it. I daren't say anything, about how I've got a stomach-ache and 'Why don't I drop you off. You can get a cab back. I'm really not up to it.' 'You shouldn't have eaten all that mullet,' she'd say. 'You should have come home. I cooked it for you.' No point. Because I'm 'always complaining you never meet my friends. Just relax. You'll like them. They're terrific.' But I know they won't be.

The truth is, I'm scared of what I might uncover. It could take me another step closer to finding out, if one of them knows. I'll be measuring all their reactions, I'll be listening for a change of subject and watching for a blush or a fidget, a guilty exchange of looks.

'Here we are,' she says.

'Is this it? Christ.'

'Don't blaspheme. You told me not to.'

'Sorry, it's just, well . . . do people live here?'

'It's all the rage.'

'It's derelict.'

'It cost a fortune.'

'So?'

'Oh, Des is here.'

'How do you know?'

'That's his car.'

'That? Jesus.'

It's a Bentley, a Mulsane Turbo. Turquoise blue and with leather cream interior. If you've seen one, you'll know it's a wanker's car. If you haven't seen one, take it from me, it's a wanker's car.

'Come on, Artie, loosen up. And don't let me down.'

You'd think that if she'd paid all that money for the place it would at least have a lift, but no. As far as I can see there's no-one else living here and Brenda's on the top floor. When you get to the top of the iron steps there's no hall, or door. You're straight into this old storage loft, the size of a football pitch. No paint on the walls. There are lights that come down in banks from the ceiling that's twenty feet high, like a snooker hall, but with bulbs of red and green and yellow. No snooker tables. The minute I see it I want to go, but Madelaine's already hugging Brenda, for longer than is necessary. They're kissing each other, which she never does to people she knows in Slipp. I'm left to look around while they tell each other how terrific they look, and by the time Madelaine unlocks from her clinch to say 'and this is Artie', I'm miles away, working out how she empties her bins and how the post gets delivered.

She kisses me, and I pull away, but she's holding my shoulders and bringing her lips onto my other cheek.

'Oh Artie, Madelaine's told me so much about you. But you're much more handsome.' By the time anything else is said my stomach has gone light, and I can't tell if she's joking when she says, 'only joking', and she turns to Madelaine 'hmm, delicious', and they both giggle. 'Come and meet the rest of the gang.'

Rest of the gang? I can't see anyone, but she leads us round an area with an oven and cupboards and sink which she describes as her 'food station'. I want to tell her that a gang is something that burns buses on the Nelson Estate and barricades itself in against the police when it's taken as much as it can stand. But I don't. I remember that I'm 'a guest', and to 'be respectful'.

They're sitting on enormous cushions on the floor in front of a raging fire, around a coffee table made from unfinished steel. They don't stand up, but raise outsize goblets that swirl red wine shadows on their faces in the firelight.

'Welcome aboard. Now, Madelaine you know everyone and everyone knows Madelaine,' then a sinister 'of course', and I miss the introductions because I'm trying to work out the 'of course'.

I'm getting a smile from a scrawny man with receding hair and bad skin that's perfect tanned. He's got slitty eyes I know from somewhere. He's dressed smart in a black suit that has no lapels, smart the way he was in the Dog the other night, and I can see now it's the same smile: smile-shaped but cold, empty.

'Hi Artie.'

'Hi . . .'

'I'm Des. Des Christian.'

We've eaten what Brenda proudly brought to the table and announced as Tuscan stew. 'A terrific peasant dish. Erica found it in an old recipe book when she was in Siena. She translated it from the original for me. She's so clever. I do miss her.' Peasant dish, of the Italian variety. My arse. No meat, not enough salt, just a mush of overcooked beans and lentils. Don't get me wrong, I'm no food snob, food is there to stop us starving in the first place. But don't call it Tuscan stew. Don't do that, not with all the other pretentious stuff you're doing, like eating cross-legged on the floor at the rusty coffee table. But I can't let Madelaine down. I could, but I don't feel I can afford to, not on the cliff edge at the top of the warehouse.

'Maddie tells me you're a terrific cook, Artie.' Maddie? No-one has ever called her Maddie. It's what a mother or a lover would call her.

'I wouldn't say that. I enjoy it though, when I've got the time. This is terrific. You must let Madelaine have the recipe. In English of course.'

Brenda laughs, politely, and the others look up and smile at me. It's the first thing I've said.

'Of course. What sort of stuff do you cook?'

'Oh, nothing fancy. Simple food. Fish, mainly. Madelaine likes fish.' Madelaine lifts her head and I get a smile, narrow and without teeth, but with wet eyes that glow in the flames. 'Good job really, doing what I do.'

'What's that?' asks Spike. His electric blue hair is shaven to bristle. I expected him to look ridiculous. He doesn't. He's very tall, and handsome. His face looks like a cartoon, drawn with straight lines on white, white paper.

'I'm a fishmonger,' I say, which makes them all chip in:

'Fascinating.'

'Wow, that's amazing.'

'Maddie, you never said.'

'Where?' asks Des. He hasn't spoken so far. He probably wants to be somewhere else too. I've felt his eyes on me, so I haven't been able to weigh him up. I know him from some-where else though, not just the Dog the other night.

'Slipp.'

'Whereabouts? Not the High Street?'

'Yes. That's right.'

Des stops talking. He's playing with his food, then drink-ing his wine, and he looks across to Bianca as she's about to open her mouth and the look from him is enough to make her not speak. She finishes off her glass. That's three for her, since we arrived.

'How can you handle all that dead flesh?'

'Cinnamon!'

'No, Brenda, I'm interested. All that death, those lost souls filling the space around you. Does it get to you?'

I hate this gibberish shit. The slow accentless drawl, and I want to ask her if I'd taste her name between her legs, if I went up there like Madelaine got me to do the other night. I want to bring her down. But what she's said, the meaning of what she's said, not the words she used, strikes a chord. Death all around me. Soaked into the plaster and the tiles. Bled onto the hands and arms of me and my dad and my grandad.

'There may be something in that. There is a bad atmos-phere,' I hear myself say.

I lose my body. My feet drift away from me and the food on the table at my lap seems miles away. I'm losing the certainty of my first impressions of this woman. This beautiful Cinnamon.

I can hear a voice. It sounds like the woman I'm living with. It's as though I'm under water, in the swimming baths, and she's calling me. I married her but I can't remember her name. There are people all around me, but I don't know them, or where I am. My legs feel dead and tingle, and the voice is coming at me again.

'Artie, Artie? You didn't tell me there was an atmosphere in the shop.'

'I don't mean the shop.'

'But you said . . .'

'He means around him. There's a bad atmosphere around you, isn't that right.' And I nod at Cinnamon, who looks straight at me, with white almond eyes that burn into me, unblinking, and she's looking sorry for me. She understands.

'Wow! Heavy stuff. Hey, you should go and see Cinnamon. Tell him, Cin, you could help him,' says Spike.

'I have a studio, alternative treatments. It may help. You need to get into the soul of it.'

'Artie would never go, Cin, he's such a traditionalist,' says Madelaine.

'Yes. Thank you. I'd like to . . .'

'Artie.'

'I would. Do you have a card?' I take it, and I'm going to use her. It's good to see that I can surprise Madelaine, even if she looks disappointed.

'Does that stuff of yours really work?' asks Madelaine. 'Come on, you can tell us.'

'Cynic,' says Cinnamon, not rising to the bait.

'Maddie's right. That stuff's all crap,' says Des. He's looking at me when he says it. I can see food in his mouth behind the empty smile.

It goes quiet. It's clear that they're not allowed to upset Des. Brenda says something that they all laugh at, mechanical laughs. I don't know what she's said because I've worked out where he's from. He's from our school, years above us, probably left before Madelaine came from her convent. But I can't say anything. One look and you'd see why. He'd destroy me. 'What doesn't destroy you makes you stronger,' they say. I feel weak.

Brenda's flitting to and from her food station with fruit I won't know how to eat. Madelaine and Cinnamon have gone in to help her and Spike's on all fours at the CD collection, with his bum in the air. Tight trousers, leathered taut on his long legs that are thick, muscular. He's at ease, humming too loudly to himself.

The girls are fussing with the fruit and giggling, all holding knives. All wanting a go.

'Sshh,' I hear. Then a whisper.

'Nobody can hear,' says Cinnamon. I move closer, with Spike's third world drum choice filling the room, from four coffin-shaped, steel speakers. 'I do, I think he's sexy.'

'Oooh no, that skin, it's horrible,' says Brenda, 'like a lizard.'

I can tell, with my ear cocked behind the pillar, that they're talking about Des. Des. D. With his year-round tan.

'He's all right,' says Madelaine, 'leave him alone.'

'You haven't,' says Brenda. 'You have!'

'Sshh,' comes from Cinnamon.

'How's it going, Artie?'

'Oh. Des.'

'Remember me?'

'You? Me? Oh, from the Dog, the other night,' I say, absently, swilling things I've heard around in my head.

Mixing them with information I've gathered, images I've formed.

'Not me,' he says, 'not in the Dog. Not my kind of place. School. Remember me from school?'

'School?'

'You should,' he says. Not meaning I ought to, but that it would be in my best interests to acknowledge him, his importance, which I don't. I just furrow my face, unconvincingly. I'm trying to conceal my failing grasp of his attractiveness to women.

'You've done all right for yourself,' says Des.

'Me? Not really.'

'Oh, you have. She's lovely.' He's smiling a different smile, but past me. Madelaine's raising her glass at us, and a red cloud passes over her face, from the fire through the wine. 'She's great, your Maddie. A real find.'

The fruit's gone, leaving pips in my teeth and a sour taste of bits that shouldn't have been eaten. Bianca's asleep in the only chair and Cinnamon and Spike are trying to roll a joint, except they're making it too big.

'Seven skins,' says Spike, 'I did it once.' They all start laughing.

'How are you enjoying this place, Brenda?' says Des.

'Great. I'm really pleased with it.'

'Good.'

'The light's fantastic.'

'You had any problems with the planners?' he asks, leaning back, flexing his influence.

'They're a nightmare. I tell you, you can't take a crap without permission in here. They're listing everything these days. Even that shitty factory in Slipp.'

'I don't suppose Slipp's worth preserving, is it?' I say.

'I didn't mean it like that,' says Brenda.

'Let me know who you're dealing with,' says Des, 'I'll see what I can do.'

'No, it's all right. Really.'

'Suit yourself. Call me if you change your mind.'

'Madelaine tells me you're a property developer, Des,' I say.

'Kind of. I dabble.'

'Where?'

'I've got something in town at the moment. Can't say where.'

'What about Slipp?' I say.

'Slipp? Not my kind of place. Going downhill.'

'Yeah, did you hear about the riots?' says Brenda.

'Terrible,' says Cinnamon.

'You ask me,' says Des, 'people get what they deserve. They say the pig makes the sty. You should get out of there, Maddie.'

'It's not so bad,' I say, looking at Madelaine, 'is it?'

'Artie likes it.' She's dismissive, the way she says it, as though she's humouring me.

'I wouldn't say that. It just suits. For the moment. It's not so bad on Top Side.'

'It'll spread,' says Des.

'I'd like a place here,' says Madelaine.

'Here?' His eyes unslit.

'Well, you know. Town.'

'We can't,' I say.

'Artie.'

'We can't. You know we can't.'

'It's his mum, she's . . .'

'There's nothing wrong with Slipp. Not where we are.'

'It needs some new life,' says Des, 'some outside money,

something to redefine the place. They should build a fucking great wall along the Railing Road and fill the underpass with concrete.' He's serious.

'I was born on the Nelson,' I say.

'So was I,' says Des.

'Were you?'

'I didn't know that.'

'Wow.'

He's smiling, taking the plaudits as they all chime up, as though he's some kind of a celebrity.

'Doesn't stop me knowing it's a shit hole though,' he says.

'It's not a shit hole. Treat people like shit, they'll behave bad,' I say.

'The pig and the sty, Artie. Remember.'

'That's shit.'

'Artie!' Madelaine looks at me, stern.

'Where do you live now, then?' I say, backing down, reducing the stakes.

'We've just moved into . . .' Bianca's come across, freshly woken and tottering to fill her glass.

'Be quiet,' says Des, and she does, with a cower and a flinch, pulling a face behind his back as he turns back to me. 'We live in town. Just got a new place.'

'Where?'

'We were talking about Slipp. Look at the Rainbow. They build a pub for these people, their own place, just for them, and what happens?'

'The Rainbow's all right,' I say, out of instinct, not knowledge.

'All right? You been in lately?'

'Well . . .'

'You know about the Rainbow, Artie,' says Madelaine, 'everyone knows.'

'Knows what?' I say, before I can help myself.

'I know and I don't even live in Slipp,' says Brenda. 'Aah, your Artie, he's such an innocent.'

'He's covering up. Bet he's in there every night,' says Cinnamon, not smiling. Just looking at me, almond eyes, lidding down from the dope.

'Why did you say that stuff about the bad atmosphere? And all that about the Nelson. Des is important, you know. What got into you?'

'I don't know. It's just that they're all so weird. I was just trying to fit in.'

'Oh Artie. Never mind. You were fine. Thanks, I know they're not your type. You didn't like them, did you?'

'I did, didn't dislike them, they're all right. Apart from Des.'

'Des? I thought you'd . . .'

'He's a creep, and probably a crook. I'm going to check him out.'

'Artie! You know nothing about him.'

'Don't I? Did you hear him asking me about the shop. He's up to something.'

'Don't be . . .'

'I know he is. I can tell, when people are going behind my back. I know. I'll check him out all right.'

'What are you? Some kind of detective. My little super sleuth.' She puts her hand on my thigh, squeezes it, close to the groin.

'You'd better concentrate on your driving. Two hands.'

'My virgin,' and she giggles as she puts her hand back on the gearstick, with a flick at my flies that makes her giggle burst.

It's late, gone two. We pull up at the lights, near a

taxi rank. There's a crowd coming out of a neon doorway. The people look like something from another country.
Not their clothes or hair. The way they behave, their
energy.

'Wouldn't you like to live here, Artie?'

'In Town? We're close enough already.'

'No. Really live here. Be anonymous. Do what you like,
when you like.'

'We can't.'

'You could. If you really wanted.'

'I've got you. I don't want to be anonymous. There's
Mum . . .'

'Artie. You could . . . you know. There are places she
could . . .'

'She's not even fifty.'

'You've got your own life.'

'Our life.' There's a silence, so I carry on. 'Anyway, what
was all that about the Rainbow?'

'You know about the Rainbow. You were just teasing.'

'I don't. I wasn't.'

'Oh Artie, everybody knows about the Rainbow.'

'Apart from me.'

'Poor love.' And she puts her hand back on my thigh with
two pats, then the tail lights in front get too close and the
hand goes back onto the stick. She takes us from fifth
straight to second with a screech of brakes, and the seat belt
cuts into me again. She giggles.

She looks across at me and smiles. I'm harmless and dependable, and I don't change. That's what she sees. She
doesn't see that I'm desperate to get out of Slipp. When the
conditions are right. She doesn't realize I know the damage a
place like Slipp can do, the way it can drag you down – keep
you there. It can lower your expectations, so you think you're

happy with the place, without thinking. And then something changes. You see how bad it is.

In the meantime, I'll be going to the Rainbow, and seeing Cinnamon, checking things out and catching her up, and she won't know about either. My changes are under way.

7

You'd probably know what the Rainbow looks like, its type of pub. I've not been in for years, but not much has changed from the outside. It's seventies: grey brick, with wood panelled insets that used to be painted white; big windows, and half of them wooden too, now. Standing outside, even though I was born round here, it's telling me not to come in.

I've taken my mum her lunch – a fish pie from the freezer. I got up too late for anything else. I feel bad, for putting the fact-finding first. I usually race down in the car, with some of our roast, tin-foiled and cut into bite sizes for her. I could see her disappointment when I arrived early, when the fish smells came from the oven, before she was even hungry.

It's noon now and there are five lads with wet hair and dry skin in T-shirts, stamping from foot to foot, under the

Christmas lights above the doorway. One of them bangs on the door.

'For fucksakes, Ged. Open up.'

'Freezin', Ged. Come on, lad.'

They've seen me, choosing not to return my nod. I know the faces, from four or five years below me at school.

The door unbolts, four times from top to bottom and I see Ged. It's Ged McCain, my year at school. His dad's name is above the door, the same E. McCain, that was my dad's mate. I file in behind the T-Shirts and Ged is hooking the door to the wall.

'All right Ged?'

'Artie? Not seen you for ages, lad. What you doing?'

'Oh, the same. Still in the shop.'

'No. Here. What you doin' here?'

'Come for a drink.'

'Jesus.'

That's what reunions can be like in Slipp. It could have been worse. Ged knows I'm Denny's best mate, or he's my best mate, on this Sunday after the Friday night. I hadn't thought of that.

The beer is pale, electric and weak. It doesn't take long to drink when you're not welcome. I have to stay though. As the sign says, the show doesn't start until one on Sunday dinners. Between twelve and one it fills up, with more wet, lanky hair and T-shirts that have been slept in. Slade come on three times with 'Merry Xmas Everybody' and I lose my place at the bar, ending up smoking at a table by the stage. I don't smoke. The Christmas tape shuts down mid-track and a disco beat comes in. The lights go off and three coloured bulbs are on above the stage. Three older men shuffle from the bar and come to my table. They sit down, don't acknowledge me. They're the only welcome for the young girl who climbs up, dancing in her underwear. She steps around, clicking her high heels out of time with the music. She's got bruises on her pale legs, and tiny tits – almost no tits at all. She stares at the lights above her and goes through her motions, with open, dead eyes and a false smile, the way she'd look a second after a camera had clicked.

Without changing her step, she bends down and takes her knickers off. She kicks them to the back of the stage, hooking them with the heel of her stiletto. The old men peer up, with beery leers and mouth approval. She has a dark muff, almost black and the negative of her blond hair, almost white. She's shaved herself into a thin black strip, but there's a stubble growing back, going down to the sinews of her groin. The music stops and she gives a sad curtsey. She claps her hands twice above her head, but her mum and dad aren't in the audience. This isn't a ballet exam. There's no response. She's still got her bra and stockings on. She looks like a detective kit that I once got for Christmas. She couldn't match the head and the body and the legs.

John Lennon comes in with 'War Is Over' and I go for another pint, biding my time at the bar, letting others be served ahead, because of what I'm hearing.

'Billy's still bad.'

'Heard. Fuckin' bastards. Got the brother though, young 'un'.

'Where they got him?'

'On the Estate. Got to let him go though, before he snuffs. Pigs are everywhere.'

'They won't come on the Estate. Not if they get the little cunt back. They'll piss off then, one apiece. Think it's over.'

'Johnny's back tomorrow. Coming back from Ulster.'

'Jesus. It'll kick off then, eh?'

'Brother's next they say.'

'Denny? Yeah. He was all right at school. Bastard. They got him yet?'

'Nah. Can't get off the Estate. Couple of days, just you watch, when the pigs go.'

'Pint please,' I say. They stop talking, both looking at me, then at each other. I want to let them know that Johnny McCafferey was my year at school. We were mates when he was cock of the school, before he got paid to beat people up – kill them for all I knew. I had to be all right. You'd have to be mad to come onto the Estate, if you didn't belong.

'Right Artie,' replies Ged, and they turn back to the bar, knowing Ged knows me, but not seeing the look he gives me, that tells me to keep quiet and go back to my table.

'Ta,' and I did, hearing as I went:

'Hey, Ged. Who's the soft cunt?'

'He's all right.'

'You say so.'

The next time the tape shuts down, with Roy Wood wishing it could be Xmas Every Day, a raunchy rock track comes on. There's a rush to the stage, this time by the young men. They're standing with their pints on their guts. Those who are sat down are banging their fists on the tables, roughly in time with the music. 'We will . . . we will . . . FUCK YOU!' they shout on the chorus. An older woman struts up on stage in a biker's jacket, leather bra and a G string – old enough to be the first girl's mother's mother.

Halfway through the track a chair gets thrown up on stage. She catches it and puts it down, then throws her jacket to the floor and rips off her bra. Her tits are big and swinging, with blue veins homing in on her nipples. She's on the chair with her legs stretched out: big thighs with veins showing too, going into the crotch. With two slow wags of a finger she summons an old boy to rise. He's got a gummy smile and places his cigarette in an ashtray. His fingers tremble. He leans up, stretching for the thin elastic and pulling down her knickers, twitching as he does it. I gag on my drink. I can see metal baldness in her crotch – shaved completely and the pink flesh pitted with early regrowth on the two folding cheeks: flabby and pierced and ringed, three on each. Fat-lipped oysters.

There's a buzz in the audience as the music stops and starts again, with a scratch, and Freddie Mercury was off again. 'We will . . . we will . . . FUCK YOU!' Louder than before, with whoops and whistles. She laps it up and takes a boot-lace from someone in the crowd, drawing it between her teeth, slowly across her smile. It's a full smile that sparkles in her eyes, not like the young girl who had gone before. The lace drops between her legs, where she twirls it with one hand, punching the air with the other in time with the music. The crowd is topped up now, baying as she passes the lace from ring to ring, finishing off with a bow, and a bow. Johnny Mathis comes on with the crowd still whistling. Sunday dinner in Slipp. Christmas-time on the Nelson Estate, with Mary's Boy Child.

I've seen enough, but I can't go. From what I can gather, the best is yet to come. And with all this: Billy McCafferey maimed and his brother coming over from Ulster, and Stevie Lane captive with only one eye, and Madelaine's secret life getting less secret – all I can think of is how she knew about this place when I didn't.

Half three. Both women have done another two turns. I'm pissed. Ged puts the four bolts back across the door with the place still full and the cash counting started. I go to the toilet, wondering how I'm going to explain it to Madelaine, this state of mine. Over my shoulder from the urinal there's a bang against the cubicle door, then another and the sound of a zip. Two stilleto heels pointing out from underneath. I can see the fishnet calves and the wet noises start, then an old man's groan. I can picture him, sat on the bog seat with his squinting smile of pain and the young one's greasy roots going up and down, up and down. Noises that pretend she's enjoying the taste of piss and salt and God knows what on his cock flesh, so she'll get him again next week. For a fiver. I'm learning fast, learning to picture and fear the worst.

I leave the Rainbow at four, with the tables and floor moving into my path. The young girl is still in the bog taking fivers, still needing more so she can inject her spindly arms with what she needs to perform her various acts. It's the new economy, I can see that now. Outside it's dark and damp, with the Christmas lights dull on the wet car park. Ged bolts the door behind me, but not before he gives me a look that says not to come back.

The police cars are still above the underpass and I can hear the kids fucking and blinding through the smells of burning. At the top of the steps, on the top side of the Railing Road, a copper asks me where I'm off to.

'Home. Just been to see me mum. Worried about her.' I hiccup twice and he smiles.

'Got to take your name and address, son.' Son? He's my age, but I give it anyway. He can see I'm not trouble and leaves me to go, up the hill to home, past the shop.

Past where the butcher's used to be. It was my dad's mate's: Charlie Bledsoe. In France they had a Butcher of Lyons, a serial killer. In France they eat horses, where's it *cheval*. Cheval. A Marron Chevalier would be a knight on horse chestnut. I once made the joke in French and nobody got it, except Miss Lefevre, the French teacher. She said 'You're a funny boy, Artie. Very clever.' Marron Chevalier, thank heaven for little girls, as they'd say in the Rainbow with their fivers.

There are horses in Tommy Jack's, even on Sundays now, on the banks of TV's he's got chained to the walls, high up on brackets where nobody can nick them. They're above the pinned-up form and piling ashtrays and torn losers' slips like pink straw on a stable floor. My dad used to come. He'd leave me on the step, until he had no money left. The only time for a gambler to stop. I had to stay outside. It's wrong for children to go inside the betting shop, just like it's not wrong for them to stand outside, with the high street traffic brushing your hair back, and the old men smiling as they pass you. It's not wrong for you to sit on the stairs and hear her cry and him rant when there's no money left and she says 'I want some meat. It's always bloody fish because you can't stay off the bloody horses.' 'What about the time we went to London?' 'That was five years ago. Five bloody years.' That was when L'Escargot won the National, when he didn't come last at a snail's pace. I remember my dad throwing me in the air, dropping me to his smiling face that hadn't been shaved. He caught me and I let my head bounce, to catch his mouth on my cheek and he kissed me, said 'fuckin' beauty', and threw me up again.

They have racing in France. The wives don't cook all the horses before the men can bet on them. In France they go to the hippodrome to watch and bet. Madelaine went to the Hippodrome in London while she was on a course. She loved it. Here in England The Hippodrome is a place I've heard about, where wives who are on courses can get laid by men who are richer and more exotic than their husbands, without anyone ever knowing.

I want my head to stay still inside. It's ranting and rambling, won't stop milling. And now my dad's come – walking with me up the hill past Tommy Jack's on this side and his dad's fish shop on the other. I've had him with me since last night, on and off, with Madelaine's dirty words about the Rainbow that she served with the Tuscan stew sticking to the walls of my belly.

He's got that smile on, my dad. The one that flicked up at the door on New Year's Eve, the one that was fixed when he pulled away from Mrs Sellars that night. He had his hands on her bottom and her skirt riding up under his walking fingers. I saw it all those years ago, when I left Frankie asleep, got told to 'stay put', 'be good'. Her thin, pink tongue pushing out of her skin-coloured lips. I can see it now, with her eyes closed, hands busy in his trousers. He didn't see me, and neither did she. I went upstairs.

There were three doors at the top of the stairs, just like at our house. Me and Frankie shared the back room and I knew that was where Kev would be, asleep like I wished I could be. The toilet was over the stairs, where my dad had to duck because he was too tall. There was only one door left – closed. I went up to it. I sensed an awful promise above the thud of music. I dropped the handle and let the light from the landing creep onto the wallpaper. I could hear her crying, my mum. I wanted her to cuddle me, but couldn't ask. I couldn't go back down either, not without her – my dad would hit me. I wasn't strong enough for that, so I went in. All I wanted was to be safe. She didn't have her clothes on, not properly. Her skirt was ruffled up, showing her bottom, and her pants hung off her legs. She was wriggling on top of my uncle Bob, Kev's dad. He had her breasts in his hands, and before she turned round to see me, I saw the smile on her. She was smiling at him as she made the hurting noises.

I didn't know if it was a game. My dad said it was, when he carried me home, when it was cold and it felt like my tears were freezing to my cheek. You can't rely on these things you remember from childhood. They said it was a game, but I can't believe that. A game of smiling tears. My mum slept with me that night. She told Frankie to shut up, and she cuddled me all night.

8

There's an echo in the house, slow drumming through the fog of lunch-time booze. I'm just waking up, but I can tell that I'm on my own. There's no flesh, no movement in the place to soak up my noises. I look to the clock. It's too late for her to still be out. She wasn't in when I came back gone four, with the darkness settled and the sound of carols round the corner. The singing has gone now. I drew the curtains and ignored the bell when they'd come with the Bleak Midwinter. I couldn't afford for their mothers to find out what I was like: alone with beer and fags on my breath, when I don't smoke and I'm not a drinker, and I'm married.

I check the house, moving slowly under the aching head. I should have done it when I got in, checked for an explanation. But I can't find anything. There's nothing to point where she's gone. Just a polish to the house it doesn't get during the week and I can see she's been at work. Otherwise, no traces.

There's only one thing for me to do. I don't like it, there's no knowing how it will turn out. You can't plan the reaction. I press the redial button and listen to the dread of its electric rhythm, counting down with higher and higher pitches before it tells me who she's been talking to while I was away.

'Hi.' The voice is female, which is sufficient. I should hang up. The last few drops of energy buzz out of my head. Her voice is faint. 'Who is that?' she says. It's too late now. I'll have to say something, I feel as though I ought, but I don't know who I've called. I want to laugh but it's not funny.

'It's, er . . . it's . . .'

'Who is it?'

'Me.'

'Me? What's your name?'

'Gill. Artie Gill.'

'Artie? Artie! Hi. I didn't think you'd call.' I recognize the voice, it's recent, but I can't put a face or a name to it. 'I thought you were just being polite. I'm glad you did.'

It's a husky voice and my balls go light. I can hear her breathing coming down the line to fill the silence, which is mine. There's a tremble to my mouth. I can feel my voice preparing to spring. I know who it is.

'I want to see you,' I say.

'When?'

'Any time. Tomorrow?'

'Let me check my appointments. Don't go away.'

I can see her in a loose fitting silk gown like she'd worn last night, her hair cropped short, in tight gel curls. Her skin is smooth, with its sheen the way she'll leave my body with her oils when she's rubbed them in.

'Can you make it half four?'

'Sure.'

'That's fine Artie. Perfect. You know where to find me?'

'It's on the card, isn't it?'

'Yes. You can't go wrong. Doesn't matter if you're late. You're my last appointment. Best not to hurry. I want you calm, first time.' She laughs, soft and fading to a purr. 'See you tomorrow then.'

'Yes. OK. Oh, Cinnamon?'

'Yes.'

'I just wondered . . . Madelaine, Maddie, she was going to call you.'

'She did, about two.'

I feel the need to justify the call. Even though there's no need. 'Did she mention anything about a party?'

'No.'

'Oh, right, good. I'm trying to keep it as a surprise. I'm inviting people round. On Boxing Day. For drinks. Would you come, and Brenda, and . . . anyone.'

'Anyone?' She laughs again, the same way.

'I mean . . . I mean you and Brenda. The gang, you know. I think . . . I think she'd like it. I'd like it, to meet more of her friends. Keep it as a surprise – if you can come, I hope you can. It would be nice. If you could.'

'Leave it to me, Artie. I can come. I'll see about the rest of the gang.'

'Thanks.'

'Bye Artie.'

'Bye.'

The buzzing is still there when I've stopped my talking. I don't know where all that came from. I'm regretting it already, all of it, but I can see her – in her silk, with those almond eyes lidding down. Jesus.

*   *   *

There are some venison steaks in the fridge. I took them out when we got home last night. I prepared it this morning while my mum's pie was cooking through. The marinade's done with wine and oil and shallots and peppercorns. Berries too, to tenderize and break it down so it's gamey fibres will flake in the mouth. It should have been done last night, but I let it slip. It will cook quickly, so I can't start yet. It will be the first proper meal we've had since I put the decorations up. I want it to be right.

The first Christmas we had in the house, we ate in every night – at the dining table with the silver, and candles. I had the candles in oranges with spices rubbed into the peel and pitted with cloves. It smelt of proper Christmas. Madelaine would get wine, and we'd sit for hours, with cheese smeared on the board and dribbles of port on the cloth, not necessarily speaking, but happy amongst the things that were ours and new. She'd get up and come back down in just one of my T-shirts, curling in front of the fire. I'd play records for her, not telling her what each one meant. She'd drift and jolt to sleep with me watching her from the table. It was the best time. I know you've got to go on, and find other best things to do. You can't go back. I accept that. But I'm trying to recreate it, as a start, to help things get better.

The door clicks shut. I didn't hear a key, but I hear her now. She's talking in the hall. Then it comes. What I've been waiting for. I look in the window, seeing myself. I am puffy in the jowl from drink and not enough sleep, and my eyes shine, from the white lights I put on the tree at the bottom of the garden. They're in my eyes. I'm reflected at myself above the sink and I can't see if I look sad or desperate or resigned, but I can hear the male voice that she's brought home, to tell me something. I know the voice.

'Artiee,' she calls. It's anxious, the way she says it, urgent.

I know she's not messing about. It's time. I take a breath and my heart goes slow. I feel heavy.

I can see her reflection coming into the room, going to the shelf where we keep the drinks. Another figure stops in the doorway. The worst fear.

'All right, Artie.'

'Denny, what're you doing here?'

'Sorry, mate.'

'You're going to have to go. You can't stay,' says Madelaine. I can't look at her. Even though I'm angry, I don't think I've got the stomach for this battle.

'What! It's my house, I live here for Christ's sake. This is my life, you know. You can't . . .'

'Artie, what the hell are you wittering on about? We've got a problem. You should have been here,' says Madelaine.

'That's rich.'

'Have you been drinking?'

'What if I have?'

'You stink like a brewery,' she says.

'Look mate,' says Denny, 'I'll go. I'm sorry. It's my fault.'

'No Denny,' says Madelaine, 'look, Artie, he's your mate, you sort it out, the two of you,' says Madelaine.

'What? What's going on?' I ask.

'If you'd been here, *you* could have gone,' she says. 'It's dangerous out there. The police stopped me twice – with him in the boot, for God's sake. I'm washing my hands of it. I've done my bit, he's your friend. I want him out.'

'They're after me, mate. I've got nowhere to go. The police and the Nelson, they're both after me. They burnt my mum's door down, first thing. I've nowhere to go.'

'Johnny McCafferey's coming over.' I'm turning to the chopping board and rolling the steaks over in the marinade. I'm strong now, composed.

'What? Jesus. I'm dead.'

'They're going to let Stevie go, then they're coming after you. When Johnny gets here.'

'How do you know all this?'

'I heard it.'

'Where?' he says.

I turn and look at Madelaine: She's leaning against the dresser with a gin and tonic. The muscles under her jaw are twitching. I wait until she looks up at me.

'The Rainbow. I went to check it out.'

'Oh Artie,' she says.

'It was nothing. Just a bit of fun. I've seen worse. Much worse.' I was lying, of course. But she shouldn't know more than me about such things. She shouldn't be allowed to think she knows more than me about these things.

'You went onto the Estate? Today,' she says.

'I was checking it out. Good job I did. Come on Denny. Get your drink and I'll tell you the rest. You can stay tonight.'

'Artie!'

'I know what I'm doing, Maddie. Trust me.'

And I could see her thinking it: 'Maddie?'

'Hang on, there's a problem. Shit,' I say.

'What is it, Artie?' she asks, concerned.

'The venison. I've only two steaks.'

'We can split them up.'

'No.'

'I don't mind,' she says.

She should. If she'd known the effort, and what it meant.

'I'm easy,' says Denny, 'don't worry about me, I'll have a sarnie.'

'No you won't. I can do you an omelette. I've got potatoes. I'll do you tortilla.'

'Whatever. Thanks.'

'Jesus, Artie. Call me when it's ready. I'm going for a bath,' says Madelaine.

'No, you . . . there isn't time.'

She's heard me, I know, but she's gone. I can hear the plumbing start to clunk, so the cling film's going back over the steaks. I take Denny into the lounge, so he can tell me what he thinks he's got to do to stay alive.

'They've hung me out to dry, the bastards.' He's almost crying, it's only the fear that's keeping it at bay. He's too scared to feel sorry for himself. He takes his leather jacket off. Throws it on the floor, with just a vest left on – grimy white, hanging loose under his arms. You can see the muscles in his arms and shoulders and chest. Like cable. Thin and strong. Skin that looks as though it wouldn't cut or bruise. He looks hard, like he wouldn't bleed or hurt. 'I did everything they asked. Against my own.'

'You mean Billy?'

'Everyone thinks it was me.'

'Was it?' I say.

'I didn't know he was going to be there.'

'You didn't have to do it. How could you? Jesus, Denny.'

'You don't understand.'

'Why did you start it?'

'We didn't. They did. They got greedy, came onto our patch.'

'What?'

'We were collecting from everywhere this side of the Estate.'

'You were? I thought Bruce got you in to stop the racket.'

He laughs at me. Empty and sneering, not the way you'd laugh at a mate. 'Bruce was in on it. We set them up, just to scare them. They're supposed to stay put. Stay on

Nelson. It was built for them, to keep them there. It's a fucking zoo.'

'We're from there.'

'We got out, Artie.'

'Who were you working for?'

'You're better off not knowing.'

'Why don't you just nick off? Back to the Gulf.'

He brings the laugh out again. 'I've not been diving for three years.'

'What?'

'Diving. Lost me fucking nerve, didn'I.'

'I don't get it. You're always loaded. Out of the country.'

'You work your bollocks off Artie. You're a shopkeeper. You're lucky. There's no men's work around any more. Where the fuck does a *man* work round here, these days.'

'Why did you give up the diving?'

'Me bottle went.'

'What?'

He's lighting up, leaning forward with his head down. His voice goes quiet, dull and deep in the carpet.

'Three of us were down. Sixty metres, like a lily pond. Flat calm. Then this swell gets up, and they call us up. Twenty metres at a time.' He draws on his cigarette. His hands are shaking. 'You got a drink?'

'Sure.'

'The swell's picking us up and dropping us. More and more, the closer we get. I can hear this banging, louder and louder. The boat's being lifted up and dumped. We're twenty metres off it and this shadow of the hull's coming down on us. Then the boat comes right through. Right through its own shadow. Fucking unbelievable sound. Twice it happens and there's nothing you can do.'

'Here,' I say.

'Ta.'

'Go on.'

'Three of the lads lose it. They go for the surface, but the hull gets them. The water goes brown, and the fish, they lose all their colour, in the dark, just shapes, like, flapping around me legs. They felt wet on me legs, even though I was in the water. Then it's quiet, and the shadow goes. The water's red and just me left. These guys, they died. They can save your life one day, for nothing. Not a cent, their families got. Not a fucking cent, and the bastards wanted me out again next day. Fuck that.'

'Jesus, mate. I'm sorry, but it doesn't make it right though, what you've been doing.'

'It's all I could do, diving.'

'Even so. The other night . . .'

'Oh yeah? And what if I hadn't done it. The problem would have gone away, hey? Don't be soft Artie.'

'So what *is* wrong, in your book, Denny. What *wouldn't* you do?'

'There's only one set of rules. Doesn't matter a fuck, what me and you do. Think I wouldn't work in a foundry? Or a pit? 'Course I fucking would. There aren't any. This is Slipp, Artie.'

I can see his desperation. His eyes are flitting everywhere, not resting on me. I can't trust him. You've heard his deceptions. Three years he's been lying to me. He does it too well. He's a danger. I was right. I'm learning. At least he's here for me to keep an eye on.

Meantime, there's more work to be done. You can't allow yourself to be distracted. I'm waiting for Madelaine to come out of the bathroom. There's time before dinner to make an adjustment to the database. I've got to raise a new card: Christian, Des.

* * *

'We could have a party. A drinks party,' I say, getting into bed with Denny's snoring humming up, under the carpet from downstairs.

'What?'

'Not family, just our friends.'

'Artie. We don't know anyone, not drinks party people, not *our* friends. It would be a disaster.'

'Leave it to me.'

'You're a nutter. You're a . . .' and she leans over me, under the covers in the warm fug of our bodies, 'a bloody nutter.' She kisses me, with juniper strong and sweet on her breath. It makes her mouth cool and wet, kind of new. She thinks I haven't noticed, but I have. I'm alert to things that used to pass me by. There's new stuff on the floor. She wasn't wearing it when I left this morning. She'd called Cinnamon and she'd got changed after I'd left.

Her arms are coming round me, on my chest with a hand going down.

'Are you still going to that thing in Wales?' I ask.

'I don't know. Probably.' She's gone serious, tensing up.

'I want to come.'

'You!'

'Yes, me. What's wrong with that?'

'You won't know anyone.'

'All the more reason.'

'It's a memorial service, Artie. What's the problem? It's only for a couple of days.'

'You've never been before.'

'I know.'

'So what's different about this year?'

'Forget it, Artie.'

'I could run you down, wait for you. Bring you back. We could have a break.'

'What about the shop?'

'Sod the shop.'

'Artie, this isn't you. You never shut the shop. What about your mum?'

'Frankie's coming up.'

She's got her hands back on me and her chin on my chest, at the top of the covers. 'Just leave it, eh? It's only for a couple of days. Did you get the johnnies?' And a giggle spills out, naughty.

'No.'

'Oh well, let's improvise.'

But this time I take her, by the shoulders, pushing her into the covers. I'm doing this my way, before she gets herself onto me, but she swivels as she goes down. I'm making a real effort here, but it seems to come so naturally to her – these moves she hasn't practised on me. I can smell her as she comes round, gluey on my chin and circling for my mouth, with my cock already in hers. It's hardness vibrates under the sound of 'mmm' that she's making. Then her thighs close in on my head and all I can hear is the noises of my own insides, like the sea coming in.

She's asleep straight away. After. The way women snigger about men's response to hormone release. In my case it's Madelaine's mouth that tastes of drink. Madelaine who's asleep straight after and leaving me to think it over.

She's calling all the shots. Last month she came home late, said she'd been to the doctor.

'I'm coming off the pill, Artie,' she'd said. 'The doctor said I should, for a while. He said . . .'

'He?'

'Yes, he . . .'

'You talk to a man about . . . did he . . . did he?'

'Examine me? Grow up, Artie. He's a doctor. What does it matter?'

'Nothing, I suppose. I just . . .'

'Anyway, I'm coming off it for a while. You should be pleased. It'll help when I want a baby. If you're on too long it can be bad. I thought you'd be pleased.'

'When *you* want a baby?'

'Me, us, whatever. You'll have to get some johnnies.'

'Madelaine!'

'That's what we used to call them, remember?'

Of course I do. Like when we went to Stratford, the Easter before she left me, that first time. She sent me in for a twelve pack. 'Someone's in for a treat,' the man in the shop had said, with Madelaine waiting outside to giggle as I brandished them in the High Street. We were like honeymooners, except that it had been an end, of sorts, not a beginning.

'What about, you know, something else.'

'A cap? Nah. Tried that before, it was a disaster.'

'When?'

'I don't know, when I was at Bristol. It kept popping out.' She's giggling. Giggling with the wrong person. 'Remember?'

'No.'

' 'Course you do. You're going senile.'

I'm not, but in any case, she's trying to get me to wear rubbers, 'for a few months'. Like the way you'd protect someone you were probably still fond of. She had put herself on my mouth, and I'm not sure if you can get it like that. I'll have to check. With her being drunk, she might have forgotten, or not bothered, or risked it. Whatever, there's plenty to worry about.

9

'Don't be ridiculous, Artie. It starts at seven thirty.'

'You could come home before you go. I would. We should eat together more often. We used to.'

'We'll have breakfast together, then. Do us a fry up.'

'That's not what I mean.'

'What do you mean, Artie?'

'It's only half an hour, anyway. Less the way you drive.'

'Half an hour each way, and I'm busy. There's some shopping I want to . . . fuck it! I don't have to explain. Drop it Artie. Just stay out of my way. Sometimes Artie, I . . . I . . . fuck it.'

I'm not going to cook her breakfast. Sod her. I've got to check the bag, which isn't a problem because she'll spend forever in the bathroom. I shouldn't. I'll be better off not knowing what she'll be showing. Practically everything from the look of things, in something she's never worn when we've been out.

I never used to do this. This sort of thing. I'm only responding to the need, which I missed for all that time. There's nothing weird about this. It seems weird, to see it in black and white. But it feels right, justified. She's providing the need. I don't know when the need to do this started, only when I picked up on it – with the letter, and the postcard, and all the obvious things from further back, and the truth underneath what's going on now. Was there a single point? When I should have noticed? I'll know soon.

Don't you think I'd like to see her look this way? Wearing these things she has prepared, pre-packed for an evening away from me. An object of desire. Of course I would. I want to be proud of her again, like I used to be. All I want is how it used to be. To have a chance of not doing whatever it was I might have done to set it off. I can't have that chance, though. But now it's done, you can't ignore the signs. You've got to do what you can to stop it being worse.

There are stockings in the slim box that should have said 'tights'. Ten denier, 'midnight gossamer'. I mean, what does she need with those if nothing's going on. I've got my hand in, making my arm, which is more or less completely hairless, look sexy. I think so. I check the box. 'Stay-ups, for maximum freedom, for all occasions.' What the hell is that supposed to mean? The bathroom door is opening and I'm into her top drawer with a panic, taking a box off the top. 'Tights,' that's good enough. No time to check the denier but the box is going into the bag which zips too noisily.

'What are you up to?' she asks.

'What?' I've still got the stocking on my arm, tucked behind my back. 'Nothing. What do you mean?'

She's gone straight to her dressing table, bending down to

the mirror and making wet noises with her lips. I can practically see her pants the way she's bending. She shouldn't be
wearing that for work, let alone what she's got planned for
tonight.

'Mean? What do I mean! What is wrong with you. What
are you up to?'

'What?'

'Today! Jesus, Artie. What are you doing today?'

'Oh, nothing much.' I've got the stocking off my arm,
under the pillow. I remember Cinnamon – my secret
appointment. With Madelaine still on my tongue and in the
tiny gaps between my gums and teeth, I remember that I'm
going for my first taste of therapy today.

'Get up,' she says.

'What?'

'I want to make the bed.'

'I'll do it.'

'You won't.'

'I will,' I say, blundering excuses to myself, working out
how I'd explain why the stockings are there.

'Make sure you do. Are you all right?'

'Fine.'

'If you say so.' She's got the bag, bending down to kiss me
on my forehead, matter-of-fact, the way she does it.

'Don't wait up, and don't forget my present.'

She's gone, leaving me in the trail of her expensive scent
which was spiced, with lemon cutting through. A smell you'd
want to get onto yourself.

I got her present weeks ago for Christ's sake.

There's plenty to do, now she's gone. I'm running a bath,
and filling in the Lane, D card. I'm not ready to relegate him
to the safe zone, yet. Not while he's so handy, under both
our noses.

The water's scorching, too hot to get into. So I get in, letting out a shriek and feeling my blood rush. I run the hot water again, to a count of five, so it's too hot to bear. I can feel my pores opening up, like steaming clams. I've got to be clean. No smells, anywhere. I don't know what Cinnamon will need to do with her oils.

Next, I'll pack the clothes that Madelaine bought for my birthday. Trendy clothes which you'd never get for yourself. 'Sometimes', she'd say, 'I think your mum still gets your clothes, while I'm not looking.' I wish she did, but it's all down to me, these things that disappoint her about me. But today, for her friend, I'll be wearing the clothes that a man she'd fancy would wear. Clothes she had bought me, to improve me, when Madelaine and a glitzy assistant talked about me in a public place as though I wasn't there. A shirt with no collar and linen trousers and a waistcoat that has lapels. This is what I'll be wearing by the time I leave the shop.

Next, I've got to deal with Denny. I know what I'll do with him. It's a deceit – exciting, like a game we'd have played when we were kids. It's not a game for Denny. The stakes are too high for him, if they find him here. And me, come to think of it.

'Jesus Denny, what've you been doing in here?'

'Sorry mate, not been eating right.'

'Open a window, will you. Listen, you know Madelaine wants you out.'

'Yeah.'

'Well, you can't can you? There is nowhere, right?'

'Right.'

'You can stay. Upstairs. In the loft.'

'She'll know.'

'No she won't. As long as you don't move round when

she's in. She's out tonight anyway. It'll be OK. Just keep quiet in the evenings, when she's here.'

The things that Madelaine doesn't know about me are expanding, multiplying. I'm on the move. I'm changing.

The bell jangles. I don't know why I'm coming in two days before Christmas. No-one in their right minds is buying fish today. There's been a frost overnight and the shop is freezing cold. It's even money for a white Christmas now, according to the radio. There is nothing on the steel and marble to soften the chill, just blades and stainless steel dishes and trays. In the back I flick the heaters on and scrub down again, until the water runs hot and my arms go red, with a grey face in the mirror, between the mottles. There's no point putting too much out, so I just get some cod and plaice and haddock from the freezer. I'm done in ten minutes, ready for action, ready to wait, so I put on a tape in the back and leave the door open so the King's College choir can soothe my silence with their carols. It makes me feel sad, but I leave it because I don't feel Christmassy yet and I want to. It's a way of coping with the situation. You can make it better by getting it to be melancholic. I like the word.

It's quiet, too quiet. My mind's on the wander again. Ranting at itself, so I get some herrings out. I can fillet them, get them into some oil and lemon and dill, for the buffet, on Boxing Day. They're fiddly to do, even for me, with their tiny bones. But mainly it's their oil that makes life difficult. They're viscous. I slide the knife through the skin and the smell releases. I put my finger into the slit and its flesh swells around me, skin peeling back. I probe, slowly. My eyes have closed. Its juice is slick, sliding me over the ribbing of its bones. It could be cartilage. I open my eyes.

The way I've cut it, not right through, like a gash, it could be . . . It could be.

The bell jangles again, and in comes Nana Gill, cursing behind her walking frame, moving slowly with her six legs in no kind of sync. She's banging it into the glass panels of the door – on purpose is my guess.

'Hi Nana.'

She grunts, coming to a halt, puffing her cheeks and pointing at the street through the plate window with a jabbing finger. This is all I need, but I can't say 'no'. No-one says 'no' to Nana Gill. Complete strangers might try it, once, but you don't really get them in Slipp, and Nana has never left town, ever. So I take the chair round, with the cushion under my arm, and I try to help her sit down, but she pokes me in the ribs with her blue, chicken-skin knuckles, which is what she would have done if I hadn't tried to help her.

'Outlive you, soft lump. Off me.'

'How are you, Nana?'

'Friggin' police. Big ones. Black ones, with fences.'

'What?' So this was where my mum was getting her language.

'Friggin' big with fences. Not when your dad were lad.'

I could drop it, and leave her to build a fury while I found something to do in the back, or I could let her know I couldn't understand her, which would make her angry anyway.

'What's got a fence?'

'Daft lump. Like *his* wife. Mother. Where you get it. Should never've. Never've.'

My dad was forty when he married my mum: Mary O'Brien, twenty-two and me inside her. By forty, I now know, he had screwed practically every woman in Slipp under the age of fifty, and some over. God knows how many he'd got pregnant. I suffered tales at school and on the corners, when they'd tell me my dad had been with so-and-so's mum or sister, before I was born and since. I played football and had fights with the sons of mothers who'd let my dad have them. My mates would slouch off to houses my dad had been to, when he closed early, before and after my mum had got caught. But he was a popular man, outside the house. 'Life and soul' they'd say. 'Good lad, Pete.' He looked eighty years old on the day he died. A year before he'd have passed for forty. The ageing came to me in freeze-frame snatches between the first dates with Madelaine. Then exams, and I'd see him less and less. The changes got bigger and bigger. He got smaller and thinner. His viciousness faded. He didn't have strength for his anger. Then he died, on the day of my interview at the college I never went to.

But he chose to marry my mum, with me inside her, the first born – the one who agreed to step into his shoes, when he asked me with his dying breath to take care of things. When he abdicated the responsibilities he never had. She'd been a virgin moments before she'd got caught with me – so I overheard my Grandma Delores say. They were arguing when she'd been called round to patch up her daughter. She'd been a respectable, Catholic girl. My dad wasn't forced to marry her. He wanted to, for some secret reason that stayed his secret. Whatever, he got to bring us both up: me and Frankie, his two little 'papist bastards'.

My dad told me once that Delores O'Brien was a 'prossie'. He said they ran her out of Ireland when she got pregnant with my mum, but I wasn't to tell my mum that I knew. He'd forgiven her, and so should I. Lovely bloke, my dad. He was vindictive enough to die before his mother – this Nana Gill he's left behind for us to look after. My mum is good to her, says she's an old character and I should listen to what she says. It's OK for her, I'm the one who has to listen to how my mum ruined my father's life. When I can understand what the hell she's talking about. She's barking mad, the old woman on my father's side. It could skip a generation. You could build a genetic case for the way I am, the way I sometimes feel I could be.

They gave me my first guilt, these grandmas of mine. For liking the one more than the other, which I would have thought is a pretty unoriginal sin. My mum told me I was bad, that there was something 'unnatural' about me to be like that – as I kicked and screamed my way to the Gill house. She slapped me for saying I didn't like my father's side. Easy to see now why she'd do such a thing.

'Back! Back here. Cars, big. Big!'

'What?'

'Big car fences.'

'Oh Jesus. You mean the police vans. They've got grilles on the windows. To stop them getting smashed. There's been a big fight, Nana. On the Estate, you must have heard.'

'Friggin' police.'

'What do you want? What fish?'

'What fight?'

'On the Estate.'

'Far away one? Which way one?'

'Don't worry, Nana. It's on the Nelson, not near you.'

'Big one?'

'Yes, that's right. Look, I'm going in the back. Do you want some tea?'

'Soft lump. Like his mother.'

I go into the back, and check the clock. Too early, but I take the rum down from the cabinet and pour a tot into my mug. It has a picture of two teddies inside a heart. They are kissing. Madelaine only used it once, and the handle had come away. I found it in the bin one morning.

'Haddock!' Jesus. At least this meant she'd be going. 'Do right. Like your Grandad. Soft lad. No bone ones.'

I know she doesn't want haddock. She hasn't eaten it since the last of her teeth went. She'll only eat yellow fish now, the colour of the whites of her eyes and the thin hair that is stuck to her scalp. But I can't be bothered, so I do her a bit of haddock and take it in the back, where I drink the rum without bothering to pour coffee over it. I take a vacuum sealed bag from the freezer with the yellow fish and a nob of butter inside. I'm putting it into a bag and going back to see her out of the shop. As she goes, she's saying 'friggin' police on the big one. Friggin' fences.' And then 'me do, me do, leave! Soft lad', when I try to help her up to leaning on her frame. She goes off, crumpling into her frame and out again, like a caterpillar. Like a mental, moaning caterpillar someone made from wool and metal. Do caterpillars have teeth?

Three fifteen and I'm clearing away, two hours early and with less than twenty quid in the till, so my conscience is clear. My conscience *is* clear. I'm only going for some oils and a bit of therapy. That's as much as I know about what Cinnamon does. With the trays empty and shiny, and the shutter pulled down, I've got forty-five minutes to change into what Madelaine would like me to look like, and to do my hair the way she says I should. There's nothing wrong with it, what I'm doing, because it's Madelaine's friend that I'm trying to fit in with. In this particular case I'm making changes she'd approve of.

Four o'clock and I'm ready, as ready as I know how to get myself. The rum has been in and out of my mug twice, without coffee, to relax me. I flick the switch from tape to radio and listen to an arts programme that Madelaine would listen to when it's repeated tonight, except she won't be in tonight. I'm killing time before I can go to Jasmine Cottage, between the pylons and the motorway. It's only three miles along the Railing Road, on the way to Town. The last thing I want is to be early. I want to do this properly.

The bell goes out front, as I'm about to slip out the back, to my car. I should leave it, but it might be a regular. They'd deserve an explanation at least. I can't let them see me like this, so I put on my coat and button it up, and pull my hair forward against the grip of the gel that makes me feel fake.

I shouldn't have bothered. It's not a regular. It's a man, for starters, and wearing a long, woollen coat, expensive, so it can't be one of my customers. He's got his back to the door and I could leave it. I should, but I think about it for too long, because he turns round and I get caught, looking furtive, probably. I know him. But he recognizes me first with a wave and three moves of the mouth which probably say 'Hi, Artie.'

'Des. Sorry, I was just off out,' I say as I unbolt the door, stepping back to let him come in, which he does, with a swagger, his cashmere tails brushing past me.

'Trade not so good?'

'Sorry?'

'Shutting up early, aren't we?'

'It's Christmas, slow time of year. I've got plenty to do.'

'Good to see you, the other night. Didn't realize you were married to Maddie. Different name, eh?'

'I don't follow.'

'Lots of women do it these days.'

'Do what?'

'Gill. She didn't take the name, not at work anyway.'

I didn't know. Such a basic thing, and a tosser like Des could swan into my shop and let me in on the secret.

'Why would you . . . why would you know my name, hers, anyway?'

'From the rent roll. I'd have remembered. Gill, I know. Hesketh I know. What I didn't know was that Madelaine Hesketh is Mrs Arthur Gill.' He laughs and I smile, out of politeness even though I don't want to. He's smoking a cigar, and the cold air is filling up quickly. A grey wafer of ash falls on my clean floor.

'What rent roll?'

'The one you're on, from the parade. You're the only one left. Easy to spot.'

'You're my landlord? Jesus. You're the one who's trying to get me out?'

'I wouldn't put it that way.'

'I'm not going.'

'Slow down, Artie. We can talk about this.'

'No we can't. Look I'm in a hurry.'

'Twenty-five grand you can have, and a year rent free in my development in Town. You know the Phoenix. Nice units they are.'

'I've got to go.'

'And I'll forget about all the dilapidations too. As a favour for Maddie.'

'What dilapidations?'

He's handing me an envelope with a smile on his face: a slit of a smile more like a grimace, that shows no teeth.

'They're scheduled here. It's just a draft. Didn't want to embarrass you with anything too official. Twenty grand's worth according to my man, could be more. It's down to you. You've let this place go, Artie. You'll be better off in a new shop.'

'I won't. And I haven't let it go. This place is immaculate, it's been in my family for sixty years.'

I hand him back the envelope, but he's playing with the buttons on his coat, leaving me standing there feeling small with my arm extended and my hand beginning to shake.

'New Year's Eve, Artie. I need this place empty and your lease surrendered. Me? I'm not that fussed, but my accountant says I'll save a small fortune in tax if I can free up the site this year. He makes the decisions, you see. I just make things happen. The small things. Like this.'

'I'm staying.'

'Calm down. Face up to it, Artie, you're going. Look, because you're Maddie's bloke, and if you're out by New Year's Eve, I'll give you thirty. How about that.'

He's stepped up towards me. I can see the pits in his face. He looks unclean, up close, but it's a look which I know is attractive, to a certain kind of woman.

'No! Now go.'

'OK, OK. I'm going, but make sure you behave. Do the right thing. Be sensible. This isn't a legal matter. I need the site. Whatever the lease says, or the schedule, or the amount of money, you'll be out by New Year's. Accept that. It's a fact. You may as well make a bit of cash out of the deal.' He pats me on the cheek, twice and hard with a slapping sound. His hands are warm and clammy as he does it in the chill of the shop. 'Be a good lad. You can have a clean start. Merry Christmas.'

Clean start? What does he mean, saying it as though he knows my situation. And what would I do with a clean start anyway? It sounds good. Is there such a thing, after all this time, so much mess to leave behind. It feels too late for a start, clean or otherwise. The shop's all I've worked for, it's the bad lot I've made the best of. I can't leave Slipp anyway, with my mum the way she is. Nothing clean about that kind of start. And then there's Madelaine.

The real problem with Des's offer, is it's exactly what I want, what I know I need. An impetus to move away. It doesn't remove the real obstacles though, which have nothing to do with money. Even without my mum, if I did leave, it would set things in motion. I'm not ready for that. Not until I can gauge Madelaine's reactions.

No shop, no Madelaine, and still stuck in Slipp. What kind of a start would that be?

He's gone. Left me to my thinking, which I can't get in order. He's made me late too. Late for Cinnamon now. She wanted me relaxed and I won't be.

10 _____

Des has made me late, which annoys me. It annoys me more than his threats, which I'm realizing are serious. He's made me rush, against the headlights and weaving through traffic to get there on time, but I'm already late, which will make me late later on, and there's plenty to do. I have to be on time to observe my Ms Hesketh.

Going north to head south, the way you have to in order to swing round onto the Railing Road, the police are flagging me down. They want me to join a queue of cars, waiting to be searched. Now the car is stopped I can see that the rain is in fact snow, weak snow that won't stick but I stop my wipers to give it a chance, and I turn up the music. It's a chant that I lifted from Madelaine's car, to see, hear, what she gets up to. It's soothing, and forms a thin wall of sound, many-layered but brittle, and too precious to fend away the impatient revving and radio crackles outside.

It's not long before I have to wind the window down, but not so soon that the flakes are beginning to stick, good for them. They pucker up like the penny falls when I lower the window.

'Artie lad, how you doing?' It's Benny Unsworth, my year from school. 'Not seen you for ages.'

'I'm all right. How about you? Still wed?'

'Yeah. She's due in Feb.'

'Well done, mate.'

'How about you?'

'Me?'

'You got any kids?'

'No. Not yet.'

'You do right, mate.' What does he mean by that? 'Seen your missus, 'bout half hour ago, come through the block. She's changed.'

'Changed?'

'Don't get me wrong, looks cracking, she always did, lucky bastard. Hey up lad, better keep this moving, on you go. Come up for a drink, after Christmas. Friday, eightish, we're having a do. We're on Helvellyn, number twenty-three.'

He's as good as said it, in the way he'd said it, what I've always known and never heeded: that you don't marry the pretty ones.

'Hey, Benny? What's all this in aid of?'

'Oh, they let young Stevie Lane off Estate dinner-time. We're making sure the lid stays on. They're saying Johnny McCaffery's back.'

'I heard.'

'It'll kick off if he is. You ask me, sooner he catches up wi' Denny the better. Else it'll be a bloodbath.'

'Benny?'

'Yeah?'

'What, what's behind all this? The rioting. Really.'

'Jesus, Artie. Not here. Come on, best move this line along. See you Friday.'

He's laughing, but it's not funny. Denny's in my loft.

I can't believe what's happened.

It's ten o'clock. I've found the wine bar they're in. I've got a long wait ahead, which is bad because there's too much to think about, four hours on from when I left Cinnamon's place.

She was waiting when I got there, opening the door as I locked up the car and waiting in the doorway in a thin, flowing gown that the wind blew against her so I could see the outline of her body: thin legs and a small curve for her belly, and the triangle mound between. The snow left wet flakes on me and she patted them away from my shoulders and hair, on tiptoes and smiling.

'Can I get you anything?' she'd asked. 'I'm doing some tea.'

'Please. Whatever you're having.' She showed me into a room at the back, along a passageway with tapestries on the walls, and candles flickering from green metal brackets on either side of each door. The doors were painted in bright colours of purple and orange and turquoise. There was a light smell of patchouli in the house, and a different, earthy smell on her. She left me in a room that was panelled in light oak, stained green, with the same bright coloured doors, and stained glass windows, cushions everywhere. There was a long bench by the window, covered in creaseless white linen with a pillow at one end. Quiet music from the east came piping in from somewhere – voice noises without words, and instruments I couldn't place.

She returned, carrying two steaming, irregular-shaped mugs.

'Here you are. It's camomile. Hope you like it.'

'Hmm. Thanks. Maddie has it.' It tasted better than when I'd had it before – cleansing and bright.

'How do you feel?'

'Feel? Oh, fine.'

'Good. You're not tense?'

'Me? No, not at all.'

'Good. I thought we'd start with some cards. It's a way of relaxing, to a higher state, while we get to know each other. It helps me connect, with you, part of the undressing,' she said with that purring half laugh.

She brought the cards to a table that had an iron chandelier above, with candles which she lit. The cards were in a carved, wooden box and wrapped in black silk. She said a rhyme of foreign words as she unveiled them.

'Put the light off, please Artie. Over there.'

She sat me opposite her and explained how the cards worked, which I didn't hear, because all the time she was talking and laying out the cards she didn't take her eyes from me, which scared and excited me. It left me concentrating on how not to look away, or blink. I felt myself going tense, stiff.

She set out the cards in a strange pattern, one face down in the middle. She flinched when she turned it over.

'What is it?' I asked.

'That is the Querent card.' She pointed at an image of a handsome man, suspended by one foot from a tree. His face was serene. Coins spilled from a purse he was holding.

'Who is the Querent?'

'You are.'

'What is he doing?'

'It can mean many things, depending on the other cards, and you.'

'What is he called?'

'He is the Hanged Man. It's not important, without the other cards.'

'The Hanged Man? Sounds grim.'

'No. Not at all. He signifies sacrifice. Dedication to a cause.'

'Is it . . . is it, a bad sign?'

'No, not on it's own. Artie, what is your birth sign?'

'Pisces.'

'Ah, water.' She smiled, and took another card. Her almond eyes locked on it for an instant and released, but with a furrow left behind. She turned it over to me, to reveal the image of another man, in a cloak of feathers, with piles of coins around his feet. 'The Knight of Coins,' she said. 'An earth sign. The sign of a practical man, gentle and kind and dependable. Are you starting a journey, Artie? It could be . . . a change in your life?'

'No. Not that I know of,' I tried to smile, but she looked stern, concerned.

'Is your life in a rut, Artie?'

'No.'

'You have to be honest. Come this way. We've gone far enough with the cards. Are you relaxed?'

'Yes.'

'Totally?'

'Well . . .'

'There are some exercises we can do. Undress. I'll prepare the oils.'

'Undress?'

'Your shirt, and trousers.' I expected her to smile, but she didn't. She left the tension, untouched.

There's some activity outside the wine bar. The sound of laughter comes into the car, through gaps in the thin-walled chant. Men in suits and girls in short skirts come spilling onto the pavement, some going away down the street and leaving two pairs that go into clinches. They're kissing with windmill arms that ruffle hair and coats, and they lean back, against the walls, with the girls' legs straddling. They syncopate, in two slow grinds, edging like crabs into doorways where hands disappear into clothes. One of the couples break off and smile, look into the next doorway and walk away down the street. The other pair moves more quickly, with the girl's legs off the floor. He's got her bottom in his grip. She's looking down the street with her hands pushing down on his hips, quicker and quicker and quicker until she cranes down to kiss him, on the mouth. I can see him check his watch. She doesn't see.

It makes me want to go inside, to find Madelaine and tell her that something terrible has happened to the house, or to family, that she has to come with me. I would like for there to be something wrong that would bring her away. And there is, but I can't tell her that.

*   *   *

When Cinnamon came back, with her oils in blue bottles, I was standing by the crisp linen table, wearing only my underpants and wishing I hadn't come – to find out I was a Hanged Man in a rut, and to lie practically naked on a table in Madelaine's friend's house.

'Good. Lie on your stomach please, Artie, to start. You look tense. Hmm. Very tense.' She traced her hands over my back and shoulders, gently with her nails swirling light patterns, making my back and arms feel like liquid. 'That's better. Much better.'

I could feel my back getting warm and full, moving to the shoulders and down the arms, then from the back to my hips, down into the legs. I couldn't recognize the smells of the lotions: complex, many-layered. My eyes went heavy. I felt my pelvis sink into the linen, melting into its coarse, random fibres and making it heavy, making it swell down towards the floor. Cinnamon murmured a soft rhyme. It repeated as she ran her hands deeper into my tissue and her voice came at me, distant. 'Turn over,' she said. I couldn't move. I felt her slide a hand between me and the linen and I rolled over. My eyes were shut and I wanted to open them but couldn't as her hands came into my chest and stomach and the front of my thighs, and the insides, with her breath chilling on the oil that was all over me.

'Does that feel good?' A slow smile spread across me. Her voice sounded distant and dull, echoing through empty halls far away. I wanted to nod, but couldn't. She asked again, this time with her breath on my face, and a wetness on my mouth, opening with a sweet tongue inside. Me not moving at all, and her mouth moving down with a whispering rustle of silk and a purring sound. The table creaked, with more silk rustling, then it came onto my chest cold and peeling away, with a new smell coming on me, with her taste, which was just like cinnamon and a warmth now, wet on my cock which I could feel rising high into softness, then falling and rising. A syrup in my mouth and a brushing on my chin, faster and deeper, then slowing, with a gliding wetness on my lips. A slow spasm and a pulse, with colours of orange and yellow and purple trailing on the back of my eyelids, which flickered, light coming in, then a shadow, and a kiss as I opened my eyes and saw hers – dark and wide and glistening, with almond tears in their corners.

I know it happened, because it left sweet stains round my mouth. I thought it might have been a dream, from the trance. But not when I saw her, going away from me with tears in her eyes, and gathering her robe in a hunch that looked like shame.

'Go,' she said. 'You'd better go now. It was my fault, not yours. I took advantage of you. I'm sorry.'

I did go, dressing quickly and shaking. She curled in a cushion on the floor, not seeing me to the door. Then the worst.

'Can I . . . can I, see you . . . come here . . . again?'

'I don't know,' she said with me not knowing why I'd said it and hating myself already.

That was before I'd stopped at the petrol station, and bought toothpaste and deodorant and scoured her from me. Before I came to watch Madelaine – which I still had to do, despite my aberration and the guilt. I have to do it, this catching up, because, you see, nothing has changed. Whatever I may have done, it wouldn't stop her from being able to break me. It doesn't make me any more able to survive her leaving.

*   *   *

I'm trying to push away the sad, dirty thrill of it. I can't rationalize it. I can describe it. I've got words for what happened, to let you know what it was like: the unreal sensations, the awful thrill of it. Pulsing, gush and come; flesh, hair and essences; smells and silk and skin. In my nostril hairs; gelling with my spit; rustling sounds, bouncing in playback. The warm germs and salt of someone else's mouth in yours, the powder of their flaked flesh on your palms, under the finger nails, the glow of used skin.

What I have no words for, what is my pictureless image – is the guilt I can't articulate. It is formless. Nowhere to send it, nothing inside to absorb it. No faith, no vocabulary. I feel contrite, but don't know what contrition is. I feel like a hollow cross. I would echo if you tapped me. What does Madelaine feel like, when . . . when she's done it? But it's not the same. It doesn't change anything.

*   *   *

The man from the doorway is back, the one who checked his watch. He's with a girl, again. A different one, and I think she's one of the ones who left about half an hour ago. They go past the wine bar, and he stops at the doorway. It's 'Pipers', the 'Gentleman's Tailor', where they sell clothes that even the old people don't buy any more. My dad was well dressed, but never from the Gentleman's Tailor. He had seven Sunday suits which he wore in turn. When he got a new one, from his friend at the undertaker's, it would go in the loft for a year, until the smell of embalming fluid had gone. Then it would come down and he'd select one to pass on, to a mate who wouldn't have to go to Piper's.

He's trying it on again, in the doorway, with a coaxing stroke to the head while his other hand is working, lower and lower until she pushes him away with a laugh, and she walks off down the street with him following, his hand straight on her arse when he catches up, and this time she lets it stay.

I read somewhere that men are more promiscuous, un-naturally monogamous, because the male orgasm is less satisfying than a woman's. Women can come all the time: for ages, riding on the edge of it, and again straight away; they can 'go off like a fucking rocket'. Some even cry or grunt or miaow. They say that for most women it's enough to have one man. I don't know about that. For men, who when they do come it is brief and then over (you can even see, measure it, in cc's or fluid ounces), it can't be allowed to be the main thing. So they say. It has to come with a chase and some danger and variety – a naughtiness. I can see how that could be the case. So that makes it all right for the man in his doorway, maybe. But it doesn't make me feel less bad about earlier, because I'm not supposed to be like that. It makes it harder to expect Madelaine to be good. If I, who am happy with my lot, and don't even want other women, can do something like that, what about Madelaine, who is changing before my eyes, and in everybody's estimation.

There's a crowd coming out of the wine bar: three men in black shirts, and tieless, with baggy trousers, and ponytails. Three women follow in long, straight black skirts and close-cropped white hair. They're in a bundle, the six of them and followed by three others. They look right together: Madelaine and the two men she's talking to, one of them with electric blue hair and a chiselled face. He's wearing a shirt with no collar and linen trousers and waistcoat with lapels, like she bought for me. I slide down in the seat and pull my woollen hat low over my eyes, just seeing Spike from the chest up. The six walk off, shouting down the street while Spike hails a cab for Madelaine and the other one. All options are open to all of them.

It's different for men, it's different for girls. They're all the same.

11

'What about Madelaine? What if she comes in?' says Denny.

'Sod her,' I say, for the second time in a day. I don't mean it. I just want her to come home, away from temptations I can't imagine her resisting.

'Artie, what's going on, man?'

'Pass us the booze. Ta. What's this stuff again?'

'Mescal. Whoever gets the last slug has to eat the worm.'

'What's the worm?' I ask.

'It's got mystical powers, hallucinogenic.'

'Jesus. That's the last thing I need.'

'What's wrong?'

'Ah, nothing. What time is it?'

'Three.'

'She's having an affair.' I regret it as soon as I've said it.

'Madelaine? How do you know?'

'I know. What would you do, Denny? If . . .'

'She's not, don't be . . .'

'If someone was threatening you.'

'What?'

'You'd kick shit out of them, right?'

'Artie. What the fuck are you talking about?'

'They're trying to get me out of the shop.'

'What? Who is?'

'Des. He gives Madelaine money for her plays. And he's trying to get me out of my shop.'

'Des you say.'

'Yeah. Christian. Des Christian. You know him?'

'Nah. Give us a swig.'

'I saw you, and him, the other night . . . he was in the Dog.'

'What?'

'You *can* help me, can't you Denny?'

'What are you talking about, Artie lad?'

'You're my best mate. Do you know what that shop means to me?'

'It's only a shop, Artie.'

'I gave up everything for that place. I stayed in this fucking shit hole and I made it work. Pass us the bottle.'

'Here you go,' he says, leaning forward on crossed legs and falling off balance. 'You're just being paranoid, mate.'

'Oh no I'm not. It's real.'

'Just leave, then.'

'I gave up everything. Got stuck here. But I've made something of it. If I went I'd have nothing.'

'What? You got plenty Artie. Take his money and go.'

'Money?'

'Yeah. Didn't you say he was giving you money. He must be, for you to be going. Yeah?'

'I didn't say anything about money.'

'I just assumed,' he says.

'What would I do if I left this place. If I didn't have the shop? What about Madelaine, my mum.'

'Madelaine would leave. She hates Slipp.'

'Hates it?'

'Always has.'

'She didn't used to.'

'Come on, Artie. It's time for a change, mate.'

'Don't you think I want to. I'd love to get out of this place.'

'Well do it,' he says.

'I can't. The time's not right. I need your help, Denny. He's going to get me out before New Year. I've got to hang on, just for a while.'

'I would, mate, but . . .'

'It's OK.'

'I would, it's just that . . .'

'It's OK.'

I let it go. He's my best mate. Even if I'm not his; even if I could tell that he was lying about a few things. I'm getting clued up on deception. Picking up on it, around me. And after what happened at Cinnamon's, I'll be needing some of my own. I can see now that each one, each small deception can have a thousand repercussions, touching every bit of your life. They can ambush you any time – ricochets from any-where. The only shield is another deceit, then another, trenches around the truth. Too many and the whole day could become a lie. I'm beginning to see how clever you'd have to be, not to get caught. And you've got to lose respect, too. Respect for yourself. You've got to acknowledge there's something wrong with your life, something that needs to be hidden.

Denny does know Des. He knew I'd been offered money. He wouldn't have helped me, even if he could, which he knew damn well he could. He wants me to leave. He's got some kind of vested interest. And now he knows my suspicions and dilemmas. I'm getting sloppy, giving too much away, because of the drink, with its mystical worm.

* * *

The birds are cooing under the eaves, but it's not them that have just woken me up. It's the sound of a car in the driveway, then the door shutting and the rapid fire clip-clop sound of female heels to the door.

'Fuck it! Denny, stay here.'

'What?'

'You let me fall asleep up here, you dozy git.'

I drop down from the trap door, replace the cover and dive into the loo as she follows the sound of her calling, up the stairs, banging on the door.

'Artie! Where have you been?'

'What? That's rich. Where have you been?'

'I've been out.'

'I know that.'

'What are you doing in there? Come out.'

'Where've you been?'

'For bacon and eggs. I've got a hell of a hangover.'

'You stayed out all night, what the fuck do you expect?'

'Artie. What are you talking about? And why are you swearing, it's not like . . .'

'You go out all night and . . .'

'I was back at four. We went to a club . . .'

'It's half past ten,' I say, losing track and groping for facts, pulling the chain, getting some time.

'Where have you been?' she asks.

'What?'

'Where were you all night? There's a change of clothes in a bag downstairs. Artie, what is going on?'

'Just a minute.' I should tell her that Denny's upstairs and that's where I was. But she'd kick him out. He's my best mate, and I want him here for observation and possible help. And you can't let people down like that.

'Come out, Artie.'

I'm trying to catch up, to get a grip on what's been going on. I'm opening the door. She's glowing, dishevelled, with her eyes smudged black and wearing a pair of my jeans, belted tight and gathering her into a two-lipped bulge that straddles the button seam.

'Artie, what's wrong?'

'Can we go to bed?' She's come up to me, hugging me. I can smell the night on her, under recent perfume.

' 'Course we can,' she says, pulling away and hitting me in the chest, playfully I think, 'but you were a bad boy last night.'

'What?'

'Last night. I had this dream, a horrible dream. You were a right old bastard. Come on.'

I can smell her on the unmade sheets, and I know she hasn't been lying to me, about coming home. I want Denny to be able to hear us, so he thinks there's nothing in the drink talking. Which isn't drink talking at all. But there'll be nothing to hear. She's fallen asleep on me. That's the way it sounds, so I curl into her and wait for myself to cave in.

* * *

It's Christmas Eve. More than half the day's gone without me realizing. I'm lethargic from the drink and the grease of Madelaine's well-meant, badly-cooked breakfast. The snow is falling again, still trying to stick, and the radio man tells me all bets are off for a white Christmas, which should make me feel happy. But the build up has been spoiled: no busy streets and carols and lights; no men on buses, drunk and unthreatening. Traditional things you haven't been able to get in Slipp for the last few years. It's all in the mall between here and the city. They pipe it in, portion controlled. It makes me mad that people fall for it, but they do.

'Let's go to the Phoenix,' she says.

'I hate it there, you know that.'

'There's nowhere else. There's still a few things I need to get.'

'I thought you were getting them last night, before the do.' And that is enough to burst the bubble, to bring back the man in the doorway, and her climbing into the cab with two men, probably showing her knickers to whoever sat opposite.

'I didn't have time.'

'You came back here. To Slipp, didn't you?'

'What? How . . .'

'I saw Benny, Benny Unsworth. The copper, our year, came to our wedding.'

'Yes. I know Artie, I *was* there.'

I waited for her to explain why she had time to come to Slipp, when she was supposed to be in the city, when she didn't have time to see me. If she'd told me, I would have cancelled Cinnamon, which would have been better all round. For everybody. Instead, there's a price to pay for that deception, for which she feels no need to explain. I don't know if that's a good thing or bad. Do lots of little deceptions make a big one? I think so. I don't think you can have one without the other. They go together like a horse and carriage.

'Artie!' She says it loud and looks annoyed. 'You're not listening to me, are you?'

'I'm tired.'

'What do you expect. Out all night, God knows where, with that wastrel friend of yours.'

'Sorry.'

'So, we'll go to the mall.'

'OK.' Which makes her smile. A moment earlier she had darkened eyes that were narrow, scanning for an argument. Now it's forgotten, which pleases me, sort of, but I don't like the way she can change her feelings so quickly.

'I'll buy you lunch,' she says.

'No, I'll buy you lunch.'

'Oh Artie. Sweet, the way you fall for it.'

'What? Fall for what?'

'You can't bear the thought of me supporting you, can you?'

'You supporting me?'

'If the day ever came.'

'What do you mean?'

'Relax. I don't mind. I like you looking after me.'

And the craziest thing is: if you'd seen her, saying it, you'd have believed she really meant it. Despite everything.

We passed a shop on the way into the mall: 'Dental Repairs, While U Wait.' It puzzled me. It made me wonder if I was missing something. If it's me that's crazy.

I'm watching us in the windows. Seeing her linking me, with her head on my shoulder, as we walk slowly in half-falling, lazy step. Our separate tirednesses are feeding each other. They're compounding, making us more listless, for each other's different reasons. It could be a trick of the lights, or a warp in the surface of the plate glass, but she seems to have a smile on her face: a soft, half smile. She must feel safe here. She wouldn't want him to catch her like this, with someone else – certainly not a husband she had grown apart from, who she was still fond of, but had stopped loving.

'What about something to eat?'

'Sure. I'm whacked,' she says without moving her head. Her breath is warm on my neck, and malty from drink, still. It smells illicit on her, making me treasure her more: for being something she shouldn't; something other people, who saw or half knew her, wouldn't think she was.

'Over there.' I nod to a set of empty plastic chairs cordoned off, with looping plastic chains, from the slow-moving tide of people. All the other cafés and restaurants have queues, waiting 'to be seated'. Anybody could see us here, marooned.

'Ma Tucker's? Oh Artie.'

'What's wrong with that? She used to be in Slipp, before they moved her out.'

'What about Le Croissant?'

'They've dumped her in here, after a lifetime. And when her rent free years run out, she'll make losses and they'll have her out.'

'I fancy a cappuccino. Let's go to Le Croissant.'

'I want some parkin. Some of Ma Tucker's.'

'Parkin?'

'You know, the taste of winter, bonfire night, the run up to Christmas.'

'You can get mincemeat filled croissants now, you know. They're gorgeous. We get them delivered at work.'

'What's wrong with mince pies?'

'Oh, go on then.'

There is no queue between us and the sad-looking woman in a chef's hat, behind the counter that's too high for her. She's aged ten years in the six months since she left the High Street.

'Hi, Mrs Tucker. How are you?'

'Artie! Madelaine, how are you both?'

'Fine. We're OK. How are you, you look well.' I can't stop it from sounding patronizing, because it is.

'Oh, middling. You still on the High Street?'

'Yes.'

'You stay there, lad. Don't fall for their blarney. They don't come here for loaves, or fish, or bread. All that's in the supermarket. I'll be busted in six months, when I start paying me rent. Forty years, for nothing. Five thousand they give me, for forty years. Stay put lad. Someone's got to dig their heels in. What can I get you?'

'Parkin. Two please, and teas.' I can feel Madelaine squirm as I order, but I give her a squeeze which is enough to keep her quiet.

The parkin comes, after two minutes of me saying how good it is, how you can't get it like this in the supermarkets. Ma's brought it to our table with a beaming smile and refusing to take our money.

'Made my day, seeing you both.'

The parkin is crisp and bubbly on top, dense at the bottom, where it still tastes of the bowl, not properly cooked and I get the taste of ginger and cinnamon and nutmeg in dry powder clumps. I force it down, but Madelaine practically spits out her first mouthful. I can't work out if it's always been awful and I've changed, or if Ma has lost it – the will to do it right.

'What was all that about, Artie? Before, about digging

your heels in. They're not trying to move you out are they?'

'Don't worry.'

'It wouldn't be a bad thing. A place here.'

'Not at the moment.'

'Why?'

'It's not the right time.'

'Wouldn't you love to get out of Slipp. We could move anywhere. Town, or into the country. A cottage.'

'Like Cinnamon.'

'Cinnamon?'

'Oh, I . . . Look, I don't want to move. I can't.'

'Artie, your mum would be all right. We'd make arrangements . . .'

'Leave it! Please, I'm sorry. It just wouldn't suit. What about *your* job, anyway?'

'My job?'

'You tell me nothing about what you get up to.'

'You're not really interested.'

'I am.'

'What do you want to know, then?'

'I don't know. I . . .' She's fallen for it. I do know what I want to know. '. . . what about that bloke, what's his name? The bloke we met the other night . . .'

'Des?'

'That's him. What does he do? He's not the theatre sort is he?'

'It's just a vehicle for his company, I guess. He's just a sponsor. Probably gives him a kick, too.'

'Why do you have to get involved with him?'

'It's my responsibility. People like Des are important these days. We've got to keep the sponsors sweet.'

'What a bummer.'

'Not really. He's quite fun, actually. He's a bit rough, but he's OK.' A bit rough. It appeals to some women. I can see that. 'I can see you're not really interested.'

'I am.'

'If you say so.' She's fidgeting in her bag and looking round. 'Why wouldn't you come here, to the mall? You'd do well. It's more lively than Slipp. Wouldn't be so lonely for you. You're the only one left now . . .'

'I've said. This place is . . . I just don't like it. I'm staying in Slipp.'

'I just thought you'd like a change.'

'What, like Ma Tucker. I wouldn't let them get to me, the bastards.'

'Who? What's going on, Artie?'

I've been sloppy again, letting too much out. She doesn't need to know any of this. It will make it easier for her to go, any disruption. Clean break.

'Hey, let's try out one of those croissants, yeah?'

'Who is trying to get you out, Artie.'

'No-one, no-one love. But if anyone did, well, I wouldn't want to go. Come on.'

'OK.' And it looks as though she believes it, which is surprising, because I'm not really the deceitful one.

I've got some of the base of the parkin stuck to the roof of my mouth with its spicy glue of oatmeal and nutmeg and treacle and cinnamon.

12

It's snowing. Hard and sticking, with a clean crunch underfoot when I go outside to get the coal. Which is unnecessary, because we've got central heating, and we're going out so we won't need the glow. But it's Christmas and having a fire is the way I want it to be: the building of it and the burnt winter smells it will make for the moments before we go.

There's an orange streetlight glow: big skied and muffled quiet by flakes in the air, dulling everything. Inside, there's an unwatched TV buzz while Madelaine gets ready for the table she was lucky to get, at Rascals. Rascals is the only wine bar in Slipp, which is as bad as you could probably imagine. We're going, even though it's not Madelaine's kind of place, and certainly not mine. 'At least we can walk home,' she'd said, 'we'll never get a cab on Christmas Eve.'

She's down from upstairs, looking terrific. The way you'd

be happy for your wife to look. No make-up, so as you'd notice, and nicely dressed. She's wearing a long skirt that hugs her bottom and thighs, but not showing anything, and a silk blouse that's loose and hanging from her breasts in watery folds. By the time we get there her nipples might be showing through. 'She's got great nipples your bird, Artie.' Johnny McCafferey had said it, ten years ago. 'How do you know?' 'Saw them in art. She was bending over. Blouse were open. Great nipples, like fucking saucers.' We'd just started going out and I didn't mind hearing it, quite liked it – the praise. But things like that, even said in the past, can be hard to live with. They repeat on you, once something's wrong. But at least she looks too good to touch, which is just as well – because later on she'll want to dance, and I won't, and I'll have to watch her from the table.

'What are you faffing with the fire for, Artie. We've got to be there in half an hour. It's Christmas Eve. They'll let the table go.'

'In Rascals? It's a dive.'

'I went to a lot of trouble to get it, Artie. I had to ask Des.'

'Des? I didn't know he owned it.'

'Didn't I tell you? He bought it a couple of months ago.'

'Oh.' It's all I can say.

'What's wrong?'

'I don't want to go.'

'Artie!'

'I don't feel so good.'

'Bloody hell Artie. What's wrong with you?'

'What's wrong with *me*?'

'Yes. What's wrong with *you*.'

'Nothing. I'll be all right. Come on.'

'Jesus Artie.'

*　　*　　*

We're wrapped up warm and it's good to be out. Slipp looks as grand as it gets, below us, scratching its way up the sides of its basin: lines edged with dark shadows on the snow. On this side, Top Side, it has shelved itself in channels of triangle roofs that come up the hill in steps from the High Street. Trying to get up the sides, not making it. It's like the teeth on a saw. To the left is the foundry, with its passed-over grime hidden away, for now. Far away, like building blocks, is the Nelson Estate set out in its crescent formation, like a sickle in cotton wool.

To see it from here, snowy and harmless, you'd never guess what the cold was covering up. What you can't see is that underneath, on the sloping cobbles and round the garbage greens, there's no money or jobs or peace of mind. Things are all right up here, on the private estates with our neighbourhood watches. We can keep an eye out from the ridges that circle it, far enough away not to hear the sirens. The rioting from the Nelson comes through radios, not curtains, which is why Madelaine and I almost busted ourselves to get up here, before I got the shop working properly.

It's fifteen minutes going down, to the top of the High Street where there's Rascals, an estate agent's, bank, post office, accountants, restaurant and beauty salon. Nowhere to buy anything. For that you've got to cross the divide, the no man's land ruled off with wire and boards and signs. If you want to buy anything, other than a stamp or wet fish, then it's in your car and off down the Railing Road. Even for the Nelson, whose cars balance on bricks above patches of oil. The Nelson had a shop until a year ago, when Mrs Blakeley finally left her son's dad, and a Patel from the city moved in. Nobody told him. He lasted a week, then they fired it.

Ryan Blakeley was in my class. Mrs Blakeley's son, he was

a bastard, technically. The teachers thought so and Thunder-cliffe would call him one. He didn't care that Ryan had to answer the door to a string of calling boyfriends, while she was in the shop. While his dad was in bed upstairs on rubber sheets because of what happened when some of his neighbours broke into his shop.

'What are you thinking about?'

'Nothing.'

'Liar. Your mouth was hanging open,' she said, laughing. Infecting me with it.

'Ryan Blakeley. Remember him?'

'Of course I do.'

Of course she does. But I'd hoped she'd say 'no', or at least hesitate.

'He was the first boy I ever kissed.'

'Oh. Right.'

'Jealous.'

'Me? Nah.'

'Liar. Anyway, he wasn't as good a kisser as you.'

Which isn't a great thing to say, because of course he wasn't. She chose me, didn't she – to go out with. If he was a better kisser she'd feel the need to assure me he wasn't, like she's just done.

'Anyway, what about Mandy Price?'

She's got something to be guilty about, because she's watering it down with my early history. Except I never kissed Mandy Price. It was Rebecca Tait, my first kiss. Prim and proper, she should have been pretty but wasn't. We just rubbed our shut mouths together when we were left next to each other at the Valentine's disco, when everyone else had copped off. There'd been open mouths and circling heads all around us, and some even going outside. I told Madelaine it had been Mandy Price because I knew Ryan Blakeley would have tried to go too far, the way Mandy Price would have expected, and by all accounts demanded. I'm not sure if Ryan Blakeley did get Madelaine outside. Chances are he did, because she doesn't know it wasn't Mandy Price, which she would if she'd have stayed inside. That little lie, which was told out of vanity, not fear, will be eleven years old in seven weeks.

'How far did you get, with Mandy Price?'

'Madelaine!'

'Go on. You told me once that you, you know . . .'

'What?'

'Don't come the innocent.'

'What are you on about?'

'So cute. I knew you didn't. I was your first.'

'I . . .'

'Don't deny it. So sweet. My virgin.'

'Shut up.'

'Your first. Your only.' She's linking me, with her snow damp hair in my collar and cheek. We're walking in falling step with the slope, and she stops, pulls away. 'I am the only one, aren't I?'

'"Course you are.'

'Liar.'

'What?'

'Oh Artie.' Her hand is on the back of my neck and pulling me down to her closing eyes, opening mouth. When she pulls away she's smiling. 'You're such an innocent.'

'Me? What about you?' Why say that. What a blunder.

'Me?'

'It's OK. I trust you. Don't answer. I'm sorry.'

And she doesn't answer. She does as I say, when she shouldn't. She doesn't get indignant the way she should. And we're walking in silence now. Hand in hand, limp. Just enough for things not to get bad, and letting the hill take us quickly away.

Rascals is heaving. It's so crowded you can't even tell it's a doss hole, which I can when I pass it every morning. Then, its plastic pine walls and garden furniture get their just deserts in the broad light of day. This is what Des thinks the people of Slipp deserve: the better off in Slipp at that.

He's here to greet us. 'Hi Maddie.' Her first. No surprise that he's leaning past me to take her by the hand, not stopping there and pulling her towards him with a kiss to the mouth, which I would say is more than a peck. She closes her eyes as she does it.

'Artie.' He's squeezing my hand. It's smaller than mine, but strong. He's not looking at me as he does it. He's following Madelaine as she hangs up her coat. 'We'd better have a chat, later on. You know,' he says, still looking at her.

'There's no point,' I say.

'Don't be silly, lad. Just a quick chat. No joke, Artie.'

But I'm walking away, into the music, which is too loud for the speakers and past its sell-by. White soul crap that matches Des's white tux with the wing collar shirt and red bow tie. He looks like what he is.

We've got a table on a platform at the side of the dance floor. The turkey and chips is brought to us in plastic baskets lined with kitchen towel, sodden waxy with grease. The turkey is cold in the middle and neither of us eat it. Madelaine makes some kind of an excuse for it. She sees a need to defend it.

Benny Unsworth is coming across, taking the next table. His wife follows him, pushing out her swollen belly in proud carriage of their unborn child.

'All right Artie. Madelaine.'

'All right Benny, Tricia,' I say.

The girls nod at each other. Tricia is glowing with achievement. Me and Benny know the girls don't get on. Tricia used to be a slag, and she knows Madelaine knows. Marrying Benny shook it off for most people in Slipp, not Madelaine. Having the baby doesn't carry weight with Madelaine, who had saved herself and isn't forgetting.

'You've not forgotten Friday night. Coming, aren't you?'

'Sure, thanks.'

We're having to shout, above the music and the Hi Ho singalong from the floor. It's ten o'clock and the bouncers are double-teaming on the door. There's a turning of heads to a mêlée at the entrance. Des moves across behind two other lads in dinner suits. A gap clears and I see a big and familiar frame leaning down, with his hand on Des's shoulder, whispering in his ear.

I can't help smiling. This is bad news for all of us trying to enjoy Christmas Eve. But it's worse news for Des, because it's his place that'll get wrecked. He knows this, but he's having to let them in, and to his credit he doesn't look fazed. In fact he's doing the whole thing through a knife-edge smile that could go any minute, a smile you don't return.

'What's going on Artie?'

'It's Johnny. Johnny McCafferey, you know . . .'

'Yes, I know. Bloody animal.'

'We used to be mates.'

'I know. Thank God some things change. Let's dance,' she says, knowing I won't. I never have. Some things never change.

'Nah, I'm all right. You go.'

'On my own?'

'You know the girls,' I say, nodding towards the floor

where there's half a dozen young women shuffling in a circle, ignoring the gyrations of two older men in moustaches.

'You don't mind?'

''Course not.'

And she's away before I've said it. She steps into the circle with the rhythm of the song and she's away, eyes half closed and moving her hips in wide sways to the back beat, which is a wall of chords from a guitar band and the first decent music they've played all night. She's got her head up high and arms behind her back. Different class from the rest of them. I can't keep my eyes off her. I know this will become obvious if it lasts much longer but if you could see the coming and going of the backlit venus gap at the top of her legs, you'd stare too.

'All right Artie.'

'All right Johnny.'

'Your missus?' He nods towards Madelaine, on the dance-floor below, 'Still with her, eh? Nice one.'

'Sorry about your kid,' I say.

'Yeah. Fuckin' bastards.' His throat swells, with a rise and fall. There's a glaze to his eyes and he blinks twice, swallowing. 'You got a minute?' His voice breaks on its edges.

I turn away from Madelaine, away from the nudging attentions of men in moustaches. 'Yes. No problem,' I say, following his nod to the back room.

He's got me walking towards an open door with voices on the other side. I can't see round him, just the bristling back of his shorn, fat head that slopes straight to his shoulders, which will just about get through the door without him twisting. Inside the door, he peels to one side. There's four shavenheads sat at a table, playing cards amongst empty bottles and full ashtrays. I can't say if I recognize any of them from the Dog the other night, but that's only because they all look the same without hair labels. Smaller versions of Johnny. Less expertly tattooed. These were the guys who couldn't even get into the army.

Johnny turns round, with a weakness in his eyes I'd never seen, not even when the whole of the Skanckhouse crew came to meet him from school one summer night. Then, he just went into his bag and pulled out the bicycle chain he knew he'd need. Swinging it round his head, he scattered them with a wailing charge. Different now, he had a lost look, a tiredness in his voice.

'Sorry 'bout this Artie. We're mates, yeah?' I nod, wishing I hadn't come in, wishing my knees would shore up and not knowing how much fear was showing on my face. 'This him, lads?' Johnny scours the four pissed faces for a reaction and gets three slow shakes of the head.

Then I recognize a high-pitched voice that says 'yeah, that's him'. I'd last heard it round the pool table in the Dog, minutes before Denny waded in with his bottle and changed Christmas-time for the worse.

'You sure?' asks Johnny, going into his back pocket.

'What . . . what's this about, Johnny? What's going on?' I say.

'Where's Denny?'

'Denny?'

He doesn't wait, doesn't 'fuck around' like he's telling me not to, now with the blade catching the light and coming through the smoke, bigger and brighter until it's close enough to feel, cold on my flesh then gone, with a hot pulse under my eye.

'Jesus, Johnny. What the . . .'

And he's telling me again, this time shouting, not to fuck around. 'Where is he, Artie? I swear, I'll rip both your fucking eyes out if you don't tell me.'

'You can do what the fucking hell you like, Johnny.' This isn't me talking. It's a streetwise someone who's got into my body. They're using my voice to fuck me up. And it's carrying on, this demon who seems to know what he's doing. 'I don't know. If I did know I wouldn't fucking tell you. I don't like what Denny did, but it was a fight. He's my mate.' It's for the shavenheads twitching, playing with their cards and bottles and fags and knives. 'We don't choose our mates, you know that Johnny. You stick by them though. Don't you. We're mates, Johnny.'

'Were.'

'No. We're still mates, Johnny. You know that.'

'I can't let this drop, Artie lad. He did it. He's got to pay. You know the score. You've got till tomorrow night. Six.'

He's nodding at the door and puts a hand out towards the table where two of the shavenheads are standing up. I want to say 'Thanks, Johnny, I'm sorry for lying and hiding the man who blinded your kid brother. Your kid brother who was weak and intelligent and had got out of Slipp with his brain, like you weren't supposed to', but I say nothing, just let the adrenaline dump down so I'm shaking all over when I close the door behind me, dabbing at the blood on my cheek, with my legs twitching as I walk.

The music is slowing and the DJ says it's time to 'grab that girl now, for your early Christmas present'. I stop at the bar, rather than sit on my own for everyone to see. I can see her, on the dance-floor, leaning across with her ear on Des's mouth and smiling as he talks, putting his hands on the smooth silk bulge of her hips. She looks round, first at our empty table, then quickly scanning the room, not catching my eye and nodding as he nestles into her with a sway to the slow moving rhythm of the music. He's got both hands on her hips. They're talking into each other's ears. They're shuffling in slow circles and she leans back to put both her hands on his shoulders. He comes towards her with his mouth. She gives him a playful slap on his chest and he pecks her on her cheek with them both coming away smiling, then her looking around the room again.

'Hello there, lover.' It's behind me, the voice that sounds too young to be in here. 'Remember me?'

'What?' I say, with her black-rimmed eyes coming big into view as I swing round.

'You were in the Rainbow, Sunday dinner.'

'Oh, right.'

Her eyes are brighter. She looks older, and pretty. But she's too thin in the arms and shoulders that stick out bony from her grown up black dress that might be her mother's. But the sad thing is, she looks as though she knows that this place, which is a dump, is too good for her. Some people can think they're over-reaching themselves even in Slipp.

'You got a car?'

'What?'

'We could go outside.'

'No thanks. Look . . . here . . .' The song is coming to an end, and Des is making more moves, this time getting a kiss on the mouth then moves behind another shuffling couple, one two three four five six seven eight nine ten eleven, and I can see them again, still close, but not kissing. Des is smiling and Madelaine isn't, and he follows her off the floor with a palm on her hip as if to guide her, but dropping and letting her bottom glide over it as she walks with her silk riding over his hand. She sees me, and waves, turning to say something to Des, who's not happy any more.

The girl is still next to me, looking at the fiver I've taken out of my wallet. I can see it shaking in my hand.

'There you go,' I say.

'I can give you a hand . . .'

'I don't want anything. Please go. It's just a present.'

'Thanks.' She's on her tiptoes and kissing my cheek. 'How d'you do that?' she's asking, touching my fresh cut with Madelaine coming up the steps through the crowd.

'Never mind. I've got to go,' I say.

'Merry Christmas.'

I've gone, meeting Madelaine halfway.

'What's that?' she says.

'Oh, just a cut.'

'No. That,' she says, smudging a finger on my cheek like my mum looking for dust. 'Jesus, Artie. I dance for ten minutes and you're in a fight and snogging some teenager.'

'What?'

'Dark horse.' She's drunk. No wonder she let things slip, in front of me, and everyone. 'She one of your friends from the Rainbow?'

'No. What about you?'

'What?'

'Why d'you have to dance with him?'

'Oh, Des. He's a laugh. Don't know why you don't like him.' She's shouting, over the music, but louder than she needs to and I'm worried someone might hear.

'I thought you were dancing with your mates, the girls.'

'They're not mates, Artie. Jesus, I haven't spoken to them for years.'

'They were at school.'

'I bet she is.'

'What?'

'From the Rainbow. I bet she is. Your little friend.'

'What?' I can't look at her now, or think of anything to say, even though there's nothing to be guilty about, and I'm not the one in the wrong.

'I don't know, what have you been up to, Artie Gill?'

'What?'

'That cut. What've you been up to now?'

'Nothing.' I can see Karen Dugg, with husband Carl on her shoulder. They're talking to Des, who's looking at Carl, not her, the way he didn't look at me when I was stood next to Madelaine. He's talking to Carl, but it doesn't stop Karen trying to get his attention. I can't help feel a buzz, from having her near to us: me and my Madelaine, who was in Wales and still my girl that night in the Masons. That was eight years ago, and still giving a thrill. Imagine the buzz from getting away with it, under the nose. All that secrecy, getting hot under the collar and stiff in your trousers. Imagine the explosion of coming there'd be for the two of you, getting away with it like that.

Des looks across. This time looking at me. His face spreads, unsmiling. There's a glint in his eye. I want to flinch, but I don't. I take a step towards him, with Madelaine's hand in mine.

'Where are we going?'

'We're having a dance,' I say.

13

Christmas Day, the way it's been for hours since I realized there'd be no sleep for me. Not with pictures of Des and his hands on Madelaine; the sounds of Johnny's threats on tape loop. One is scarier than the other. Sticks and stones can break my bones, but fists and blades can't hurt me. That may not be entirely true. It's the combination of time and threat that does the damage. So you can form pictures of what might happen, of the scars that will hurt beyond the pain. Johnny's blade had flashed from nowhere. The wound pain was gone before I knew it was there. It wasn't like the film where they cut off a bloke's ear: you can hear them do it, but only see the shape of it in shadowplay. It's worse when you have to colour it in for yourself.

I'm making her breakfast rather than watch the guy on the telly with the big hair and the super-groomed beard using kids in hospital to make us say what a good bloke he must be. I'm doing the eggs the way she likes them, too well-done so they won't run, but the way she likes them anyway.

There's a busy day ahead. We're off to Mrs Hesketh's for Christmas dinner. I wanted to go to my mum's, which we're doing tonight, but as Madelaine said, 'We always go there. My mum's on her own too.' Mr Hesketh won't be there, of course. Not with that Mrs Hesketh at any rate. He's got a new one, only three years older than my Mrs Gill. Josie will be there, Madelaine's younger sister: not as pretty, but pretty anyway and giggly with a dirty mouth that will make us laugh, while her mum's in the kitchen fussing, the way I am now. Then it's back here for a break before I take Madelaine off to her mother-in-law's. Frankie's coming up, which will be awkward and almost certainly end in tears.

I can hear Madelaine patting around upstairs. She's mumbling in curses and bound to be in a bad mood from the drink last night. She's been drinking too much recently, more than she used to. Maybe it's Christmas. Maybe it's something else. I'm putting on the radio to dampen her sounds.

. . . but unfortunately, the season of goodwill has not carried as far as Slipp, where the riots of last week were rekindled last night in a fresh wave of violence. Police made sixteen arrests in the early hours when fighting broke out as attempts were made to remove the barricades which have made the Nelson Estate a no-go area since the brutal maiming of Billy McCafferey. In sub-zero temperatures, hoses were turned on the rioters and we understand that the situation is now under control.

Denny! I've forgotten all about him. And Johnny McCafferey's words in the back room at Rascals. He's still in the loft. I've not been up since yesterday morning. He'll be starving. There's no way I can get up until tonight, and by then my time will be up. But I'm not going to panic. Whatever happens, I won't give Denny away. How could I?

On a lighter note, bookmakers all over the country are counting the losses of the recent cold snap. The central London weather centre has just confirmed that we've got a white Christmas, so here's wishing you all the very best for the festive break. More from the news desk at nine o'clock and in the meantime let's set you on your way with that yuletide classic from Bing Crosby, dedicated to William Hill and his friends.

'Christ I feel awful. That wine was like piss.'

'Madelaine!'

'Oh bacon, fantastic. You're an angel, Artie. Shall we take it back upstairs?'

'It's Christmas Day.'

'So?'

'We've got the presents to open.'

'They can wait.' She's got her arms wrapped round my waist and her head is heavy on my back. 'I feel randy, Artie. I think I'm still pissed.' A giggle gushes out with wafts of drink. She's behaving like a tart when all I want is for her to be excited by her present, which I've been bursting to give her for weeks.

'Don't you want to give me my present?'

'Oh,' she says, downcast. 'I'm sorry, I didn't know what to . . . I'm sorry Artie, there was nothing I . . .'

'Doesn't matter.'

'You don't mind do you?'

'No, it's all right.'

'You sure?' She's kissing my neck. 'Come upstairs, I'll give you a special Christmas treat, I'll . . .'

'Stop it! Just stop . . . stop being like . . . like that.'

'Like what?'

'Like, like a . . . I don't like it. You go up. I'll bring the tray.'

'OK, Mr Prude.'

And she's off, upstairs, mumbling a song that tells me everything here is less important to her than to me.

'Tah Dah!' she shouts, making me jump, spilling the orange juice.

'What the . . . ?'

'Here you are, you moody old bastard.'

She's jumping up and down on the bed and smiling under a mop of tassled hair that's not woken up yet. Her make-up's dark and smudged black round her eyes, but her big lips are stretched taut over her teeth and there's a sparkle under the glaze of her eyes. She's got a bundle of wrapping paper in one hand and a long, broad-bladed knife in the other which she's waving around, and now jabbing towards me.

'Get on the bed and rip your keks off.'

'Madelaine!'

'Do it.'

I sit on the edge of the bed feeling the mattress flex with her bouncing. I know I can't be in any danger. I know she's not serious, that there's nothing to be scared of. Not like that. But I'm scared anyway – at the wild look on her face, at her abandon that's total, not just down to the drink.

'You'll do some damage, put it down.'

'You soft bastard. Here.' She throws the paper at me and jumps in the air, landing in a lotus position and bouncing to stillness with the knife pointing up from her lap, six inches or less from my rib cage. 'There you go, lover boy. You try wrapping the bloody thing.'

I've got the knife in my hand, with a brass plate inlaid

on the veined bone handle. 'Something Fishy from your Madelaine.'

* * *

I've driven us to Madelaine's mother's. It's further on up the hill and out of Slipp where you can't see the houses from the road. They've always lived here. They managed to keep the house even when Mr Hesketh's kitchen empires kept going bust. Madelaine had to leave St Ursula's and come to the comp, but three years at the convent had been enough to set her apart. To her credit she stayed the distance at the comp even though Thatcher gave her dad a leg up, so she could have gone back to the convent – after we'd met. But she didn't, even though her father wanted her out of there, and away from me.

He'd talk to me, while I was waiting for Madelaine to come downstairs to surprise me: with what she was wearing, the way she'd done her hair; with her combinations, her infinite varieties. He'd talk to me about the 'British Disease.' His backside would be roasting in front of the fire, a glass of gin and tonic in his hand, in the front room and I'd have to listen to him going on and on about the laziness of the working class.

I don't know about Mr Hesketh's British Disease, but he was selling the same kitchens then as he had been ten years before, according to my dad: 'except this time the fuckin' banks are queuing up to lend him money. No difference, same old wanky kitchens. Half a million he owed last time and they let him do it all over again.' Our parents never got on, even though my dad was a shopkeeper, just like Mrs Thatcher's dad.

Mrs Hesketh doesn't use that room with the big fireplace

any more, because the house is too big and he got better lawyers than her when he traded up to the new Mrs Hesketh. According to Madelaine and Josie, the new Mrs Hesketh is a tart. She's common. She's vulgar, only interested in money and showing it off. From what they'd say, you'd think she could be working class – but that wouldn't make sense.

Mrs Hesketh opens the door and the smell of damp hits the snow chill. She can't afford to heat the place now. She won't move though, she's got to believe it was a victory – getting the house and nothing else.

'Hi Mum.'

'Madelaine, merry Christmas darling.' They kiss. 'Hello Arthur.'

'Hello Mrs Hesketh.' We don't. 'Merry Christmas.'

'Yes. Come on in, Josie's been here ten minutes,' she says, really meaning to say 'you're ten minutes late'. 'You smell peculiar, darling.'

'If the truth be known, mum, I'm still a bit tipsy from last night. Artie took me out.'

Oh yes, sure, I took her out, it was my idea and I forced drink on her.

'You should take better care of her, Arthur. Have you hurt your face?'

'Oh he won't tell you about that. Those friends of his from school, you know what they're like. Always in trouble.' She turns and gives me a wink, thinking it's all right to do me down in front of her mother, and I smile back letting her know it's all right, that I don't mind. But I do.

'Come through, we're in the back room. I prefer it in here.'

Madelaine and Josie are unlocking from a full embrace by the time I follow Mrs Hesketh into the airless calor heat of her back room, which is even more crowded with the fuss of ornaments and furniture than it was the last time I came. She's got all the decent stuff from a ten-room house in here.

'Hi Artie.'

'Hi . . . ooh, Jo . . .' she's thrown herself at me, with arms on the back of my neck and wet lips on my mouth, '. . . sie.'

'Oh Madelaine, I want him.' She looks up at me and says, 'I want yooo,' and kisses me again.

'Put him down, Josie, you little strumpet. Get a fella of your own.'

'Oh but I have, and he's almost as nice as yours. And an animal, ggrrrrr.'

They whoop, and Mrs Hesketh goes out to 'put luncheon on'.

I sit down and watch the girls, and catch myself smiling in the empty TV screen, that has round corners and dials. The bastard even took the Trinitron.

'Hey, Artie, I've got a bottle of bubbly in the fridge,' says Josie with her arm round her sister in a giggling hug.

'Oh go on, Artie. Give us a few minutes,' says Madelaine. 'Let us girls catch up on our gossip, be a mate. I could do with topping up.' I'm smiling as I lean up out of the chair, watching myself in the dead telly, which won't get turned on in case it claps out before the Queen's speech.

'He's a sweetie,' I hear Josie say as I leave them to it.

'Sometimes,' Madelaine says, and they laugh as I shut the door behind me. They don't really want the champagne. They want to tell each other secrets. They don't know I know this, which is my secret. What Madelaine does know, though, is that I'll say, as I do, when I go into the cold and enormous and once-plush kitchen: 'Mrs Hesketh, do you want some help?' and that she'll say: 'No, I'm fine thank you Arthur,' thinking that I'll think she is, but I'll insist anyway and it'll end up, as it does, with: 'Oh, go on then, there's a pinafore on the back of the door,' and 'I hope you're taking care of Madelaine, she takes a lot of looking after you know . . .'

And all the while, they're in a huddle and talking about God knows what and not even bothering that the champagne is still in the fridge. As it happens, it's a good job I have come in to help because she's about to put the veg on at the same time as the six pound turkey is going in the oven. There's no prospect of a sauce or trimmings. So I'm turning the heat off on the stove without her noticing and gathering wine and stock cubes; the flour and butter for a roux, to make at least something go right on Christmas Day, but not everything, because as I watch my hands go into action with their expert flicks and turns, my mind is folding over last night's leftovers.

* * *

After we'd had our dance, we went back to the table, for more wine and stilted conversations lost in the music. Madelaine would jump up every twenty, then fifteen, then ten minutes, because 'Ooh, this is one of my favourites, you don't mind?' Eventually, she just stayed there, on the floor with the shuffling girls and the mock-grind lads, in the danger zone.

I recognized him from what he said, Des, the kind of thing he would say.

'She's terrific isn't she? The way she moves. She's talented too, at work. Done wonders.'

'What do you want?'

'How do you get a girl like that?' Meaning 'how do *you* get a girl like that?'

'Haven't you got things to do?'

'Oh no, no.' He sat in Madelaine's chair and waved at the floor, to where she was smiling up at us, him. 'No, Artie lad, told you before, *you're* top of my list.'

'List?'

'You're my number one priority. I said to Santa, please let no harm come to Artie this winter, that's what I said.' He was laughing with himself, at me through glazed eyes. A bloke in a dinner suit came to stand behind him. 'Heard you had a run-in with Johnny. Not good. Not very bright, that. I've just had a chat with him myself.'

'So what?'

'So he's part of the team now.'

'Tell someone who gives a shit.'

'I think you do, Artie lad. I think you do.'

'You're wrong.'

'I've got Denny. Your mate.'

'What?'

'Everyone knows it was him that did for Billy. So I've offered him to Johnny. Like a, what you call it, a signing on fee. Yeah, Johnny avenges the maiming of his brother, and I get Johnny. Everyone gets what they want. Make sure you don't miss out, Artie lad.'

'You don't know where he is. Nobody does.'

'Nobody? I think you're wrong. I know where he's been.'

'What do you . . .'

'A little bird told me. A gorgeous little bird, matter of fact. And I think you've just told me a bit more. You're sweating lad. Oi, Decko. Get the lad a cold beer. Sharpish.' He got up, out of the seat, just as the guy in the dinner jacket came back with the drink. 'Nice talking to you, Artie lad. Wise up. You're out by Wednesday, like it or not. Johnny's staying. I'm buying him out of the army. Better do as he says.' He was laughing as he left me. I followed him across the dance floor, past where Madelaine was pushing a shavenheaded groper away.

*　　*　　*

It's too white outside and there's steam on the window, so I can't see me in the window. But I know I'm worried. I can feel the slow bead popping on my brow. I can almost see the time passing, see the fuse burning to six o'clock – when they'll do something about my sheltering him.

What's also got me worried, with the butter too cold to meld properly with the flour into a good roux, is how Madelaine could betray me like that. I could melt the butter over a heat, or in the microwave, but it would congeal. It wouldn't be right.

With Madelaine still on the dance-floor, Johnny had come over after Des had said his bit.

'Des had a word, yeah?' he'd said as he sat down, drinking mouthfuls from his lager. 'We need a little chat.'

'OK.'

'I should have done you in there, you know that.' I shrugged. 'Fucksakes, Artie. This is no joke. I can't piss about, the whole of the Nelson is waiting for me to sort this out.'

'It's nothing to do with me.'

'You know where he is, don't you?'

'No.'

'He's a waste of space, Artie. He's lost it. He'd sell you down the river soon as wink, you know that.'

'He's my mate. Anyway, I don't know . . .'

'Des can hurt you all sorts of ways. He will.'

'Let him.'

'Denny's been ripping him off. You know that?'

'What!'

'He was working for Des. He's been in Des's pocket for years.'

'So what?'

'So he's scum, Artie.'

'That makes Des responsible for your kid.'

'Denny went too far.'

'How can you work for him?'

'Jesus, Artie. You can't not work for him.' He leant across and spoke into my ear, under the music. 'You can't do anything about him. 'Course he's a bastard, but you can't touch him.'

'You could have him any day.'

But Johnny's looking sad, and shaking his head.

'Fucking listen, Artie. Do what he says. I'm working for him because if I didn't I'd never have made it back from Ulster.'

And he said it in a way, with flexing muscles and fear in his eyes, that made me believe him. It was the first time I'd seen Johnny scared. Some changes you just can't fail to spot.

14

Dinner was late, so we missed the Queen's speech, because I'd been 'faffing about' with one of my 'damn sauces'. Mrs Hesketh fell straight off to sleep. She was twitching, her head jolting like a baby's. Then she farted, which sent Madelaine and Josie into a fit of giggles. To me it just capped the sadness of her plight, her slow, flapping flight from the woman I'd first met.

Madelaine and Josephine were watching a film on TV and passing the champagne between them, drinking from the bottle.

'You watching this to the end?' I said.

'Of course.'

'I think I'll go for a walk then.'

'A walk?'

'Yes, the food's slowed me down a bit.' But they hadn't

wanted an explanation. Madelaine was questioning my sanity, not my motives. My motives didn't seem to hold any fascination for her, which is a shame, because if she knew where I was going, and why, it would surprise her. That would be good.

Even before I've got the key out of the door I can tell he's come down. There's a crust of fresh nicotine in the hall, and a soft chorus of canned telly laughter. From the door, I can see through into the kitchen which is more littered than when we left and as I shut the door and move to the lounge door there's a sound of quick clothes noises.

'All right mate, how you doing?' Denny's lying awkward on the sofa, with his shirt lap out and a fluster to the way he's pushing his hair around.

'What are you up to, Denny?'

'Nothing, I . . .'

'This isn't a doss hole.'

'I know, I . . .'

'I'm sticking my neck out for you . . .'

'I know, I . . .'

'More than you know.'

'What?'

'You could show some respect.'

'Sure. Sorry, I . . .'

'Take the cans away.'

'You OK Artie?'

''Course I am.'

'Good. You, you just seem, I don't know . . . different.'

'I might be, maybe it's time I moved on, got some new mates.'

'Get out of it, Artie. Just a few fucking cans, mate.'

'Yeah? Well get them shifted, and open some windows.'

'Sure,' and he goes off, leaning over as he walks and furtling in his shirt, taking a can from the pile on the coffee table.

'Put the kettle on, will you?' I shout and I can hear him doing it straight away, as I'm picking up the cushion he was leaning on. The pants are familiar: small and black and gluing. What this tells me is that she's a figure of desire for him – forbidden, illusory, fantastic. I can't attribute the blame to her. What can she do? But it is a further violation – not so much of her, but of me and Denny, which by anybody's reckoning would have to be a friendship that ought to be on its very last legs. I drop the pants onto the pile of cans, where I'm going to leave them without comment. It's time *I* started fucking people up, don't you think?

I go into the kitchen, taking none of Denny's mess with me. I give him what I hope he sees is an empty look.

'Clear your mess up, Denny and get back upstairs. I don't want you downstairs again.'

'All right, all right, you don't know what it's like up . . .'

'Not my problem.'

'Are you all right, you seem . . .'

'I'm fine.'

'How do you get that cut?'

'I saw Johnny last night.'

'McCafferey?' he's gone pale, he actually has, the way they say frightened people do. 'Shit, you didn't say anything did you?'

'He's going to catch up with you, Denny. Sooner or later.'

'You didn't say I was here did you?'

'He's working for Des.'

'Des? Shit.'

'Is that bad news? I thought you didn't know him.'

'I don't. Just, like, you know. Heard of him. Sort of. He doesn't know I'm here though? Does he?'

'Clean up. Everything. The way it was. Everything.'

'You wouldn't let me down?'

'Betray you? Me?'

'Jesus, Artie. You're being weird mate.'

I'm walking away, playing with the keys in a jaunty way that surprises me. I know what I'm going to do, I think. I'm going to burrow away and set some tests for them all, and doing something about it makes me feel bright, without any of the fear that I ought to be feeling. Maybe I *am* going a bit weird.

'Just as you found it, Denny. And keep out of my way.'

I can't hear what he's saying, just the desperation of the way he's saying it. I'm going upstairs, locking the bathroom door, and getting the panel off the bath. The database is up for revision. Lane, D. is back where he belongs, low priority in view of the trail he's left. He's no threat. As one door closes, another slams in your face, so I'm taking out the latest card. It's new, and straight in at number one. With a bullet.

I can't be paranoid. The threats are real. I'm not frightened of them all, though. Not really afraid of Johnny's blade or Des's threats. Sticks and stones. My body's made for healing. I know what can really hurt me. And the evidence is there. You can see that. Can't you? I've somehow lost, over the years, the strength to be on my own. The resolution and fortitude you need. Faith. Words that mean nothing. Particles of soil and stone, flaking from a riverbank – real changes you can't see. I'm clinging on.

Madelaine's not keen on going to my mum's, but I'm in-sisting because I don't feel like coping with my mum coping with Frankie on my own. We're already late, which means the first row should be out of the way.

I'm taking the slip road onto the Estate, but Benny's there, in his uniform, flagging me down with a grim look on his face.

'All right, Benny.'

'Artie. Madelaine.'

'Bad luck, mate. Working on Christmas Day.'

'Yeah, been here since this morning. Calmed down now.' He's downbeat, which is unusual, for him. 'Can't let you on the Estate with the car, Artie.'

'Where should I leave it?'

He nods at the scrubland between the slip road and the fences where the riot vans are parked. But he's distracted and sad-looking. 'Should be all right there.'

'Cheers,' I say, revving the car back up and working on the steering wheel.

'Hang on, Artie. I'll come with you. There's been some trouble – at your mum's.'

'What?'

'She's all right. No harm, just a bit of upset.'

He won't tell me any more and I don't push it because I suppose I don't want to know.

'What is it?' asks Madelaine. We're walking through the entrance to the Estate. There's nobody about, and as we turn the corner, with Benny not answering her, there are wet ashes matted onto the green and a ring of charred car shells. Benny's walking quickly, towards my mum's house with his head down, and as we get near I feel my stomach drop and then jump.

'Jesus, Benny.'

Madelaine is shaking and saying 'bastards, bastards', over and over.

'Why didn't you stop them?'

'They're watching the house. We can't go near until Denny's been found.'

'What? You're the police for fuck's sake.'

'Artie, it's . . . it's . . . we've got family, mate.'

'Who's said you can't. Johnny?' He shakes his head, embarrassed. 'Des?'

'Des?' says Madelaine. 'What's he got to do with this?'

'Shut up,' I say.

'Artie?'

'I said shut up.' I take Benny by the arm, and turn him away from Madelaine. 'Why can't you do something about that bastard?'

'Drop it, Artie. Just give 'em Denny.'

'What? They'll kill him.'

'He's dead anyway. Good as.'

'Look, you're a fucking copper. You know who's causing this. Just arrest the bastard.'

'Drop it.'

'Come on, Madelaine,' I say.

She's shaking, nestled under my arm as we pass the big tar cross they've daubed on the door. Glass is crackling underfoot. Shards snap and small pieces crunch, going back to powder. I go down the side of the house, through the arched passage that separates it from next door, and into the shed.

I've got a handful of wood and nails under my arm, which will have to do, until I can get someone to come and put new windows in.

It's taken about an hour, and the shavenheads have been watching me all the time, jibing and chanting. I'm one of their own. I can see their point of view. I can see why they're angry, but we don't deserve this. There are four young ones coming close, with balaclavas and T-shirts in the freezing cold. There's a wail, then a whirr of shadows across the streetlights and a thud on the grass in front of the house.

The balaclavas are sneering a new chant and jumping, then turning and running away. They've seen me see it. They've seen my reaction to Monty's split belly, his matting fur, his splayed legs, his open-mouthed, broken-toothed dead smile. His scared eyes are open. His final breathing horror is preserved for ever, at least until he decays. By the time I've got him, heavy and wet in my arms, looking up at me with his eyes I can't close, the young thugs are back. They're jumping and waving from a safe distance. It's difficult not to blame them and I know that as long as I've got Denny in my loft, there's nothing I can do about it.

Inside the house, my mother is in the kitchen. She looks up, hunched in her chair, with red eyes that are dry now, and puffy. Madelaine's got a bottle, which she's opening for her.

'Where are the glasses?'

'There aren't any,' I say. 'She uses mugs. Up there.'

'Frankie's home,' Mum says, with a sniff that she's using to try to raise her spirits, and she raises her voice to try to let some of the misery out. I know these things: these manner-isms of hers, these techniques that stopped her falling apart when my dad was alive, before Frankie took over with the task of making her life a misery. 'Got a new girlfriend.'

'Jesus.'

'Don't be like that.'

'Where are they?'

'In the front room. Be nice, Artie, there's been enough upset for one night.'

'Artie,' says Madelaine, coming towards me, handing the mug down to my mum as she passes the sink, 'I'll come with you.'

In the hall, where there's an old smell of burnt food that I couldn't smell in the kitchen, Madelaine takes hold of my arm. She looks desperate, with the giggles of the car journey buried deep and I feel guilty for bringing her into this family.

'Stay calm,' says Madelaine. 'Just say, and we can go. Don't get angry.'

'I won't.'

First thing I see when we go into the front room, kept for best, with dusty antimacassars and an old stereogram, which is playing one of Frankie's old punk records that my mum would hate, is Frankie's girlfriend. She's pretty, but with greasy skin. That's my first impression. I can see that she's wearing a dress, which is unusual for Frankie's partners, but with motorcycle boots more steel than leather, which is par for the course, but that's as much as I can take in. That's the extent of my first impression, and I'm trying to be polite, but it's difficult because I've just seen Frankie.

'Frankie.'

'Artie.'

She's smiling, my sister. Smiling, despite what's just happened, because after all these years of surprise and control, she can still spring a shock. She'll be able to see it on my face. It makes her smile, joyless. Her hair is shorn, closer cropped than normal, and there's some new holes in her face: nose (three); each eyebrow, and one above her top lip, on the upper edge of her bad tooth smile that's got something new. She's got a beard. Thin and wisping, shaped into a goatee, she's got a fucking beard.

'This is Isabella,' she says.

I nod, but can't bring myself to speak.

'Hello,' says Isabella.

'Hi,' says Madelaine, 'I'm Madelaine.'

'Hi Madelaine.'

'Hi Frankie,' says Madelaine, coming up behind me, with a kiss on the nape of my neck. 'Artie. Can I get you a drink?'

'Yes, a rum please.'

'How's the world of fish then, bro?'

I wait for Madelaine to leave the room.

'What do you care?'

'Don't be like that.'

'Why do you bother?' I say.

'What? Oh, you don't like my beard?'

'I think it's cool,' says Isabella.

'Artie's a bit reactionary,' says Frankie.

I know that I've got nothing I could possibly say to, or learn from, these people, but I can't go. I want to, but I've got to be here, for Mum, to help her through the visit.

'Anyway,' I say, 'how are things in London?'

'London? Fine. Seems like this place is only changing for the worse. If that's possible. Anyway, you don't care.'

'I'm being polite. You are my sister. Mum worries about you. You didn't have to do this.'

'Do what? Oh this,' she says, fingering the growth on her chin.

'They're quite popular now, in London,' says Isabella. 'Dead easy.'

What I want to say, but don't, is: 'Fuck off Isabella, let me guess who the man is in this relationship.' But thinking it, just the thought of how the two of them get together, is enough to drop my eyes to Frankie's baggy denim crotch, and I'm wondering if you can change your hormones, to grow facial hair, without it altering the whole kit and caboodle.

'Madelaine's looking good. She's changed.'

'Changed?'

'Yes. She's, she's less . . . less Slipp, less girlie. She looks good.'

And all I can say to get at her, which I want to do, is 'They've killed Monty'.

It was her cat, before she left me, then Mum, to look after it. I tell her this and watch her choke and gag on the full-time sneer that's dropping. She's crying, for the first time ever as far as I'm aware. I can see her losing the fight to keep the tears away, relinquishing control. I'm getting a glimpse, from this side of the broken windows, of the power of evil.

'You bastard,' says Madelaine, coming back with my rum.

'I know,' and she takes me away, into the hall where she's hugging me, sheltering my shame.

So where Frankie and I used to sleep, until I was seventeen, and her sixteen; where I used to wake in the night to the sound of her discovering herself, she and Isabella are doing God knows what. At least my mum's asleep – in her chair, with her boozy snore that would muffle anything that Frankie could muster from above. We tried to get her to come to our place, until the troubles calm down, but she won't.

'Who'll feed Monty?' she'd asked, with a thin, forgetting smile, and as she said it I could picture her in the morning, on the other side of booze, wheeling herself out to call her cat, and the neighbours sniggering at the mad old woman, who isn't actually old but who can't remember that Monty, her sole companion, was killed only yesterday.

'What a day,' I say, breaking under the strain of the quiet in the car.

'Christmas. Jesus, why do we bother looking forward to it.'

'Do you think this would all seem less bad if it wasn't Christmas?'

'For Christ's sake, Artie. This is serious. I don't know, it just seems . . . you let things wash over you, I don't know how you do it.'

'Maybe it's a good job. Maybe I'd go crazy if I didn't.'

'Maybe you are crazy.'

'Oh no. I'm all right.' I shouldn't be driving. I've had too much rum and my tongue feels loose, but I won't let it. No more slips. 'No, I'm not crazy.'

'God knows, I could understand it if you were. Dead cats, your sister's got a goatee beard, and cooped up in that bloody shop all day, with all those old women and their bags on wheels. Jesus Artie, I'm not sure I can take much more of Slipp.'

'What choice is there?'

'I feel like getting away.'

'A holiday? You're going away in a week.'

'Not that.'

'What about me? What would I do?'

'Oh, forget it, Artie. I'm tired.'

'You can't leave me.'

'Leave you?'

'I couldn't manage.'

'You'd adapt, maybe it's what you need.'

'Don't.'

'I was going to tell you, but I've been putting it off.' There's a buzzing in my ears and her words are coming in with an echo, loud and like when your ears have just popped. Loud against a blanket of dullness. 'I've been offered a job, a new job.'

'Where? Nearby?'

'No, not nearby. Drop it. I knew you'd be like this.'

'What do you expect?'

'Let me out of the car. I'll walk.'

'I'll be quiet.'

'Good.'

'Did Des get you the job?'

'For fuck's sake Artie.'

'Did he?'

'Stop the car.'

'I'll be quiet.'

Did he?

Did he?

'Course he did.

I could tell her it's him behind the riots. The tar cross, and the broken windows and dead Monty. She'd say, 'Don't be ridiculous Artie.' Then she'd ask him straight and that would be that, like Johnny McCafferey told me – last night, and again today with their tokens.

No, I'd best keep quiet and get her home. We've got a party tomorrow. Now that'll be a surprise. For her.

15

'What are you up to, Artie?' says Madelaine.

'Just sorting something to eat, for later on.'

'It's only two o'clock.'

'The game's on telly. Save me bothering later.'

'Football? Oh great.'

'We used to go, Boxing Day, every year. Remember? All the O'Briens.'

'I remember.'

'And Delores O'Brien would come too. She'd say "sod the cooking", and Grandad would have to go at half time, rush home to make the turkey sandwiches.'

'I remember.'

'I used to love that. Didn't you?'

'No.'

'What?'

'I didn't like it.'

'I thought. You said . . .'

'I used to like being with you.'

'Used to?'

'What are you making?'

'Just a few canapes.'

'Canapes?'

'It's easy. We can pick at them during the game.'

'A sandwich'll do for me. I still feel crap. Hey, I fancy a kebab.'

'Madelaine! You've been drinking too much.'

'Can you blame me?'

'More than you used to.'

'Leave it out, Artie.'

'I'll just finish the food.'

'Have you been opening the mail?'

'Why?' I say, struggling to recall exactly where I've secreted the envelope. 'What? . . .'

'That medical report, from the psychiatrist.'

'What's the hurry?'

'I wanted it sorted out. They can't settle with the other side without that. I'll have to call them tomorrow.'

'No need for that. I called them the other day.' The lie trips out smoothly, as though I've been doing it all my life. Maybe it's catching. 'You should have it in a week or so.' I'll re-seal the envelope. Soil the postmark, and tear it with the letter inside, so the date disappears, so she can't trace back to when it was sent. 'You're not desperate for the money, are you?' It's in with the rest of the stuff. I'm sure I filed it away.'

'No, I'm not desperate, I . . . Artie! I'm talking. Where are you going?'

'Just . . .'

'There's the door. You get it,' she says.

'No, you, I'm . . .'

'Jesus, Artie. Artie! Bloody hell.'

It's going to be a disaster.

'Thanks, Artie.'

'You glad they've come?'

'You're an angel. I didn't think you were serious, when you said the other day.'

'I know.'

'I'm glad you like my friends.'

'Here, take these in,' I say, handing her a place of Eggs à la Russe.

'OK. Don't stay in here all day. Come and have a drink.'

'In a minute.'

She goes out, smiling without a care for her hangover or the fact that she didn't have time to change or do her hair. She's different. The words she's using have changed, and her mannerisms. The breadth of her smile, tight lips across her teeth the way I don't see so much.

'Hi Artie.'

I thought I'd prepared for this, but I haven't. I deluded myself, having a party. Inviting Cinnamon. Letting myself go off half cock. I let it gather its own momentum, beyond my control, getting out of hand so I couldn't stop it. I couldn't throw a decent party to save my life. I can see that now. I can feel myself slipping, feel my face burning up, giving myself away.

'Cinnamon.'

'Maddie's delighted. Great idea.'

'Hmm.'

'What are those?'

'Devils on horseback. Prunes wrapped in bacon.'

'Sounds gross.'

'Try one.'

'Go on. Hmm. Nice. Hmm, yeah. How are you, anyway?'

'Me?'

'After the other night. At my place.'

'Oh. Right. Yeah, fine.'

'Good. You still look a bit, I don't know. Tense. Come again. I was thinking about you. I think I've got just the thing. Let me take those in. Hmm, nice. Oh, hi Spike. Try one of these. Devils on horseback.'

'Devils on horseback. Love it. Hmm. Delicious. Salty. Sweet inside.'

'You devil,' says Cinnamon.

'I don't think so darling. Artie, any more of that Chablis, delicious.'

'Sure. Here you go,' I say.

'You OK in here? All locked away with the dishes. Let me take over for a while,' says Spike. He looks hard, but you can see he's not – from the way he moves, the way he talks.

'I'm fine,' I say. 'Did you have a good time the other night?'

'I always have a good time.'

'At Bacchus. Your Christmas do wasn't it? From work.'

'Oh that. Boring.'

'Late finish?'

'No, no. Not me. Tucked up in bed by midnight.'

'Oh. I thought, I thought you and Madelaine, the gang, I thought you, Madelaine said . . . you went on somewhere didn't you?'

'No, straight back home for me.'

'Oh.'

'I think some of them went back to that awful place of Des's, up this way somewhere. Maddie dropped me off on the way.'

'Rascals.'

'Too right. Pissed as farts they were, the lot of them. You sure I can't do anything?'

'No thanks.'

'OK then, Cinders. Catch you later. Oh, hi Maddie. Just trying to drag your man out of the kitchen.'

'Can I help you, Artie?' she asks.

'I'm all right.'

'Here, have a drink. Hey, this food's terrific.'

'Spike seemed to have had a good time – the other night. Said he went on to Rascals.'

'When?'

'The other night, you know. Must have been after your office do,' I say.

'Not his sort of place. No, I think he went home early. He's in love.'

'He said some of you went. Did you?'

'When?'

'Artie.' The voice is new and familiar and behind me. It's a voice from school that should be in my loft.

'Denny!'

'What the fuck. What's he doing here, Artie?' says Madelaine.

'I . . .'

'Any chance of a drink?' says Denny.

'I said I didn't want you here, Denny,' says Madelaine.

'Don't be like that, Madelaine,' I say.

'I can be like anything I fucking well . . .'

'All right Cinnamon,' says Denny.

'Denny?'

'Yeah. Geeze, I've not seen you for ages. Didn't know you were mates with Artie.'

'She's not. I mean, she's Madelaine's friend. Mainly,' I say.

'Artie, can I have a word with you. Out here,' says Madelaine.

'I've just got to sort these out. In a minute.'

'Make it a minute.'

'OK. You two know each other, then?'

'Yeah, sort of. Me and Cin,' says Denny.

'It's a long time ago.'

'We were, what would you say, Cin? Mates?'

'Mates? Never.'

'Maybe you two would like, you know. Look. I've got to . . .'

'Don't go on my account, Artie. I've got to get this wine to Brenda. See you, Denny.'

'Christ, Denny, what the fuck . . . what are you . . . I didn't know . . . how do you know Cinnamon?'

'Three guesses.'

'You and Cinnamon?'

'Hmm. Sweet.'

'Look. You can't stay here. What are you playing at? How are you going to get back upstairs now?'

'I'm not. I'm moving on.'

'You can't. I need . . . I want you to stay, Denny. We're mates. Best mates, aren't we?' He's different from yesterday. Something has happened. He's reclaimed his cockiness, turned the tables.

'I've got a job.'

'You won't get past the High Street.'

'Oh, I think I will.'

'Johnny Mac's after you. So's Des.'

'I know.'

'You know?'

'It's sorted. Trust me, Artie. I'll be fine.'

'I don't see how you can be. Look, this is no joke. My

mum's last night – they broke her windows. Every fucking window. They killed Monty.'

'Jesus. I'm sorry, mate, I . . .'

'I don't know what's going to be next.'

'It'll be all right now.'

'They want you – Des and Johnny.'

'It's not a problem. It's been sorted. I've got one last job here, then I'm off. I'll be gone by New Year. Spain. Great, eh?'

'Denny . . .'

'Relax. I'm off to say bye to Cin,' he says, with a smirk, 'and Maddie, of course. You got any beers?'

I can't stay in the kitchen any more. It's getting embarrassing, and the longer I leave it, the harder it'll be, the further behind I'll be, with their conversation and drink, and the hardness of the edges to the circles they'll be forming. So I'm going, into the lounge, and the first thing I see is Denny still there, perched on the arm of the chair where Cinnamon is sat. He's talking to her and Madelaine, who doesn't seem so pissed off that he's still here. To look at him, you'd think nothing was wrong with his life.

'Artie lad, come and sit down. Here you go. I'm going for a leak,' he says.

I catch Cinnamon's eye, with Madelaine looking away with her eye on Denny as he leaves the room. Cinnamon's telling me to sit alongside, perching above and probably touching her arm with my hip, and Madelaine cross-legged on the floor beneath us.

'Come on, Artie. Sit down. Have a rest,' says Madelaine, 'I'll load the dishwasher.'

'We can fix up another appointment,' says Cinnamon, with Madelaine getting up to go out of the same door as Denny, but still in earshot.

'Another? You two have got together? I didn't know,' says Madelaine, turning with a smile.

'Oh dear,' says Cinnamon, 'I've breached client confidentiality. Hope you don't mind.' She doesn't see the seriousness of the situation, or maybe she does. Sees it as an opportunity for fun, dangerous fun.

'I tell you, Cin, he's a mysterious soul just lately. Hope you can plumb his depths. As long as you tell me what you find.'

'There'll be nothing,' I say. But they can't hear me under their laughing, which is at my expense and which I don't think is a laughing matter.

'Oh dear. So, when *are* we getting together again, Artie?' says Cinnamon.

'I don't know. I wish you hadn't mentioned it, though.'

'To Madelaine? Why?'

'I don't know. You know, it's just . . .'

'We're mates. You know what girls are like.'

'It's just, you know, a kind of private thing. Isn't it?'

'Depends what you're talking about.'

'I didn't know about you and Denny.'

'There isn't a "me and Denny".'

'There was?'

'Kind of. Few months back. Don't tell Maddie.'

'Why?'

'Just don't.'

'It's over now, then?'

'Oh yeah, it's over.'

'Good.'

'Thought you two were meant to be mates.'

'We are. It's just that he's, you know, a bit rough. He can be violent.'

'That would have been nice. No, I can handle myself.' She

lowers her voice, theatrically. 'Tell you the truth, a bit of roughness wouldn't have been a bad thing. Between the two of us, he's a bit of a disaster in that department.'

'That department?'

'Hmm. Fast, and not nearly furious enough.'

'Denny?' I ask, but she can't hear me because she's started a dirty giggle, to herself more than anything else, and she's looking over my shoulder.

'Hi Denny,' she says. 'Just talking about you,' and the giggle starts up again, louder and dirtier, and Denny gives her a look which is dirty in a different way, and then me one that's embarrassed.

'Charming,' he says, with his jacket over his shoulder. 'I'm off, Artie. Thanks for the tucker . . .' he's looking round, with Madelaine coming back into the room, preening herself, changing the shape of her hair.

They've eaten all the food, which I thought I'd prepared too much of, but they're still here, with half a case of the cheap wine left, and a group of them smoking dope in a circle in the lounge with no gaps now between the laughter. Maddie's in the thick of it, and she looks happy in a way I'm not used to – an abandoned kind of happy with a fixed smile and heavy eyes that shine when the lids rise.

I'm feeling kind of light and confident, talking to Brenda and a couple of her friends, whose names I've forgotten. They're talking about some clause or other that's somehow going to affect the rights of gays. Something to do with the army.

'It's just another way of limiting us, another way of grinding us down. It'll affect us all, not just in the services,' says Spike.

'Serves them right,' says one of the girls – a pretty,

mousy-looking girl in dungarees that drown her, 'I've no sympathy for anyone who gets paid for killing people.'

'That's not the point,' says Brenda, and the others are agreeing with her as I stand up, with no will to talk about this, and failing to catch Maddie's eye with a warm look that wants to let her know that I think we're going to be all right. She's looking at Brenda, listening to what she's got to say and nodding with a glint and she looks totally happy. I need her to know that I wouldn't choose these people as my friends, but I think I can live with it, that I'm going to change, to keep up with her. But I can't catch her eye, to give her a warm look. I feel strange, detached.

Up the stairs, and I can see Cinnamon's silk trail, hanging from her slim hips, and the rest of her comes into view as I round onto the landing.

'Hi.'

'Hi.'

'What are you doing?' I ask.

'Waiting for the loo. Spike's in there – keeping it for himself. Tight bastard.'

I nod, as though I know precisely what she's talking about, not just the gist of it.

'So, when are we going to get together again?' she says.

'Any time. I'd like to.'

'Good.'

'I . . . I enjoyed it, the other night. All of it.' Which isn't entirely true. Not true at all. But I can see why I allowed it to happen, why someone might go looking for it.

'Artie . . .'

'I'd like to . . .'

''Bout time, Spike.'

'Can't rush the good stuff. That wouldn't do,' he says. 'There's more. For later.'

'I'll be watching. And waiting. Wanting . . .'

And Spike goes down the stairs, sniffing, and humming a song from a musical that I can't place. I'm not really trying to place it, I'm trying to catch Cinnamon's eye, but I can't because she's on her way through the door, so I touch her hip and as she turns back, I lean down towards her, locking a look onto her lips, which blur and go dark as I close my eyes.

'Ar . . .'

The rest is muffled and warm in my mouth, and I search in her wine taste, for a second or two before she pushes me away. She's left me stooping, waiting for a shame which won't come. She's talking to me, in soft tones that I can't hear, and all I can see is moving pictures of Madelaine, at the door, turning round before kissing him, long and hard, him with his hands inside her jumper and a bent knee appearing from between her legs. I'm nodding at the movement of Cinnamon's lips, not knowing what to do with my hands or my stance, and this image of Madelaine at the door, and Cinnamon's earlier words, about Denny, coming at me through the fuzz. 'Don't tell Maddie . . . just don't.' It's not difficult to work out why she wouldn't want Madelaine to know about her and Denny, but it's not Denny I can see. He's smaller, with slicked-back hair and slanting eyes. He's got more to offer than Denny.

16

There's burnt herbs in my mouth, coming through the glue taste of dough and tomato paste. This much I can make out. And guilt is there too. I want to, but can't, get to the bathroom. There's a searing in my head, damp on the pillow that's still wet from the towels I wrapped around my burning skull during the night to stop the throbbing. Her T-shirt is on the pillow next to me, but she's not here and the wardrobe door is open. No sounds from below, so she's gone. Without waking me.

She'd gone to bed before me, but not before I'd started to lose it, with the dope I'm 'not used to', that I didn't 'go easy' with, and the tequila I'd gone for with Spike, who was used to it, even though to look at him you'd think he wouldn't be.

I've got to get up and away from the thing with Cinnamon, its shabbiness. I've got to move, to walk it off, get into the day so things can start coming at me. Until I do, they'll just get bigger and darker, these moving pictures of Cinnamon's mouth when she pushed me away, with the sweet taste of her wine going sour. I can feel myself cringe, here in bed, when I rebuild the nervous looks I'd given her through the evening afterwards, those silent pleadings.

The snow has thawed to slush. My feet are wet and I'm only at the top of the hill, looking down to the High Street. Madelaine's out here somewhere. Doing something she obviously doesn't want me to know about. So is Denny, skulking around in some kind of hiding, unless you believe him when he says he's cut a deal with Des. They're all out here, going round in circles, not making life any easier. You can see the towers in Town today, now the snow's stopped. You could almost reach out and touch it. From here, Slipp doesn't look so hard to get out of.

So I'm on my way down, to colour in the day, and taking stock of the shop for the year end. The first time my dad let me do the stock-take was a New Year's Eve. We'd get there early, eightish. He'd take a bottle of Scotch, which he'd open at a minute past midday, ''cause only sad bastards drink in the morning'. They were good, those seldom days, so far as they lasted. The togetherness of it. No women, for once. My friends would go to the match with their dads: uniforms of colours and tactic-jargon; or fishing: the mischief of early mornings before the milk float, with all the tackle and kit. I didn't have that. This was all I'd had, the only thing we did together. They call it bonding now, on the telly and in the papers. I can't remember there being a word for it then, but it doesn't mean the lack of it wasn't a problem.

The last year we did it, two years before he died, he didn't bring the Scotch. At five to twelve he said, 'You know the ropes, son. Just popping to the Dog for me dinner.' That was the end of our little bit of togetherness. He never made it back from the Dog, and I've been doing it on my own ever since.

The door jangles. Inside, the air is brittle thin. There's a letter behind the door. Brown, A4, 'By Hand, Urgent, Strictly Private and Confidential', 'Neville Neville Solicitors' embossed on the flap. That's a lot of information for the outside of an envelope. I can guess what it is, which makes me not want to open it. Neville Neville, 'fuckin' mason' according to my dad, isn't a *firm* of solicitors, he *is* a solicitor. His mum and dad, Mr and Mrs Neville just had a sense of humour, which he's using to his advantage. Because some people actually think he is a partnership. He sends me my leases, anything to do with the shop.

I'm not wrong. At the top of the letter, underneath his Gothic lettering that tells me his registered office is at 48 High Street, Slipp, just across the road, is a heading. 'Schedule of Dilapidations'. It goes on to tell me that Neville Neville wants twenty-seven thousand pounds off me, on behalf of their (his) client, Magnate Property Holdings, whose registered office is not in Slipp, but in Panama – at PO Box 100879 to be more precise. Des was born and schooled in Slipp, just a few years ahead of me. He owns shops here, and lives nearby, and this is where he tried to get off with my wife (if he hasn't already). This is where he has been getting off with my wife, for longer than I'm able to fathom (probably). But if you want to communicate with him, you have to cross the bloody Atlantic. But what it also means is that Johnny was right. 'You can't touch him.'

I'm drawing up my own Schedule of Dilapidations, which I haven't done since I decided to stay here, in Slipp, and take the shop on.

Good Things about My Life
    Madelaine
    Shop
Bad Things about My Life
    Living in Slipp/people here, e.g. Des, Johnny Mac
    Family – Frankie (love Mum though)
    Friends – Denny (Have I got any??)
    Madelaine (?)
    Shop (?)

It doesn't make me feel any better, which it never should if you do it properly. You're only doing it in the first place because you're fucked up. I mean, nobody stops in their tracks on a country walk with the one they love and says, 'Right, hang on a sec, I'm going to calculate just how good my life is, I'm going to do a good/bad list.'

So I'm putting 'DEFINITELY' next to the two items in 'Good Things', and crossing 'family' out of 'Bad Things', and deleting 'love Mum' because everyone loves their mum, even my dad for Christ's sake. I know that this is what they call fudging and it makes me feel worse, that I'm actually trying to cheat myself. If you lie, or need to be deceitful – as I've said before – there's something going wrong in your life. What if you lie to yourself? Jesus.

I'm angry again, with the coat going on and a pen in my hand that's making a big and diagonal, capital 'FUCK YOU' across Neville Neville's letter, which is on its way up the street to go behind the bar at Rascals where it'll get to Des a sight quicker than Concorde can cross the Atlantic.

Back home. I've abandoned the stock-take. I'm at work on the Cinnamon guilt. Except it feels as though I actually quite like her – at least the newness of her, to me. This much is fine and understandable, except it can't be, because I've kept it from Madelaine. I'm trying to.

I'm moving round the house, from room to room. I'm mooching, with her all around me. My Madelaine: on stage with people you might vaguely recognize, but wouldn't be able to name, from the telly, pointing and smiling, having a good time even though she's supposed to be at work. She's elsewhere: soft-focused and posed; or in stark flashlight with peoples' arms round her, some of them men, and sometimes kissing. She's everywhere in this house, and nowhere to be seen.

It's difficult if you marry your first. Madelaine seems to have created opportunities to herself. But for me, there's been none of the discoveries my mates have always been having in pubs and at discos; and the holidays where that's all they're after. And in Slipp, if you're not going out with them, they're not around – in the Dog or the Masons. They're in the Rainbow of course, but that's different. There's women in the shop, but that's scripted. In and out. Three or four minutes and even then it's only the weather or the buses or the council, unless they're ailing or know someone who is. Where do you meet women, unless they're friends of your wife's? In which case they'd be her friends, which I'm beginning to see doesn't have to mean they can't be yours, unless you blow it.

Madelaine has managed to make friends out of men, though, without them being mine first. Probably because she's not stuck behind a counter all day with a stream of old women, or men in her case. If she was, she'd probably still make some headway, the way the barmaids and girls in the bookies do. For example: Mrs Sellars comes in the shop, she's not going to say, 'Looking good today Artie', and start nudging Shelley Blakeley when I turn to fillet her plaice. Is she? But get Mr Sellars going into Tommy Jacks's, with Madelaine behind the grille in a clingy top – he'd come out with something. And even if she didn't fancy him, there'd be some young lad in the queue to catch the glint in her eye and see his chance. Before you know it there'd be a comment, then conversations, a rapport. A week later there'll be a 'What time are you having your dinner' and an 'I shouldn't' and not long till there's quick drives to neutral pubs, then shorter drives to the woods.

So imagine the chances she gets in the city in a job that's full of actors and stage hands and delivery men and catering people. Imagine that – I am, but I'm saved by the bell.

I pick up the phone, but can't pick up the voice, until he tells me. We've never spoken on the phone before.

'It's me. Johnny.' He sounds surprised by the sound of his own voice, as though he's not used to the telephone.

'Johnny? Oh, right.'

'Look, Artie, I . . . I shouldn't be talking to you. I'm just sorry, 'bout your mum's, the other night.'

'Did you do it?'

'Don't matter. Just do as he wants, lad. It'll be for real next time. Look, I shouldn't be telling you this. But we used to be mates. You know, the stuff you said the other night. I feel shit about this. Your mum, she won't talk to mine. They been friends forty years.'

'Denny's gone. Left Slipp.'

'No he hasn't,' says Johnny.

'He has. Last night.'

'Anyway, this isn't about Denny. It's the shop,' he says.

'The shop? What's that got to do with you?'

'You're going to lose it. One way or the other.'

'No way.'

'No helping it lad. Just let him have it.'

'It was my grandad's. It's all I've got.'

'Get what you can for it and leave.'

'What can they do?'

'Can't say lad. He'd kill me.'

'You can tell your boss I'm staying put.' I'm trying to get some conviction into my voice, so I'll believe I'm strong enough for standing up to them. I can hear him breathing at me down the line, then a sniff and he speaks.

'They're going to fire it.'

'What?'

He's gone. By the time I've got the phone back onto the hook I can't hold my hands still. It's come too close, close enough to shorten my breath and to make me ask what I would really do if I had to confront them. Handing the envelope back was easy enough – an unopposed act. More foolish than brave. But they're coming now, to get me. I can feel it, see their sticks and stones; their knives and petrol rags.

Madelaine's driving onto the path as I leg it out through the door and I'm ignoring her shouts as I race off the Close and onto the hill. Slipp is juddering in front of me, up and down and out of kilter to the sound of my breathing, which is out of step with the rhythm of my strides that are too fast and short because the hill is sliding with the slush underfoot. I'm going too fast to slow down and I won't be able to change direction, but all that matters is getting the envelope back, the 'fuck you' fire warrant, before it gets to Des. The cold is in my eyes, and by the time I get to the High Street, with Rascals in my blurry sights, there are tears on my cheeks and thin snot dripping from my nose. I'm not crying. It's just the cold, but I could easily be, when I see a turquoise Bentley parked out front with the driver leaning on the bonnet, smoking and burly and liveried.

I'm diving into the doorway of the Estate Agent's, opposite Neville Neville's place, in time to see Des walking to the car behind someone twice his size. The big guy's staying on the kerb and nodding as Des is talking up to him, getting into the back of the car with a clenched fist going up and down like a workman's hammer. The big guy's blowing out with puffed cheeks and a mop of the brow, even though it's freezing cold. The driver's taking Des past me. There's a phone at his ear and his narrow mouth is making small spitting shapes. His staring eyes that look like shutters to whatever kind of soul he's got.

My breath won't slow down, can't get enough air to stop the fear tightening me up. Too late. It's on its way to Neville Neville's in the hand of the big man who you wouldn't mess with, but who does as Des says. He's got them all doing as he says now. Since that night in the Dog. I'm leaning on the plate glass to shore up my knees and the Bentley is away up the hill, in double vision in the thick plate glass that's showing Brenda's flat. 'Luxury Dockside Apartments'. They're probably Des's too.

Something formless is making me giddy, not angry. I can't say what it is. Like when you read a sentence or a paragraph over and over, narrowing it down into phrases and words you know should mean something but which make no sense. You know it's making you happy or sad but the meaning's not there.

I'm crossing the street and looking up at my shop, with its sign that needs painting but which otherwise is in perfect nick. It's immaculate. Despite what the schedule of dilapidations says, I've done everything that's needed to be done. Roof, pointing, damp proof. I even reinstated the plaster-work, the only one on the row, despite Madelaine telling me

I'm 'bloody mad, there's no need'. Stucco they call it, and I did it to make it look like it was before, in the photos from when my grandad had it. My mum's got the photos at home, with men in tunic suits and bowler hats sat outside on benches playing cards with their lurchers curled in front. Straight backs and handlebar moustaches, Sunday best in camera. The whole row was the same then. I've even kept it the same inside, with the big tiles and their blue and green swirls in deep relief; the contoured wood, and marble surfaces; the stained glass inset panels above the plate. It's a conservationist's paradise.

I'm running towards my mum's, further on down the hill where the shops peter out to the Dog where I vault the walls to its forecourt, and out the other side to cut the corner and over the barrier to the Railing Road with a run to the central reservation where I'm stopping to get some breath. There's a gap in the traffic so I'm off again and vaulting the wall to the Estate, which is too high so I scrape my shins on the top, but without any pain, just a glow by the time I'm across the green and in sight of my mum who is scrubbing the tar from her door, reaching up in grimaces from her chair with the neighbours watching, arms crossed under their apron breasts, grim-faced. I should help her, but can't. There's too much to do.

'Artie! What are you . . . ?'

'Nothing Mum. Stop that. I'll help you later. Back in a sec.'

But I'm not, because I'm straight into the front room where I've got the drawer from the sideboard on the floor.

'Do you mind?' says Frankie. 'We were trying to listen to . . .'

'Fuck off Frankie. Why aren't you helping Mum?'

'What?'

'Just fuck off.' And I'm smiling. I can see it in the polished silver frame of the fire that's electric barred and never used. 'Front room's for best. You know that, so piss off into the back.' It's tradition, you see. You should respect tradition. I always have, which I've always seen as holding me back. But I've got the photograph now, and I'm on my way back, with Frankie muttering.

'See you Mum. I'll pop round later,' I shout as I run across the garden and onto the green.

'Artie!'

But I'm gone. The words on the advert are coming into focus as I'm back over the wall with the traffic cutting across me. I can see the shop again, up the hill, sticking its stucco chest out from the modern grime, like a fish out of water.

```
         Two units left in our Exclusive Dockside
                     Apartment Block
    Unique City Centre Location in Historic Listed
                        Building
            Heritage Approved Development
         Acquire all the luxuries of Modern Living and
                a foothold in your history.
```

And I know it's all more or less true, from when Brenda showed me round her place. So proud, she was, of the original beams and the windows and the pillars and the grain elevators which all had to stay. 'Can't touch a thing. You can't take a crap without permission in here. They're listing everything these days.'

Back at the shop, across the road and looking up at it, breathless, I take it in, then look down at the photo, and back again. Shop photo, photo shop. Perfect match. It's quarter to three, still plenty of time – to go down to the council offices to do what's necessary. In photographs there's a chemical called fixer. It stops the image fading in the light. We did it in science. Protects it from the passage of time.

I'm looking for a taxi, which could take some time, so I'm walking down to the carriageway where I'll stand more chance, when past comes the turquoise Bentley. I'm diving into Tommy Jack's doorway, with the warm fog clutch of tobacco and the blanket sound of horses' names and cursing. But not before I've seen the brake lights glow red and my Madelaine in the back.

17

There's good news from the planners, who were very interested to hear my case, and who are implementing emergency procedures to safeguard the site in the short term, even though they're on a skeleton staff. They can see the urgency of my position. But the bad news isn't any better, with Madelaine in the house when I got back but volunteering no kind of explanation of why on earth she was in the back of the Bentley.

'You've not forgotten it's Benny's party tonight have you?' I say.

'No.'

'Aren't you getting ready?'

'You go on your own.'

'I want you there.'

'I don't fancy it.'

'What will you do?'

'Do? I don't know. Have a bath, watch telly, sleep. Get my vibrator out.'

'Vibrator?'

'What the hell do you think I'm going to do, Artie? I just want a bit of peace, that's all.'

'I'll stay.'

'Go. I want some peace.'

'You didn't wake me this morning.'

'I'll tidy up while you're out.'

'Where did you get to?'

'It's still a mess from last night.'

'I saw you in the High Street,' I say.

'You can't have.'

'In a car.'

'Oh.'

'What were you doing?'

'Just get ready and go, Artie.'

'You want me out of the house.'

'Too right.'

'You shouldn't just drop people. We've known them fifteen years. I make an effort with your friends.'

'I know, and I'm very grateful. It's sweet of you.'

'Sweet? It's loyal.'

'I just don't fancy it.'

'You should stand by your friends. Stand by each other.'

'I just want to stay in.'

'Why?'

'For fucksakes Artie, just go. I don't like the people.'

'So you're not going to make the effort.'

'No.'

'I'd make the effort for you,' I say.

'I know.'

'How can you . . .'

'Shut up!'

'I love you.'

'Oh Artie.'

'As much as I ever did.'

'What's going on?' she says. I think: going on? With *me*? 'I . . . I didn't want to mention this,' she says, getting out of her chair, 'I was going to let it lie.' She's off into the dining room, through the archway where I can still see her, and she's going to the cupboard in the dresser, the one that's full of junk, and she's burrowing to the back with old bills and dead plugs falling on the carpet, which she doesn't bother picking up. Her voice is deep and echoing from inside the cupboard. 'I was getting ready. Except I couldn't find something.' She's standing up, and walking towards me. 'These.' She drops the loose leaf knickers and stockings and the football sock onto the coffee table. 'What are you up to, Artie?'

What can I say? What would you say? 'What are you doing rummaging through my drawers? Is there no privacy in this house?' She's saying nothing, which is making the silence big and wide so I have to say something, which I do, but I don't know what it's going to be until I say it.

'I . . . I just found, I don't like . . . them. They're vulgar. You shouldn't . . .'

'This is too weird, Artie. Look, I've been trying to tell you. I want to get away for a bit. A few days. The play's working fine. Spike's happy for me to take some time.'

'Spike's happy? Oh great. No problem then. What about Des?'

'What?'

'Nothing.'

'I'm going the day after tomorrow.'

'You've got the service. In Wales.'

'I know,' she says.

'Still going?' She nods. 'So you'll be back, New Year's Day. I'll take you down. Wait for you, nearby. Like we arranged.'

'We didn't arrange.'

'We . . .'

'I'm not coming back.'

'Not coming back?'

'Not straight away.'

'You're leaving me.'

'Artie! I . . . oh Jesus!'

'You've outgrown me, haven't you?'

'Artie, for Christ's . . .'

'You never used to blaspheme,' I say, thinking of the present I bought her, the one it took me months to find.

'That is my business.'

'Where's the rosary? I've not seen it since I gave it to you. That was a present, I gave it a lot of thought.'

'It's safe.'

'You're supposed to carry it. It's supposed to . . .'

'I know what it's supposed to do, Artie. I *am* the Catholic, was, remember? It's very nice, Artie, but it's just an ornament.'

'An ornament?'

'If you've lost your faith.'

She's faithless. Faith*less*, not necessarily *un*faith*ful*, though you could be forgiven for confusing the two.

What is beyond doubt is that she's found my secret trove. She's also not carrying the rosary that was supposed to stop her changing. It was supposed to push her back towards the faith she had when I found her. Adultery is a cardinal sin. But she's lost her faith.

'You can't just drop people when it doesn't suit you, you know,' I say.

206

'You go, then. Apologize for me.'

She's too clever for me. Too strong. I haven't got the fortitude to ride out the silences that would squeeze the confession from her. I'm in the quandary of wanting to search but not wanting to know. Wanting to know but not know – if it's bad. Little bits of truth that I want is what I want.

I don't want to go out, but my weakness will be flaunted if I stay, in front of a programme she doesn't really want to watch, or a record she knows I don't like. No, I shot my bolt when I mentioned that I'd seen her in the Bentley. It didn't stand up in court, sloppy. A thousand excuses would have filtered down by now, and she knows I won't follow it up. There is little doubt in my mind that she's aware of how much I want to not find her out. She must be, but what she probably doesn't know is how much I'm prepared to do to gather the evidence.

I'm on my way out, to Benny's party, even though the time we'll spend apart is precious, because her leaving of me is only three days away. By the time I've shut the door behind me, which breaks the silence of her not saying good night, I'm realizing that I can't face the party. So I drift down the hill to the Dog for the first time since the fight. It's not a good time to be going. But I need some kind of an end to be brought closer. I'm wanting a resolution. It's that time of year.

Dead Christmas is in the pub; the aftermath of too much drink and smoke and even though it's half empty and the lights are low, it hits you with its beery, ashtray smell. There's dirty glasses on all the tables and crisps and pie crusts on the floor. Bruce is not behind the bar, where he should be on a busy night. He's sat in the corner, letting it all go to rack and ruin while he's all over a middle-aged woman who I've never seen before. Her eyes are almost closed, mouth hanging open and Bruce's hands on her legs, near the top. You can see she's lost the will to push them away.

I've ordered my drink before I realize that I don't want to talk to anyone. I can't sit down because I'll look like a weirdo, on my own where I know people. So I'm sticking at the bar, which is bad because it leaves me wide open to anyone coming up for a drink. I can check them all out from the bar, with some mirror peeking between the peanuts and the optics. Which is important, because when you're stood at the bar on your own, there's a risk that you'll drift off, through the lack of things to stop you daydreaming, and when you come round – with a nasty thought or to the sound of a voice, there you are: staring at the barmaid's tits. Which would give people the wrong impression. You can go from looking for a bit of peace to being a perv without even trying.

'All right, Artie.'

I know the voice, but I've drifted off, the way I said I wouldn't and as I'm placing it I've got the barmaid giving me a bad look, which is understandable, because she probably gets it all the time, with having such lovely tits.

'Denny. I thought you were leaving.'

'Nah. Something turned up,' he says, shuffling from foot to foot and sniffing, looking at me briefly, then away, focusing on the mid distance where there's nothing. He's wearing the same white vest he's had on since the last time I saw him in the Dog. Dark hairs wisp up to his neck. There's a sheen on his skin, a glaze in his eyes. 'I'll be off soon.'

'What about Johnny?'

'They've all gone to the game.'

'Lucky for you, being in here.'

'I'll be all right.'

'So how are you?' I ask, but he's got his drink, still looking away. Hasn't heard me.

'Sorry mate,' he says, without looking. 'I've got to sort something out. See you in a bit.'

'Fine.'

It should suit me, this being left on my own, but it doesn't. A thin rejection. Worse than a row, this indifference from someone I'm stopping liking, but who is still, in the absence of real challenge, my best mate. I follow him, between the optics and the peanuts, in the ersatz mirror which advertises Player's Weights. It took me six months and eventually a dictionary to trace the meaning of that word. Fake, cheap, inferior, an imitation of something long-standing and established.

When I see who I think he's gone to talk to, I do a double take into the mirror. It is her. Off her pitch, but then so was Rascals, I suppose. Bruce doesn't seem to mind what's going on in his pub, after all those years of pride and defiance. He's glued to the old girl's mouth now, which I can see through the other mirror, the Ovaltine one that shows his blowing sucking cheeks going in and out as he gets every drop from the woman who can't be far from losing consciousness. This might be the best chance he gets for quite a while. But the main event is going on through the Player's window, and there's shrugs and pleadings being made, with Denny turning away and the thin young girl taking his leather sleeve, and turning him back, with a whisper to his ear and a finger swirling on his T-shirt nipple. There's a look of intent from her and a slow smile spreading on him. He's giving her something, a little plastic bag. He's tucking it into her bra with a furtive look that doesn't stretch as far as the mirrors, beyond the sad old men at the bar who've got their backs turned. They go out.

I give it a few minutes and finish my drink. It's my third and enough to dizzy me up a bit, and send me out the back with the confidence to see what they're up to. I push the cross bar, 'IN CASE OF FIRE ONLY', and go into the car park. I've seen it before, from all angles. Her black leggings are gathered small around her ankles and her legs are bowed, with him going between them, against the bonnet of Bruce's Austin Princess. Denny's pawing at her tiny tits, which I can't see now, but which I know are almost completely flat, but with pale, fleshy cone nipples the same colour as her skin. She leans up, but still with an arm on the bonnet to support herself. She clasps his arse with the other hand, and gives two rapid, violent thrusts with her hips and Denny's head drops, with his knees giving way.

He's stopped the mauling of her breasts, putting himself back into his flies. I look up, from the action area, and she's looking at me, with a fixed smile and tears in her eyes, and she brings up her hand from the bonnet, wiping each eye in turn with a fist that's letting go of a little plastic bag that's gone empty.

Second time today, I'm walking across the green to my mum's. The door is half clean, half tar, and I realize I didn't come back to help her scrub it. Turquoise Bentleys and black lace knickers, and Denny's white buttocks in the dark car park getting in the way. It's no excuse.

I'm here to tell her what I've decided, what's been decided for me. But I'm not going to be able to give her any answers to the questions she'll ask. I can't tell her why I'm getting rid of the shop, or what I'm going to do instead, or what I'm able to do, or where I'm going – which I don't know, and won't know until at least New Year's Day, and only then if I've got my wits about me, and keep up with Madelaine wherever she's going. So, on balance, I'm not looking forward to seeing my mum, but I've got to grasp the nettle.

As I get to the gate, I can trace to the music that's been drifting from off the crescent since I came onto the Estate. It's coming from my mum's house.

> *The boys in the NYPD choir*
> *Were singing 'Galway Bay'*
> *And the bells were ringing*
> *Out for Christmas Day*

It bursts out louder as cousin Declan opens the door, with a can of lager in his hand and love bites on his neck.

'Artie lad come in and get yourself a drink. Great to see you. How are you doing?'

'All right, Dec. How are you?'

'Great. Great. This is Monica. We're getting wed.'

Monica is drunk, hanging onto Dec's shirt for grim death. I can smell the night cold on them both. They're been outside, out of respect for my mum and her upstairs.

There's baseball bats in the hallway, propped up against the understairs cupboard, with a crowbar and long-handled hammers.

'Come prepared, eh Dec?' I say.

'We'll have the cunts, if they show again.'

'Take it easy.'

'They won't fuck with Town. There's ten of us here, more waiting if it kicks off.'

I can see them, in the front room, the best room, which I've never seen full before, and the music goes up a notch, with Declan's mates swaying to the sound of Shane McGowan and Kirsty McColl.

> *I could have been someone*
> *So could anyone*
> *You took my dreams away*
> *From me when I first found you*
> *I kept them with me babe*
> *I put them with my own*
> *Can't make it all alone*
> *I've built my dreams around you.*

I go in the back, where the old women are sat in a circle, in gentle and earnest chatter, and my mum's crying opposite Delores, who looks no older than the daughter she's trying to comfort.

'Merry Christmas, Artie,' says Delores, 'Thanks for the present.' She has soft eyes in a hard-skin face and she's fingering the chain of the cross I gave her.

'Give your mum a hug,' says my mum. I bend down, and she makes my face go tacky with her tears as she pulls me further down, into a stoop.

'So what's to cry about?' I ask, pulling away, knowing it's just the drink bringing it to the surface. Non specific tears are these, not too dangerous to discuss, because the women are smiling with their glasses and waiting their turn to embrace the sadness in their own lives.

'Oh, just this place. This bloody place and its bloody people. I wish your dad was here.'

'You didn't tell me you were having a do.'

'You'd have only gone fussing round. You've enough on your plate.'

'Hmm. Has Frankie gone?'

'No,' she says, with the heads around the room dropping in honour of the shame her daughter's brought to our mother. 'You won't ever leave will you Artie?'

'Me?'

'Say you won't.'

I don't. I just give her another squeeze, with the smell of her face make-up strong in my nostrils.

There's fresh tears coming in her eyes, not spilling. They're pooling up, making her blink. 'I wish things were different, had been different . . . things a child shouldn't see . . . just a game. Just a game . . . the things he's had to do, all on his own.' And she's going out, with the tears bursting. She's banging through the door into the kitchen, where the chatter stops, then starts again, in a hush.

'Sit down.' Delores is talking to me, with a slow beckon of her hand, and she nods at the door, sending my aunties away, to look after my mum, leaving us alone. She pats the cushion next to her, on the settee where she's sitting. It would be a sofa in our house. Her hands are thin, with thick, greeny veins. 'You can tell me what's wrong,' she says, looking severe and with a deep, gravelly voice that's still got its Irish core.

'Really grandma, I'm all right.'

'Just have faith.'

'Faith? I . . . I'm all right grandma.'

'Sure you are, but you're wanting, I don't know, some assurance, about something. Am I right? You look lost.'

I'm nodding at her, not having the words, the vocabulary, for the conversation.

'But faith isn't that,' she says, 'it's not assurance. It's not certainty. It's a step into the dark. You might think it's a weak man who seeks faith. It's not so. It takes a strong man, to take that step.

'Your Granda was a weak man, bless his soul. I had strength enough for the both of us, I had to. He missed the war, got left with the women. Been better off fighting, he would. I never stopped loving him you know, never. I think it meant I loved him more, to do the things I did. Those things I had to do. He didn't see it that way. I was only keeping his weaknesses from the world.'

'Am I like him, Granda Sean?'

'In some ways, son. In some ways you are. But he'd never have gone. You're going, aren't you son?'

'Not yet, Grandma.'

'Not the party. You're *leaving*, aren't you?'

'How do you know?'

She looks at me, through those soft blue eyes, with her jet black hair drawn back into a scarf. They'd pass for sisters now, Delores and her daughter. Delores had stood up better to the tests of time. There's sweat on her brow. The beads cling onto her dark, tough skin that's gone scaly with age, when you see it up close.

'There's nothing I don't know about my kids. All of them. You're like him, that bastard, can't keep a lie off your face, but you're a good kid, Artie.' She leans forward and draws me down close to her with a reaching hand, that's cold, on the back of my neck. 'Always been my favourite,' she whispers. And she kisses me, on my cheek. Dry and rough. 'Don't let on though,' she says, with a glint of mischief in those eyes.

'I can't leave, though. You heard what she said, my mum.'

'She'll be all right. I know her better than anyone. She'll cope. We all will. Someone's got to break the chain.'

'Break the chain?'

'Live for yourself, Artie. This place'll drag you down. It

gets the good with the bad. But you hang on to that girl. She's all right.'

'Grandma, do you still have faith? Really?'

'It's stuck in me like a knife.'

'What about my mum. She's not got it.'

'Oh she has, lad. Oh she has. Spite of everything. I can see it. So can you. It's her sadness.'

18

'How long are you going for?' I ask.

'I'm not sure,' she says.

'You've got enough stuff.' And she has. The sofa is full of ironing – all her best stuff which she's taking her time over, with a Cary Grant film on the telly while she's doing it, as though she's escaping already. 'I said, you've got enough stuff.'

'I heard you. Sshh. I'm trying to watch this.'

'You've seen it before.'

'So?'

'So we can at least have a conversation if I'm not going to be seeing you.'

'Have a good time last night?' she asks. 'At Benny's.'

'It was all right.'

'Many there?'

'Oh. Oh, yeah. Quite a few.'

'Anyone I know?'

'You want some tea?'

'I thought you wanted to talk.'

'I'm having one. I got some of that camomile stuff.'

She's not even supposed to be going for three days yet, as far as I'm aware. She just can't wait. Normally, it's a last minute job, her packing. Up all night before we go, getting her stuff together. But it seems that she wants to be prepared for this. So I'm taking my tea upstairs, knowing her mind's elsewhere.

It's as I expected. I can't exactly leaf through the pile of her gear on the sofa while she's there. But looking in the wardrobe, and knowing her collection as well as I do, I can tell what she's taking. Simple matter of deduction. What's left, on the once-crowded rails that have now got room for the empty hangers to jangle, is her entire collection of safe stuff. Amongst it are the things I've bought for her down the years, which she's at least had the decency not to throw away, even though she doesn't wear them any more. Mainly full-length dresses, expensive ones that I rushed home from the shops with, on birthdays and anniversaries, imagining all the way what she'd look like in them, how proud her wearing of them would make me. Even the one I bought for her first production, which she said was 'lovely, Artie', but 'not quite suitable'.

She's made it plain that she doesn't want me here, so I'm going to clean out the shop and pick up something for dinner, something special and a decent bottle of wine. But there's things to attend to first. I'm taking my jacket out of the wardrobe. It's leather, and seen better days. I should get a new one really, as Madelaine keeps reminding me. But it will do, to get me through the next few days. I've got the sewing kit ready, and a swatch of leather, which I'm stitching into the lining. The knife is next, coming out of the bottom of the wardrobe where I've kept it, rather than the kitchen, so Madelaine won't notice when it goes missing. I've laid the knife down, on the leather swatch, which I'm pulling tight round the blade, pinning it into a perfect fit, so it won't jut out or make the jacket hang badly.

I'm stitching it secure, then unpinning, sliding the knife in and out, so only the handle shows. I turn it round, to read its ivory message. 'Something fishy, from your Madelaine.'

I've just finished tidying away when the phone goes.

'I'll get it,' I shout, taking the stairs three at a time to get there first, with her stood at the lounge door and watching me, as though she might have something to fear.

'Hello. Who? Oh, Isabella. Hi.' She's back in the lounge with a raising of the eyebrows and no doubt feeling relieved. 'Where is that? Let me get a pen.' I'm in the drawer of the telephone stand, looking for a pen, which I can't find. I need it because Isabella wants to meet me, which is strange. I'm definitely not her type, in every conceivable way. But she's worried about Frankie. 'Hang on.' Madelaine's handbag is draped over the bannister, so I'm scratching around in its chaos, looking for a pen. But half-heartedly, because something has gone wrong. 'Go on then, tell me again. I'll remember.' Part of the second layer of fresh skin rubbish in the bag is the burgundy shape of a passport. 'Climax? You sure it's called that. OK. In Town? Near the cathedral?' We always keep the passports, both of them, in the bureau. I'm in charge of them. I do all the arrangements for holidays. 'Six o'clock. Should be all right. I'll call you back if there's a problem.' And she's giving me her mobile number, which is a new one on me for someone in dirty skirts and motorcycle boots who lives in a squat. I'm saying 'yes, yes, yes' as she tells me the number, but I'm not taking it in or writing it down because I've got more important things to consider.

I really have got to do the stock-take, which will be my last. I've got today and tomorrow by my reckoning, because after that I'll need to be able to go, in pursuit at the drop of a hat. It's difficult to concentrate though, because I'm trying to dismiss the ridiculous notion of stopping her in her tracks by hiding the passport. It is ridiculous, because I won't be able to lie to her well enough, when she asks me if I've seen it. She'd have to come clean about why she wanted it, but I'd be coming clean about why I'd hidden it, which would ring alarm bells and allow her to get her defences up, which would spoil my chances of getting to the bottom of things. Perhaps that's what I want, but it's not what I'm going to do. I'm taking control, whether I like it or not. For better or for worse.

There's not that much to do, if only I applied myself. The freezer should only take an hour or so, and the rest is on the shelves: tartare sauce and dried peas, that sort of thing. I don't know what'll happen to it all, when Des gets it. I don't know what he'll do to these non-perishables. He could have them for all I care. I'll be out of here by then, well away by the time he realizes that these bricks and their mortar aren't perishable, preserved as they are by an order from the council that I can pick up later on today.

So I'm pushing it to the back of my head, and pulling on a top jumper to keep out the first layer of chill in the freezer. But I'm sure I can hear something out front. Can't be because the latch is on, and the 'closed' sign should be showing. But there is a rattle, I'm sure I can hear it – dull through the walls. Like someone trying the door, and then there's a jangle, so I'm rushing out, and closing the freezer door with a solid metal clunk. By the time I'm through into the shop I can hear the bell jangle again, with the front door bouncing open off the latch. I check the door, which hasn't been forced, so whoever it was must have had a key, unless I left it open, which I'm sure I didn't. There's no-one outside, no-one running away, but a car engine revs up, and disappears with a screech, down the hill to the carriageway before I can clock its number plate, but not before I've seen it's a Capri, spoilered and not that uncommon in Slipp.

Within an hour or so I've got the freezer finished and I'm getting stuck into the shelves, which will take me no time at all. I'm making up boxes as I do it, for my mum and Delores O'Brien, but not Nana Gill, who I've decided I won't miss at all, and I try to hone in on this, to make me feel better about leaving, but it ends up making me feel bad in a way I can't fathom.

The telephone blurts its staccato shrill, armalite, the way it's been since my grandad Gill amazed us all, when I couldn't have been much more than five, by being the first person in the family to have one.

'Artie.'

'Denny?'

'Yeah. Are you working?'

'Seems like that,' I say, trying to get the loathing into and down along the wires.

'Look, I'm sorry, 'bout dashing off last night. I was, like, busy. You know.'

'Sure.'

'I was wondering. Could we, have a chat, maybe a drink.'

'Why?'

'We're mates. Aren't we? Come on. I'm on my way to-morrow.'

'You're leaving Slipp?'

'Yeah. I'm off to Spain. How are you fixed?'

'Now? I'm busy.'

'Come down the Railway. Just for an hour.'

'I haven't got my car.'

'It's not far.'

I don't want to agree, to relent. But it suits me anyway. It's on my list of things to do, part of the straightening out, the finishing off.

'All right,' I say.

'Good lad. Hey, it'll be good, like old days.'

'In the Railway? It's a dive.'

'So? Remember when we used to go. Only place'd serve us. Bitter's great.'

'You drink lager.'

'Old times' sake.'

I've got to get off the phone, because I can feel myself softening.

'Half an hour.'

'Good lad.'

I lock the door, checking it twice because of what happened before, and start off up the High Street. There's two ways to get to the Railway, much of a muchness, but I'm going up, past our old school, with Denny's words lamenting in time with my step, 'old times' sake, old times' sake'. Just for the hell of it, I'm walking at a stretch, treading on cracks, the way we used to.

The quickest way to the Railway, from the top of the hill, is down through the clough. There's a seat at the top where Madelaine and me would sit until it got too cold – in summer, right up until the sun went pink and then died, over the chimneys. I'd come here on my own, after work, in the first summer she was away. At first I'd relish its melancholy, lapping it up and excitable at the thought of her visits home, which got less and less regular, until I couldn't bear to come here. Then we got engaged, and I didn't need it any more. But I'm not going through the clough, because I've got decent shoes on, and I want to go past school, for the first time in years.

They built it at the same time as the Nelson, but on this side of the Railing Road, trying to lure decent kids from the grammar school. It never really worked, which meant you'd get the rabble traipsing along the High Street and lowering the tone for everyone. It's built on the valley bottom, next to the foundry. The football pitches and playground are waterlogged now, like they always were. Thick mud that would cake on your legs after games, and which you could pick off in French or Maths if you managed to dodge the showers. French, where Johnny got to be cock of the school, for decking Denny, and splitting his head against the wall, with two slow motion kicks that sounded like the cracks of a snapping branch, even though it was leather on flesh, and Thundercliffe came running up the stairs with his face red and his fists clenched.

'Right McCafferey! This is it, you're finished.'

And Johnny just standing there, with Miss Lefevre shaking like a leaf. Like a leaf that was shitting itself. He was grinning, with Denny's blood on the skirting board and pooling slowly towards his shoes.

'Shut it, Thundercliffe. Else I'll do you too.'

Even though Denny was our favourite (of the two) and crying like we'd never seen before, we sniggered at the way Thundercliffe took a half step back and dropped his fists. He stood there, trembling, and said 'All right, McCafferey, all right. Very clever. Have it your way. We'll see what your father has to say about this.' He said it with his voice cracking and it made Johnny laugh, louder and louder, until his eyes started to water, and rubbing off on us with Denny lying there and the sound of sirens from the ambulance getting closer.

Of all the things that happened to me at school, most of them good it has to be said, I don't know why it is this that's repeating on me now, the first time in years that I've been back to the place. And rather than think of the rush of first kisses and the hidden-pride carriage of exam results, or goals scored on the football pitch, I'm looking at the scarred, peeling panels of the three-storey concrete, and digging deep for memories of Des, three years above, who must have been hard, to end up the way he is now. All of which confirms that it's got to be right to get out of Slipp now. If these are the things that have risen closest to the surface, still, after all these years of relative success, it can't be much to leave behind.

My leaving is in motion. I've got the letter to Des, my deed of surrender, and later this afternoon I get the preservation order. It's only temporary, the order, but it will stop Des from being able to do anything to the shop for now. Leatherbarrow had been more than happy to see me when I went round to the planning offices at the council yesterday. His name meant nothing to me, but I knew him to look at. Three or four years above me at school, and probably the same year as Des. He knew the name straight away, and Des's plans for the shop.

'Glad you came, Mr Gill.'

'Artie.'

'Artie. Yes, glad you came. I can see what you mean, about the shop. You've kept it well. Should be proud. We can't let our history go, can we?' But as his smile had hardened, and gone evil in his eyes, it wasn't hard to see that the shop meant as little to him as it did to Des. He was coming at it from another direction, that's all. It was a stick to beat with, in a game that Des had been winning. 'You know, the last thing we need is an office block in that location. The heart's been ripped out of the town as it is. We're very concerned about Slipp, the centre. There'll be nothing left if we don't draw the line somewhere.' He's sure of his ground, behind his desk. A wooden shield in a war waged with paper. Not the real world, of glass and steel; other weapons he feels safe from.

'The shop's been in our family for three generations.'

'And so it should remain.'

'Yes, sure. But I could get out, if I wanted, needed to. Couldn't I?'

'Oh yes. Of course. If you needed to.'

'Good.'

'Now, this will protect the building until the next council meeting. I will be recommending to the council that the shop receives a listing. That process could take some time.'

'Will they accept your recommendation?'

'I can't say for sure. But there hasn't been much sympathy, of late, for these schemes. Particularly certain developers.' His smile recharged and he leant back in the chair, waiting for me to appreciate him and his efforts. He had his hands behind his head with flakes of dried skin floating down the arms of his suit – cheap and creased in thick sweat folds with his sleeves riding up, cuffless and showing thick, pasty wrists that were mousy-haired.

'Fine. I . . . I'm in a bit of a rush, is it OK if I . . .'

'No problem.'

'Thanks, it's just that I . . .'

'I'll have the papers for you tomorrow.'

'Good. Thanks very much.' He was dragging his hair back and patting down the thick, unstyled flaps over his ears. I wanted to stop having to watch him. I could smell the smells I thought he'd have and I checked his ringless hands and glimpsed an empty, unclean life away from these offices.

'You still mates with Denny Lane?'

'You know him?'

'Sort of. And you, I remember you. You probably won't remember me.'

His hand came across the desk, and his buttoned jacket rode up as he stretched.

'I . . . I, of course I do. You were . . . you were . . .'

'That's right, three years ahead of you. Same year as our friend Mr Christian. Small world, isn't it?'

'Hmm, it is,' I said, wanting to get out and wipe my hands of his limp and soggy handshake. 'See you.'

'Goodbye, Artie. Good luck.'

Looking back on school days – walking past the place and with the Leatherbarrow I couldn't remember fresh in my mind – sets me thinking. You come off the Estate: same kind of parents; go to the same school with the same teachers, same mates. Then you split up, different directions, by chance. Some behind desks; some into the sea; some behind stages that make people laugh and cry; some with guns in other countries and me in a shop with old women, practically in the shadow of the school we all split from. Still much of a muchness, doing our different things. Even Des, with his bigger cars and sharper clothes, is more or less one of us – hasn't been able to get away, not really, any more than Carl Hubbard, on a beach in Cyprus but with his wife still shagging blokes in town like he'd never been away. What makes the difference is the people you choose, or who choose you, I suppose. This is what makes you either happy or sad, and so to that extent we've all got more or less an even chance.

Maybe Madelaine's not changing, like we're all not changing, not really. Maybe she's always been different and it's just coming to the surface. Maybe not even that's changed, maybe I'm changing so I can see her differences.

Which brings me to the Railway, by surprise the way it can when you let things float around in your head. The sky is black – heavy with snow which will be sleet by the time it gets to us, but there's a crack in the cloud, on the horizon, like it's coming away at a seam, up on top of Frogg Moor. We'd go there in cars in the fifth year, before we'd passed our tests: nicked or borrowed and turned on each other in a circle with full beams on and cider and Newkie Brown piled up in the middle which we'd pass round with rock music wailing out into the black nights above us. No girls and maybe the last perfect moments before it all started to get out of hand.

We'd come to the Railway too, round then. They'd serve anyone, because they needed the business and no-one was around to spot us, which was why they could serve anyone. Everyone had moved away from the Railway, even the railway had stopped coming. And here I am again. Six or seven years since the last time, which was with Denny too. God knows how they get the trade to be still open. Drugs, probably. It's far enough out of harm's way to be right for that.

It's not changed from the outside, but inside it's different. Just one big room where there were three or four snugs before. It's anaglypta'd in pastel pinks and greens that have gone dirty, with threadbare chairs that match. It's not Denny's sort of place. Not anybody's sort of place, nobody I know at least.

I've ordered a pint of lager, because they haven't got bitter. 'No call for it,' says the friendly and fat middle-aged man behind the bar. He's got a high-pitched voice that's inviting conversation, but I move away from the bar to wait for Denny. The lager is warm and flat, metal-tasting. There are two piles of free papers on the window-ledge: one white, one pink. I pick up a pink one and flip through it, not reading but filling the gap until Denny arrives. The man behind the bar is looking at me and smiling, about to break into chat, so I flip a couple of pages, with some kind of purpose, and start to read. My feigned interest turns real when the word CLIMAX jumps up at me from a full page ad. 'Mr Bear Heats.' It's inviting me to 'come and cheer on our regional finalists'. Climax, the place where I won't be meeting Isabella tonight. There's enough on my plate already. I want to drop the paper and leave my pint without giving offence, when I realize what's happening.

The pavement's coming up at me in jolts and I'm trying to get my legs to pump faster, driving me past the school and up the hill, along the mud track through the clough. I've got to take the short cut. Got to get back to the shop. Denny isn't going to the Railway. He never was, he wouldn't go there for anything but a fight, queer bashing. But he wanted me there, lulled me there with fake nostalgia, so he could get in the shop, the way he tried earlier.

19

The door is locked and resisting the key. The blinds are down over the door and the window, which they weren't when I left. I've got my shoe off and the mud seeps between my fingers as I take a firm hold, and twist my head away to protect my face, with the sound of glass shattering in echoes as the shards hit the tiled floor in the shop. I feel stupid, putting the shoe back on so I won't cut my feet, and undoing the snick. The smell hits me, and I know it's not stupid.

He's running into the front of the shop from the back, following the sound of the breaking glass, until he sees me. He's got an ashamed look on his face, and I can see he is lost and desperate. Despite his treachery, there is fear in his eyes, more than sorrow. He drops the can to the floor with a hollow, tin bang. Looking over his shoulder I can see he's completed his preparations. The desk is in splinters, the doors off their hinges. He's been through the plasterboard of the ceiling too, and there's a stream of petrol trickling from above where he's doused the joists, which will take. It would go up all right.

On the mad rush through the clough I'd been running over what I'd say to him. I'd got it looping back on itself, going in figures of eight and reordering itself to maximum effect, so in the end he would drop to his knees and weep and plead how sorry he was. It would be my test. A litmus on my powers of forgiveness. But now I'm here I don't know what I'm going to say.

'You're back quick,' he says with a smile that's gone before he stops talking.

'Yeah. Not so quick on the uptake, though eh?'

'You got here. In the end.'

'This is a man's job, is it?'

'Don't, Artie. Don't make it worse than it has to be. This is the only way to end it.'

'Don't lie to me, Denny. There's no need now. You're here to save your own neck.'

'You don't understand.'

'*You* don't understand. You don't know why you're doing this.'

'Jesus, Artie. I feel bad about this. You don't know how bad. Shit, mate, we're . . . oh, come on. Leave it, Artie. It's got to be done. He wants you out.'

'He wants me out all right. But he could have got anyone to do this. For fifty quid, friends or neighbours. But he chose you. Why is that, Denny? Why do you think he wants you to do it?'

'I don't know, he just . . .'

'Don't you think he might just enjoy seeing you betray me like this? Do you think he'd get more of a kick out of destroying a friendship than just torching the place? Do you think he might enjoy controlling shit like you Denny?'

'Fucking hell, Artie. You know what he's like. Maybe you don't. I had to say "yes". He'd have killed me. He'll kill me now if I don't do it.'

With the petrol smell thick in my head, getting into my throat, and the steady drip from above, I can see the bastard's going to go ahead with it.

'Why you though? Think about it.'

'You should've seen him, Artie. Look, it's only a shop. It's insured.'

He's looking at the door and digging into his pocket.

'You were working for him when it kicked off in the Dog. He set it up. It's not your fault if it got out of hand.' He's saying nothing, avoiding my look, and his hand is moving in his pocket. I can see his fear. It's something else. Not the fear of doing this or getting caught. So I beckon him towards me, with a soft smile, and he comes, slowly. 'Look mate, I understand. You've got to do this. I can see that.'

'You do?'

I'm taking his head between my hands. I can feel my smile going softer, I can feel his neck in my palms: rough and warm and strong and sweating. I tighten my grip and his eyes bulge, his breath is gusting in my face, all the way up from his balls where I've just brought my knee up, as hard as I can. His head's going away from me, in my grip with a crack to the wall, then another, and a smudging of blood on the wall, striping down to the floor where he's crumpling. I've let his head go, and I'm across to the counter and back again, with my foot on his chest and the cleaver in my grip – thick-bladed, big-handled.

'What . . . the . . . fuck.'

'Shut up. Shut up! Listen to me. You tell me why he's using you. Tell me! Or I'll kill you.'

I will, really I will. It came in a flash, the last rush of conscience deserting me. I'd kill him, then fire the place. I'm reaching down, into his pocket, and knocking away the weak hand he raises against me. I've got the lighter. I'd caught him red-handed, trying to escape. There'd been a struggle, and he fell, against the wall and banged his head. The flames were all around us. I tried to save him but I couldn't. The police would believe me: they'd be happy to be rid of him. So would Des, that's obvious. But why? Why would Des be glad? Why stitch him up with this arson job?

'Tell me, Denny. Last chance.'

'I can't.'

I've got the thick blade of the cleaver on his cheek, with my foot on his chest, trying to freshen my anger to make me cut him. But I can't. It's gone. I won't be able to kill him, so I stamp on his chest and he wheezes, dry and rattling.

'It wasn't . . . an accident,' he says, 'what happened to Billy. It didn't happen in the Dog.'

'I was there.'

'You were out cold. No-one saw it.'

'I'll fucking kill you, Denny. If you don't tell me the truth. I swear it.'

'They had Stevie.'

'Your kid? Who had him? I thought they got him afterwards. They already had him?'

'I can't say any more.'

'I'll kill you. I'll fucking . . .'

'You won't. You can't.'

'Tell me, please.'

'You can't do it, can you?' There's no smugness in his voice. Not a sneer. He's pitying me.

'I can save you though. If you tell me.'

'Save me?'

'I'll surrender the shop. To you. You can give it to Des. He can have the place. I've got the contract. You can take it back to him and you won't have to fire the place. Tell me what happened.'

'You won't tell anyone else?'

'No-one.'

'Swear?'

'I swear.'

'Where's the contract.'

'You can trust me.'

'Where's the fucking contract!'

Madelaine was out when I got back from the shop. No doubt preparing for her trip, which I now know won't just be to Wales, in memory of her friend. So there's no kind of worthiness to her desertion of me. This is much worse.

The smell won't go. I'm sat in the bath, on top of my evidence, with a whole tub of her apricot and walnut facial scrub gone, scoured into my arms and face and neck, and still the petrol is stinging in the hot water fog. I can see how desperate she is to leave. To go straight away, with a passport and a new job in a new place, with all her best clothes packed, and me on a false trail to Wales, stupid tosser as I am. I top up the bath with more hot water and lie back. The steam rises, takes the blur with it, leaving it a little more clear.

It would suit her if I was tied to the shop. You can see now how important my little stash is. How clever it was of me to keep it, even when you might have thought I was paranoid and untrusting for hiding it away. Money can't buy you love, but it helps if you want to feel it drain away slowly, until you get something else to fill up your life. You can't just let it go with a cold kiss and a suitcase, and then there's nothing. Absolutely nothing. I've glimpsed the emptiness: on a dance-floor and in the back of a Bentley, and I've heard it in small, passing untruths.

I've got to find out where she's going. So it's on the floor with everything from the sideboard, and a slow replacement, item by item. I sift all the big stuff up: hairbrushes, sellotape, crimpers, car manual, assorted belts and hairbands knotted together, and a broken picture frame. They're in a pile now, and going back into the drawer. Next is all the small crap: cotton bobbins, hair grips, gas bills from years ago, plug fuses, and a fir cone I spray-painted silver our first year together, which I'm putting to one side for the tree, later, and the rest is going in the bin. I've been waiting too long for them to find a purpose. Which leaves potential stuff. These are going back in the drawer, item by item: credit card receipts, matchbooks, business cards, folded post-it notes, theatre programmes, an old diary which I've been through before. All sorts of stuff, but nothing to help me.

Nothing. Folded post-it notes. The ones Madelaine uses all the time, going grubby and folded in onto their own gluey edge, the way she does when she's talking on the phone, with a bored look on her face, but sounding the essence of charm. All grubby apart from one, which I retrieve, and un-fold in an origami rewind, it's triangle and square pattern creases multiplying to reveal her own name. 'Madelaine 0171 638 5859', and more: 'hrow 1540'. Why would you write down your own number? Why would you have a London number if you lived in Slipp? I have no choice. I'm following her, down the line and at least one step behind, but getting closer.

I've got to wait for the line to accept the clicks, which

come in a rush before the ringing, which is short-lived and taken up by a female voice, foreign.

'Gaul Travel, Yvonne speaking, can I help you?'

hrow makes sense now.

'Is Madelaine there?'

'Madelaine is not in today. Your name please.'

'I'm calling about a flight my wife booked. She arranged it with Madelaine. I need to change something.'

'What is your name?'

'Gill. Her, my name is Gill. G.I.L.L.'

'And the destination?'

'The destination? Ah, yes it's the 15.40, from Heathrow.'

'Ah, Charles de Gaulle.'

'Yes, exactly. Paris, that's right.'

She's tapping away, at a keyboard, and talking in French to someone. I can recognize the shape of some of their words, put images to them, but there's no meaning to it. I was a 'waste of space' at oral, according to Miss Lefevre.

'Mr Gill?'

'Yes?'

'What is the problem?'

'Problem?'

'You wanted to change something?'

'Ah, yes. Of course. The booking is for two people, right?'

'Yes. Mrs Gill, and . . . Mr Gill?'

'Yes?'

'I'm afraid . . . I'm sorry, your wife will have to contact us herself. She made the booking and . . .'

Too late. For her. I'm taking the phone out of its socket, in case they call back while I'm out. Who'd have thought it? Paris. Two of them.

*　　*　　*

The funny thing is, knowing that Madelaine's got two tickets for Paris and her bags packed, leaving me behind – I don't feel too bad. Maybe this is the step into the dark that Delores O'Brien was talking about. Maybe the faith that I'm finding is in my power to recover. At least I'm not going crazy. At least there has been something to worry about all this time.

There's another end approaching me. It's sorting itself out too, with a helping hand, from Denny of all people. With my foot still on his chest and the deed of surrender in his hand, he had explained it all: about Des and the Nelson, and the Dog that Friday night.

I pretty much knew what he told me about the gangs, one on each side of the Railing Road: Town Side and Nelson. The Nelson was the Nelson, and Des had the Town Side. What I didn't know – I didn't not know it, it just didn't touch my life – was that there was more and more money passing through the Nelson. The kids needed it for their drugs, so it filtered down the High Street in burgled shipments that ended up in needles, but it upped the stakes for controlling the Nelson. It became an embarrassment for Des not to run the Nelson. It had raised him and now it was a goldmine, of sorts. The Town crews wanted to know why he wasn't taking a cut.

The Nelson wouldn't let Des into their businesses. That was when he called Denny back, to set up the ruck in the Dog. As far as Denny knew it was just supposed to be a warning. Des told him to get one of the Nelson crew, keep one of them behind to take a message back. So Denny grabbed the last one out of the door – Billy McCafferey. Denny reckons he thought twice about taking him. Billy was weak. More importantly, Billy was Johnny's brother, and everyone liked him because he'd got out, straight off the

Nelson and into university. Not by changing – just being good at the other side's game. Like Madelaine, except Madelaine was from the other side.

Denny needed Des. Des had something he wanted. His brother. He had Stevie safe, so long as Denny did as he was told. And anyway, Des just wanted Billy to deliver a message. But Denny would say that, wouldn't he? Bleeding in my shop and clutching the contract like his life depended on it, fearing for his life, but not fearing me: stood over him in the petrol smell, holding the lighter and probably looking as though I didn't have too much to live for. No, he was afraid of Des, small Des in his expensive suits, like everyone else.

So Denny gets Billy outside, in the car park, into the back of Des's car, and Billy's wedged in between the two of them. Des grabs Billy round the throat, doesn't say a word, just screws Billy's face round, so Denny can just see the back of his head. Then Des starts digging at Billy's face, jabbing him, and there's a scream from Billy, a scream that goes on and on, with blood coming onto his shoulders until Des gets out and drags him onto the gravel. Des leans into the car and picks something off the floor and tosses it to where young Billy's still screaming – like a cat. The driver starts the car and Des turns round to Denny, who reckoned he couldn't believe what was happening. Des gives him the bloody knife, saying, 'You did that. You take the rap or your fucking brother dies.'

So, Des makes his inroads onto a Nelson that's rioting because of him, and gives them someone to blame, says he'll sort it for them. He's taken Stevie's eye, which shows there's no loyalty to Denny, to keep him quiet. And just to make sure, he brings Johnny Mac over from Ulster, as his new man in Slipp. To bring peace to the province.

Torching my shop was going to be Denny's last job. He's off to Fuengirola to run a bar for Des. As far as Johnny Mac is concerned, he's been run out of Slipp, and with Des having someone catch up with him – which, I reckon, is probably the case anyway.

This information satisfies my curiosity, but is otherwise worthless as I've promised Denny that I won't tell a living soul.

A promise is a promise.

Mates are mates.

20 _____

'When do you go?' I ask her.

'I'm not sure.'

She's putting on a dress I've not seen for months, one I bought her. She's not worn it since she changed her hair, and it doesn't look right. It looks almost vulgar – even though it's long and she's wearing it with sheer nylon and court shoes the way you should. It makes me feel, I don't know, uneasy. It doesn't fit, but I smile, feeling powerful and ironic – in control, because I know what she's up to, and she doesn't know that I know.

'New Year's Eve?'

'No, not New Year's Eve. Probably not. I might go to-morrow, travel down leisurely, you know.' She's found something that needs attention on her dress, picking at the hem so she can duck her head out of contact and do something with her hands, to stop her lie fidgets. Without looking at me, she says, 'I'll be able to stop off for lunch, avoid the traffic, you know.'

'The Wye valley is beautiful. You could go that way.' I'm making it easy for her, I know. But finding her out isn't the issue here. I don't want to do her harm, make her uncomfortable. I wouldn't do that, I don't think. Whatever. That might not be true. 'Yes, I think that's a good idea,' I say, surprising her again.

'What? OK, fine. Tomorrow it is,' she says. 'It's only for a few days.'

'That's what you said. The other day. I believe you.'

'You believe me? What's that supposed to mean?'

'Nothing. I just believe you.'

'Why wouldn't you?'

'I wouldn't. Not believe you.'

'Artie.'

'What are you doing today?'

'I thought we could have lunch or something,' she says. 'You've got nothing to do.'

'How do you know?'

'It's Sunday, you're not in the shop.'

'There is more to my life than the shop you know. I've got a full day as it happens,' I say.

'Why are you wearing that jacket?'

'I like it.'

'It's scruffy, old-fashioned.'

'I like it.' I can feel the scale of the blade, but not its sharpness. My sheath's doing a good job. It's protecting me, and you can't see a thing.

'Why have you got it zipped up. Aren't you hot?'

'You were asking me what I'm up to today.'

'No I wasn't.'

'You're not interested?'

'I am,' she says.

'You're not.'

'Whatever you say.'

'I'm selling the shop.'

'Selling?'

'Yes, been on the cards for a while now.'

'We haven't talked about this, Artie, we need to discuss this.'

'You don't talk to me about your work.'

'You're not interested,' she says, not realizing how genuine my interests are, now it's almost too late.

'What will you do, without the shop?'

'I'm not sure. Something different, I think. I'm still young. College, maybe.'

'For money, what will you do for money?'

'Me? Or us?'

'Yes, us. No, I mean . . . never mind.'

'Money's not a problem,' I say, trying to be composed, cool. Trying to lull her into a mistake.

'You can say that now.'

'I thought you'd be pleased.'

'I wish you'd talked to me about it.'

'When? You've not been around.'

'Oh, Artie. Whatever you want. Christ knows what the bloody hell you do want.'

'You going out?'

'Yes.'

'In that dress? It does nothing for you.'

'You bought it.'

'I made an error. It's not you.'

'Go to hell, Artie.'

*   *   *

As soon as she shuts the door behind her, I've got my shoes on, picking up the keys to my car on the rush to the driveway where her angry exhaust is still fuming, even though I can hear her brakes padding up at the junction a hundred yards away.

I'm having to drive faster than normal to keep her in my sights. At least the roads are empty in waiting for the New Year. As I thought, she's heading for Town, turning left along the Railing Road and outpacing me beyond the speed limit. She won't know what speed she's doing, won't be able to hear the engine under the music she'll be blaring. I've got to keep up, because even though I think I know where she's going, I don't. If you see what I mean. I don't know where his house, flat, penthouse is/are. Even Denny didn't know, or wasn't telling me. Either way, it's classified.

It takes seven minutes to get from the eight mile sign to the ring road. When you take into account the traffic lights, and two roundabouts, you can see how fast she's dragged me along. Now, she's switching lanes and taking turns and doing the roundabouts at a speed which tells me she's done the route before. We're alongside the railway tracks now, on a pothole road that used to be main – when my dad brought me to see the ships, or at least put me on the dockside while he went in the Jamaica. Which all makes sense, beginning to, now I've got my bearings. Why shouldn't Des live in his own waterfront luxury apartment with a foot in all our histories.

She's parked up, and gone into the building. I crawl alongside and past her car, past the Bentley, to park round the corner, giving her a couple of minutes to get in and work her way up before I get out.

There are only two names on the buttoned, metal box with its speaker grille. 'Brenda' and D.C.' Just as I thought.

I'm not sure what to do now. I could wait, see if they come out – linking arms, or just looking good together – and watch their expressions change. But it could be a long wait, which would make matters worse, leave me with the dots to join up, and the outlined shapes to colour in: getting brighter and more complex the longer it takes.

This is another step in the dark which I've faced up to. No light in the tunnel, so I pipe some music in. But it's not music.

The rioting in Slipp appears to be drawing to an end. After a peaceful night, a group of youths wearing scarves and balaclavas dismantled the barricades at the entrance to the Nelson Estate. In accordance with the terms of an amnesty agreed with the police, the gangs on the Estate now have twenty-four hours to relinquish all arms to the authorities.

A government spokesman today claimed that 'the amnesty was a victory for common sense'. The government has commissioned an inquiry into the latest round of urban unrest and has pledged funds for regeneration, if this is deemed to be necessary.

From the opposition benches, Donald Scarr said, 'What has happened in Slipp simply maintains a seventeen-year Tory tradition of regressive social and economic mismanagement of the country'. He went on to claim that 'the riots are part of an irreversible trend of a disenfranchised working class minority seeking to regain a voice denied it in the first place by Tory dogma, and now reinforced by a rudderless opposition. Throwing money at the problem is simply another manifestation of houses for votes.'

The leader of the opposition condemned the government and dissociated himself from Mr Scarr, saying that 'the government has bowed to the whims of violence. The situation in Slipp is simply another illustration of its failure to demonstrate to the electorate that it can maintain a consistent law and order policy.'

Whatever the politics, it is clear that the people of Slipp have

welcomed the end to the riots which have blighted the festive
season in this ordinary . . .'

There's a ringing in the car that takes away my feeling of control. I'm flicking off the radio, letting the phone noise fill the car and lapse, fill the car and lapse, out of kilter with the rushing of my body pulse.

'Hello?'

'Artie.'

It's her, Madelaine.

'Hi, what . . .'

'What are you up to?'

'What am *I* up to?'

'Yes. What are you doing here?'

'Here?'

'I can see you.'

'Oh.'

'This is ridiculous.'

'What are *you* doing . . . there.'

'I was about to have a cup of tea.'

'It's a long way to come for . . .'

'. . . with Brenda.'

'Brenda?'

'Yes. You've been here, remember?'

'Oh yes. Yes, I remember.'

'I'll talk to you later about this.'

'Put her on.'

'What?'

'I want to speak to her.'

'Don't be ridiculous. Go home Artie, or wherever you're going.'

She's gone. Hung up and no doubt watching me. The two of them: her and . . . well, we've only got her word for that.

There's a tapping on the window. It makes me jump, and

243

jump again when I follow the noise to his smileless face. Up close and pitted. There's scar tissue on his eyelids, those slanting eyelids. I haven't been this close, not with the protection of the glass that's letting me weigh him up. His mouth's moving, so I'm winding the window down. I can feel the bulk against my chest, feel the weight of the blade he can't see.

'Well, well, well. If it isn't Artie.'

'Des.'

'What's he doing here? Clever boy, finding out like that. Who'd have thought it.'

'Shut the fuck up, Des.'

'Don't. He shouldn't annoy me. He should know better. I saw him, you see, sitting all on his own. Sad sight. But it made me realize, I haven't thanked him, for surrendering. No reason for him to stay now. He's free to leave.'

'I've still got a house here. We have.'

'You want me to buy that too?' He's laughing. 'Go on, sad bastard. Fuck off where you're going.'

I've got the car going, denying myself the knife, which he'd have something to match, and which doesn't feel as though it's going to provide me with much protection.

There's no time for moping. The day's piling up in front of me. I've set in motion the things I've got to do and the four hours between now and five will crumple me if I don't get on with it. They're lining up for me: people and buildings and questions and answers and forms and methods of exchange. It's just as well, because the way things went before I'd go crazy if I dwelt on it.

But I've got the preservation order from the council, getting away from Leatherbarrow double quick and swerving the drink he said we ought to go for, to celebrate. Coming back into Slipp, I'm on my way to see Neville Neville. I'm going through my list of things-to-do like a dose of salts. I take a last look across at my shop. It will be there when I've finished, still there for as long as my future's likely to pan out, thanks to the preservation order I've got and which is now registered and which neither Neville Neville nor his client know about.

It will stop being mine, once I've taken the money, which is down to twenty-five grand – a concession I've had to make for the cash I'm insisting on. The cash is crucial to the whole thing, as far as I'm concerned. Not that the shop ever was mine, not really. Or my dad's, not after he swapped the deeds for a lease and God knows how many thousand pounds that took the walk along the High Street to Tommy Jack's and the Dog, and didn't last long while trade seeped away.

It's not exactly the fall of an empire, but I can feel the guilt as I take Neville Neville's clammy palm into my firm shake and see his smile turn down as his small hand squashes in my grip. One thing my dad did teach me. 'Look 'em in eye and squeeze fear of fuck into 'em. That's what hand-shakes are for.'

'Good afternoon Mr Gill.'

'Mr Neville.'

'Take a seat, please.'

'Will this take long?'

'Not long, no. There is some signing though.'

'I've signed the contract, the deed of surrender.'

'Yes, but there's some initialling to do, to the changes. You may want to call your lawyer.'

'What changes?'

'Just the amount. My client said you had agreed. There are several references.'

'That's OK . . . Do you have the cash?'

'Yes.'

'I don't need a lawyer.'

'It's up to you. If you could initial here, and here, and here . . .'

Simple as that. End of an era. Not necessarily, because I could be back, once they realize the building can't be demolished. Not that I feel as though I'm likely to want to take it back. And Des, of course, might prefer to alter the cut of my jib rather than offer me a new lease, when he finds out. He won't be able to do anything about it. Now it's official. His usual methods, of fire and blood would be too obvious. His interests are too public, they're documented, too vested. For sure, he'll come after me, but I'm going to the travel agent's, to get to the last place he'll be looking for me, over his shoulder in Paris: a flight, a channel, five hundred miles from his power base.

It's the travel agent's next. A new shop, down the road from Neville Neville's where the butcher's used to be.

'Hi Artie.'

'Hi Louise.'

'How're things.'

'Fine. You?' I ask.

'Not so good. Our kid got hurt the other night. On the Estate.'

'It's over, isn't it?'

'So they say. You're up on the hill now, aren't you?' she says.

'Yes.'

'Nice up there, out of the road. You still with Madelaine?'

I nod.

She nods.

It's awkward. We used to be the same. We still are, but

we both know it doesn't seem that way. We're judged differently now, and I want her to know it means nothing to me, but there's no way to do it. And anyway, that's not entirely true, because I did move off the Estate first chance I got, didn't I?

'Where are you going then? On holiday?'

'No, not a holiday, not really. Just a flight.'

'Where to?'

'Paris.'

'Nice. When for?'

'Tomorrow.'

'From Town, or you can go from Heathrow.'

'I, I need to get there before the fifteen forty from Heathrow.'

'Let me see. There's the thirteen forty from Heathrow.'

'I'd rather not go from Heathrow. What about Town?'

'There's only one a day – at fourteen hundred.'

'OK.'

'I'll just check availability. Two?'

'One.'

'When are you coming back?'

'I don't know. Can I get, you know, an open ticket, or a single.'

'Open return'll be cheaper. In the long run.'

'Fine.'

'Won't be a minute.'

She was slow at school, I remember that. But easy to like. She didn't get a hard time for being slow. She had, still has, a pretty face – milky and bright with surprised eyes. She didn't mind who she went out with, didn't used to. Not a slag, she just liked having boyfriends, and all the lads liked her. They didn't rubbish her the way you'd have thought they might. She's turned out nice. Amazing she can do an office job though. I'd never have thought it, but you can't tell. Thinking about it as she comes back, with her shoulders pointing inwards and showing she's shy, you'd come here to book your holidays with her. She'd be good at talking to people, about holidays they haven't had yet.

'There's plenty of seats. Two hundred and ten quid though.'

'That's all right.'

'How are you paying?'

'Cash.'

'Oooh. Shop doing well, then?' she's saying as her clenched little fist squeezes the biro, jig-jagging fast across the form, while I fumble in my trouser pocket with one of the wads that Neville Neville gave me.

'No, not really. When will the ticket be ready?'

'You're booked on now. You'll have to pick the ticket up at the airport though, an hour before take off. Just take this with you, to the British Midland desk.'

'Thanks.'

'Send us a postcard, eh?'

'OK.'

'And take care.'

'You too.'

21

She's been a long time, she must have been, considering how much I've done, and I'm still back before her. But the speed of her right-angle turn into the drive, the not bothering to lock the car, tell me she's not calmed down. I can see her through the net curtains coming towards me, unable to see me, conceding that one-way advantage. She's coming with a home-truth walk, head down and stride too long. But I'm feeling calm, standing my ground by the table and not running to the business of my stove. The table's candlelit and linen'd up to the nines. If you had time to let your senses take it in, you'd smell the roasting pork and the sweetness of the pan-fried apples (done in the pork juices from when I flash fried the joint to seal its essences before it went in the oven). For once, I haven't prepared my conversation or anticipated her responses. I've not amended my starting position. So if things don't go well, it'll be one less reversal of fortune to cope with.

'Hi.'

'Don't give me that,' she's saying.

'What?'

'The normal bit.'

'I've done pork. Thought I'd make an effort, for our last night.'

'You not making an effort isn't a problem, Artie. You always make a fucking effort.'

'Don't be like that.'

'I want to go out. You know that. We talked about it.'

'I want to stay in,' I say.

'Oh, for Christ's sake.'

'You're the one who's leaving. You can't call all the shots. It's not fair.'

This is the point at which I fold, normally. I don't feel about to fold now, though. Maybe I've lost my bearings a little, in this darkness of Delores O'Brien's, this darkness which, I have to remind myself, is the essence of faith. Not uncertainty, but faith in the fact that if I'm myself, then that should be good enough. If it's not, then she doesn't deserve me. That's the hard bit. Seeing her here, with fire in her eyes and a glow to her skin. If you saw her, with all the memories coming to the surface, spitting and sizzling, you'd find it hard not to cling on, at all costs. But I'm trying. It's close enough to the inevitable to try something different that will rekindle whatever it was that delivered her to me in the first place.

'Don't start that. Since when did I call the shots? If I did, I'd be able to go out without having you follow me.'

'Calm down,' I say.

'Calm down?'

'You're shouting. Look, at least eat your dinner.'

'I'm not hungry.'

'Well I am.'

I'm not. But it'll throw her off balance. So I'm sitting down, pouring some wine and serving up the apples, which have caramelized the sugar I sprinkled on at the last minute. That's the part that can go wrong, but it's turned out perfectly and brings a fairground taste that makes me lose track of what she's saying. The pork's a smidgen overdone, but you can't have it too pink, and Madelaine likes the crackling, which makes it difficult to please everyone, especially with a small joint.

'Are you listening to me?'

'Sorry,' I say through a mouthful of food. The contrast of flesh and juice, of savoury animal essence and the sweet fruit, of texture and taste, is superb. 'This is very good, are you sure . . . ?'

'I'm sure. Jesus, Artie. What's wrong with you?'

She sits down, opposite me and putting her head into her cupped palms, letting it drop so her fingers seem to come up through her hair. But they're not, they're still. It's her head that's moving, and letting out a sigh.

'I'm fine,' I say, swallowing a piece of almost perfect pork, perfect but for the compromise.

'Why did you follow me today?'

'Why are you going away?'

'Answer me.'

'You answer *me*.'

'And what about those, those . . . things I found. In that sock. What is going on?'

'I've sold the shop.'

'You've *what*! Already!'

'I could fit in, with your plans. Your friends like me.'

'Why the hell did you do that?'

'Brenda and Cinnamon and Spike like me.'

'What are you going to do, Artie?'

'I can fit in anywhere, fit in around you. I've learnt how to, I've changed. I won't let you down.'

'Brenda thinks you're a tosser.'

'No she doesn't.'

She doesn't. I can tell, because Madelaine isn't coming back with a quote, which would be her style, in her hurting mood, if she had the material.

'You don't know what she thinks.'

'I know more than you think,' I say, putting down my knife and fork, feeling a little sick but having proved my point.

'What's that supposed to mean?'

'What about this job of yours? This new job that you mentioned, are you going to take it?'

'I'm not sure,' she says.

'Where is it?'

'Not in Slipp.'

'I'm ready to move.'

'You'll never leave Slipp.'

'I would. Will,' I say.

'What about your mum?'

'Since when have you been interested?'

'That's not fair.'

'Sorry. I . . . I've got something lined up for her.'

'And the house, what about the house?'

'That's your concern as much as mine. I thought you liked your job, your friends.'

'I do. But it's over,' she says.

'Over?'

'The theatre closes after this show. End of February. I can

stay on till then but there's nothing for me to do.'

'What's happening to it?'

'Des is turning it into a Game Zone, you know, virtual reality . . .'

I was doing fine. But the name has tipped me off balance. I can feel the room changing, with its shapes on the move on the edge of my vision, so I'm clearing up the plates – putting Madelaine's in the oven in case she's hungry later.

'Where are you going? Artie. Artie!'

*   *   *

'Hello?' She sounds younger on the phone. At first I think it might be one of Johnny's girls, not his mum.

'Hello, Mrs McCafferey?'

'Yes.'

'It's Artie. Artie Gill.'

'Hello Artie.'

'Is Johnny there?'

'He's asleep.'

'Asleep?'

'He was out all night, again.' She sounds downbeat. Beaten by his die-hard ways.

'Oh, right.'

'Lord knows what he's up to these days.'

'When'll he be up?'

'I'll get him.'

'Are you sure?'

'His tea's ready. Hang on.'

Her life, with its misery gone tragic, forms shapes in my head when she's gone. Pictures of her by Billy's bed in the hospital wondering if he'd slip away, and if he didn't, what he'd be like with a lopsided look. And her empty house made emptier by the fact that Johnny's back and sleeping all the days, out all the nights. I should be working out what I'm going to say to him, but she's made me feel sad with her voice, cigarette gruff and monotone.

'What you want?' he says.

'It's, it's a bit awkward, about your Billy.'

'Fuckin'ell.'

'Calm down, it's something you should know, about . . . about, you know, what happened to him.'

'I know what happened. That bastard mate of yours. Heard he's still around – in the Dog for fucksakes. Been out all night looking for the cunt.'

'It wasn't him, Johnny.'

'D'you know where he is?'

'It wasn't him.'

'That's shit. Say that again and I'll fuckin' have you.'

'Des did it.'

'What? Says who? That's shit. He wouldn't.'

'Think about it, Johnny. Who's come off best out of all this, since, you know, since it happened.'

'Sod off.'

'He's got Top Side and the Nelson now. You know it. You know how much money there is on the Nelson. Who's controlling that, now? Hey?'

'He wouldn't do that.'

'He made sure you didn't know. Tried to anyway. He had someone to blame it on, someone who couldn't tell the truth. He's lined Denny up with a job in Spain, looking after one of his bars.'

'How do you know?'

'Ask him.'

'It's crap. Tell me where he is, Artie. Fucking tell me!'

'Think about it, Johnny. Why would Denny hurt Billy?

We all liked him. But Denny couldn't say anything. Des had Stevie. They'd got hold of Stevie before they got Billy, to shut Denny up.'

It's gone quiet. All I can hear is the sound of my own breathing, loud in the earpiece and rapid, heavy. The danger of this, if Johnny doesn't believe me, is beginning to dawn. He's coming back, with a sniff, and his voice has gone dry.

'If this is crap, Artie, if this is a lie, you're both dead.'

I should have eaten more of my dinner. Not doing so has left me feeling trembly, not strong enough to keep the panic away. What if Johnny is right? What if Denny was lying – on the squirm with my foot on his chest. It makes my belly feel empty, still wanting to empty itself anyway. I've seen what happens to Johnny's threats. They materialize, in pools of blood.

I've got to find Denny, but he's in hiding. Got to find him quick, and I'm trying to catch up with my brain, which is flitting through our past: random and desperate. There's nowhere to start. Johnny will have looked in all the obvious places: his mum's, the Dog, probably even our house, without me knowing. He'll be somewhere Johnny doesn't know about, which rules out the Nelson too. He could be anywhere. On his route to Spain. Des's? Des wouldn't unclean his hands, and I'd been there earlier, no signs. Who does he know, outside Slipp?

I'm coming up blank and tracking back through time, flitting across the recent past of the shop and the Dog, my loft and Madelaine's party. Stop. Rewind. My kitchen. Cinnamon. A knowing look, and the hidden wanting from the both of them. He'd be safe there.

*　　*　　*

'Artie? What are you doing here?' says Cinnamon.

'Can I come in?'

'It's a bit awkward just at the moment.'

She's looking ruffled, the way I didn't think she could, with her olive sheen gone to grease and no life in her almond eyes. She's just wearing a T-shirt, her breasts showing through lower than I thought they would have.

'Just for a minute,' I say.

'Does Madelaine know you've come?'

'This is nothing to do with Madelaine.'

'How can you say that?'

I'm going off her. Not just the way she looks, with a dirtier self at the surface, but because of the attitude, the assumption. The way she looks, and seems – on the cold, drizzle doorstep with stale and smoky smells coming down the hallway – feels like a betrayal. It's stupid, I know, but that's how I feel.

'It's OK.' Denny is at the kitchen door, pulling his vest over his head. 'He's all right, Cin,' he says, coming towards the door with a slow, unsteady tread and a vacant look. His face is mottled, with eyes that are barely open, his mouth moves slower than the words that come out. 'Get us something to drink, Cin.'

'All right. Don't use that room though.' The cockiness has gone, no more jokes about Denny in the sack. This is the way she is. Letting herself be mastered. Denny's ability to do this, from a position of such weakness, confuses me, makes me feel inferior.

'It's the only warm room in the fucking house,' he says, shuffling into the room where Cinnamon had tranced me up with her cards and oils and hands and music.

'I said don't go in there.'

'Just get the drinks, girl,' says Denny.

The coffee table is a mess of cigarette papers and cans and ash, with an open, wooden box that Denny reaches over to close, but not before I've seen its needle and spoon kit.

'Sit down, mate,' he says drowsily. His eyelids are dark-ringed and red-sore, like they're missing a couple of layers, like a bloodless wound.

'You all right?'

'Sure I am. Fucking hell, man, I feel great.'

'Good, good.'

'How d'you know I was here?'

'Johnny's been looking for you.'

'Tell me about it.'

'I've been speaking to him, about Billy. About what you told me.'

'What?' he says, with signs of life crawling to the surface in early and weary, inarticulate stages of panic.

'I told him it was Des that did for Billy.'

'Fucking hell, Artie! You daft bastard. Jesus, man, I don't fucking believe it!'

'It's true, isn't it?'

'What? Yeah, 'course it's true. Fucking hell. He'll fucking kill me.'

'Not if it's true. He's going to sort it out. With Des.'

'I mean Des, soft cunt. Des'll fucking kill me.'

'Not after Johnny's got hold of him. It'll be all over.'

'You know nothing.'

'What?'

'Johnny hasn't got a chance.'

'What? He can have Des any day.'

'Have you ever seen Des? Have you? He's insane. I once saw him deck this bloke. He put his boot on this bloke's head, grabbed him by the throat. Pulled the fucker out, skin and tubes, the fucking lot.' He's laughing now, slow and deep, like a retard, 'Ripped his fucking throat out. Come away in his hand, tubes 'n' everything hanging out. I swear it. This bloke's scream ended up in Des's fist.' He's sitting down now, anger fading and the voice gone sad, even slower.

'Here's your drink,' says Cinnamon, bringing in a couple of cans.

'Get out. Me and Artie's talking. And shut the fucking door.'

'Thanks,' I say, taking the can from Cinnamon who's got her head down, and is slinking away.

'You said you wouldn't tell no-one. Promised,' he says.

'You let *me* down, remember. You betrayed me.'

'No choice.'

'That's shit.'

'What do I do now, eh? No Spain. No job. Can't stay here. Jesus, what you done to me?'

I'm not going to let him do this to me, let him pin this guilt on me. It's chemical anyway, this self-pity of his, and short-lived.

'Maybe we can stop him,' I say, 'Johnny.'

'No chance.'

'Let's go, Denny. I know where he'll be. Help me.'

'Let it lie.'

'Come on, help me.'

'Damage is done.'

'You're just going to sit here, doped up and . . . you haven't got the balls.'

'Get out of here. Get the fuck out of Slipp. Your shop's gone, man.' He's laughing, slow and scared, resigned. 'Fuckin' split, man.'

'I'm asking you to help me, Denny. Stay and help me. Then we can go.'

'Too late.'

'Fuck you, Denny. Fuck you!' But he's gone. There's no response, no more signs of life.

I'm on my way, through the hallway and nearly treading on Cinnamon who's curled up and shaking on the floor by the door. I'm checking against my chest for the carving on the handle and the inlaid metal of its message, the cold comfort of its hidden blade. By the sound of things it won't be nearly enough.

22

I've got to get back to Johnny's, before he gets to Des. I don't want to have things unmended, unfinished, but I don't know what I can say or do to make it better. It's not just Denny and Johnny, who got themselves into all this. I don't want to, can't, leave my mum as his only available means of getting back at me.

It's taking me to the Nelson, back to the beginning, with charred car pillars on either side of its entrance, and wet rubbish from emptied bins trying to flap in the wind and rain. There's a group of skinny youths in T-shirts and balaclavas shuffling around on the far side of the green. They're smoking and drinking from cans, doing some kind of a sentry job, and one of them waves me over. There's no time to play their urban soldier games, so I park up and step through the debris pavements to Mrs McCafferey's house, where I've not been calling for ten years and more.

'Hello, Artie.'

'Hello, Mrs McCafferey. How are things?'

'Oh, you know, surviving.'

'Hmm. Is Johnny in?'

'Just missed him, love. Went belting out. Just after you called. He's up to no good, don't doubt.'

'Oh, right.'

'You can wait, if you want. Cup of tea?'

All the misery and loneliness I'd heard on the phone, when I called her earlier, I could see now, in her hunched and weathered frame: aproned and, like all the women in Slipp, ten years older in looks than years.

'Thanks. Thanks very much. I can't, really. I think I know where I can catch him.'

'All right. Bye Artie. Don't let him do anything silly, will you?'

'No.'

'Be careful, love. Be careful.'

There's a false smile coming onto me, and I say 'he'll be all right,' with a jolly conviction that brings the danger we're both in up close. I can smell it on my own breath.

'Oi, you!' He's shivering, the teenage gangster who I'd ignored on my way in. As he walks towards me I see goose pimples standing up on his tattoo, which is blurred and cheap.

'What?' I say.

'What you doing?' He's got bad teeth that show yellow and chipped through the hole in the balaclava.

'None of your business.'

'You're not from here. We told you to stop.'

'I don't give a toss.'

'What you doing at Johnny's?'

'Do I know you?' I ask.

'Don't know.'

'Well fuck off.'

He takes a step back, as surprised by my response, as I am. 'You're not supposed to be here.'

'Listen, you little twat. I was born here, I'll come here any time I want.' I'm taking a step towards him, looking down at him, with his pals in their T-shirts stopping their slow advance, twenty yards away.

'All right. All right.'

But it's no kind of victory, and his shuffling, embarrassed return to his mates, who are only playing games, makes me feel cheap, unprepared for stiffer tasks ahead.

The Bentley's parked up by the steps outside the entrance. It's enough to put me off. It's a shield between him and the rest of us, this money of his. It doesn't fit: with our school, and the Nelson; with the size of him and the way he dresses. It's his misfitting that's making me scared. He's made himself this way, which carries a message, that there's nothing he won't do to keep it like this.

Unless I get out of the car now, straight away and up the steps to the buzzer without thinking, I won't do it. I've got to imagine it the way it won't be – with a victory of reason over aggression, but not knowing what I'll say to make this possible. So I'm racing onto the next deceit – that I'll strike him straight away, not caring how hard it feels on my fist when I pile it into his face, how loud that ugly, solid slap will sound, how I won't be put off by the sight and feel of blood and carry on with more, pinning him to the floor and making him agree to let it all lie, to call it quits. I've pushed the knife to the back of the scene, staying in its sheath as protection of only the last, most desperate resort. I'm trying to reject the bottle or blade he'll grab himself, even if I can strike the first blow. I'm trying to reject the long struggle, the unwillingness to stop, which will be his relish, not mine.

I touch the ivory handle and go blank on the wonder of whether I'll use it. Not a dead fish on a slab. That's a joke anyway. When we used to go fishing, I'd throw them back, going sick at the way the others slapped the heads on the tackle box for that final spasm. I've spent my life since then cutting them up good. But they're already dead. A giggle tries to rise in my belly as I press the buzzer next to his label, 'D.C.'. Funny if I could gut him, pare the flesh off his bones, with the knife that Madelaine gave me. Put an end to their rides and trips and God knows what, forever, on the eve of their trip, on the eve of New Year's Eve. And I'm getting a picture of his hands on her hips, getting her skirt to ride – higher than it did the other night, and with her mouth going onto his, her hands into his trousers, with a smile spreading on his scrawny face as he pulls away from her, and tells her he wants her. 'I want you now, Maddie, now.' And she's lifting her skirt, with a shimmy of her hips and her hand busy in his trousers. His slanty eyes close and he bites his lip as she . . .

'Hello.' The voice is electric, crackling and female.

'Oh, hi. Sorry, is that . . . is that Des's place?'

'Yeah, who is it?'

'Artie.'

'Says it's Artie,' I can hear her saying, muffled in the metal box. 'Come up. Top floor.'

'Thanks.'

I push the door, which is heavy and electric-bolted. My mind's racing now, flitting hyper and I grab a fire extinguisher off the wall, keeping the door ajar with my foot, and lodging the extinguisher between the door and the frame, in case I need to get out quick. In case I get out at all.

The steps take me past Brenda's landing, up hollow-sounding steps to a smell of new paint and flowers hanging from iron baskets. The steps end, with just one door for the whole top floor. The door is metal-green and unfinished, with an ornate rope with gold-flecked tassels. I'm pulling it, hearing a dull ring on the other side, then the sliding of metal.

The face is familiar. Pretty and plump with big lips, fleshy in the neck. Tabloid-pretty, obvious. She's wearing dark glasses – expensively logo'd.

'Hello. Bianca?' I say. She wipes her nose and nods her head. 'We met, at Brenda's. Downstairs? Week or so ago.' She's still nodding, stepping to one side, and leaving a sweet trail of booze. There's a stack of cases, patterned in black and beige, behind where she was stood. 'Going away?' She shakes her head and rubs her nose again. 'Des?' She nods.

'Artie.' The sound of his voice comes through the door before he does, in a black suit: tunic-topped without lapels. He's got his hair gelled back and smells, even from here, fresh and clean, expensive. 'Well I never.'

'Des.'

'Oh Artie, Artie. What have you done?' It's too late now. I know I shouldn't be here. I can see what Denny meant, the new look on his face, eyes gone soulless, smirking smile, looking up at me, then down, inspecting his nails. 'Call me a taxi. Twenty minutes,' he says to Bianca, 'Now!' She flinches and takes herself away, through an archway and into another room. 'You see, Artie, I've got a trip. This shouldn't take long, though.' He's turned his back on me, going through an archway. 'Come on, lad.'

I follow him into a large room, with four ceiling-high

windows looking across empty docks to Town with its stained towers against a black, rain sky. There are large canvasses hanging on the yellow and orange and green walls, no furniture to speak of, just a couple of iron and leather chaise longues. Johnny is sat at one of them, with his face screwed up in pain. He's sobbing.

'Johnny. You all right?' I say.

'Shut the fuck up and sit down. Over there,' says Des, still smirking his smile and taking a goblet from a cabinet made from glass bricks. He swirls the drink and takes a sip, puts it down, and picks up a pill from a silver plate, popping it into his mouth and swallowing it with a grimace, then a sip, and a wider smile. 'You've got a big mouth, Artie. Spreading rumours. I've put Johnny here right.' Johnny dropped his head as if in shame.

'Johnny, what's going on?' I say.

'I said shut! The fuck! Up! Clear?' He's taken a step towards me, hands behind his back, chin up.

'I, I . . . just want to know . . .'

'You've got no rights, shithead. Clear?' He's moved up against me now, with lemon on his breath and a wild absence in his expression. You couldn't hurt him, that's plain to see, now, up close, so I'm dropping my head too. 'I've got a flight. You two cunts are getting in my way. What am I going to do?'

He's back by the cabinet, taking another sip from his goblet, and I catch Johnny's look and I ask him 'Why? why do nothing?' with an upward nod of my head. He looks down at his legs, moves one and grimaces in pain at the other, which I can see is hanging, from the knee down – loose and dangling.

'Jesus, Des. What's going on? This has all gone too far,' I say.

'Is that you? I thought I told you. This hasn't gone far enough, that's clear, wouldn't you say?'

He opens a drawer in the cabinet – glass-fronted on steel runners, and brings out a leather tube, truncheon-shaped with a metal clink inside. He's wrapping it round his hand, twice, three times, so the leather bulges, slapping it into his open palm with dampened metal thuds.

I don't see him move, not really, just the first spin and a blur and the cracking of my leg, then the sound of my own body crumpling to the floor. No pain, just unable to move, a tingling. 'Don't move, play dead,' I think, seeing things pan slowly as he skips round me, then jumping over to Johnny with another spin that brings the leather, full orbit into his good leg with a scream that lapses to groaning and comes again.

'You stupid! Stupid! Fuckers. Oh, what am I to do.' He's pacing round the room with a manic spring to his step and pounding his palm with the leather. 'What, what am I to do? Finish it, finish it. That's what I've got to do. We all know that, but here? No, not here. Or should I?'

Johnny's on the floor now, with his legs splayed from the knees and making wet croaking noises that's him trying to breathe.

He caught me on the calf. I can move my leg. I'm making like I can't, and feeling for the knife and its ivory message, but I can't make a move with him pacing round so close.

'What's this about, Des? What did Johnny tell you?'

'You're scared, are you Artie, eh? I can smell it.' He sniffs up twice, like an animal, then he smirks. 'Jesus. I don't know what she sees in you.'

'Who?'

'Who? Stupid boy. Who do you think?' He's pacing towards the window, out of sight and clipping his heels there and back on the wooden floor, with me getting the knife out, so it's in my hand, between my chest and the floor. 'This is who.'

I look up, screwing my face across the floor and squinting up at Madelaine's face – sultry, on black satin, looking into camera with his dicky bow head smirking next to her in the flashlight. It is scrawled: 'Des, thanks for everything, love Madelaine.'

'That's who, you sad bastard. Dragging her down. Trying to drag me down with your stories.' He's turned again, placing the photograph on the cabinet, with me pulling up to sit, with the knife in my hand.

'They're not stories, Des. They're true. You know that,' I say, ready for his attack.

'Everybody knows.' The voice is behind me. Denny's voice, with Des going wide-eyed, for a second, then composing himself.

'I see, all the shit's here now, is it? Any other scum want to come on board?' he sneers, swilling the drink round his goblet.

Denny's walking towards him, not stopping, keeping going with a slow tread and saying nothing.

'You want to do this?' says Des. He spins, bringing his foot up high to Denny's face with a cracking noise that sends Denny to the floor. Des has got hold of Denny's hair, got a grip of his head, which he's banging, up and down onto the cabinet, in his lightning hands. The glass surface smashes and Denny starts groaning through blood. He's got Denny's hair in his hands again, but failing to lift it this time, releasing it slowly. It's combing through his fingers as Denny drops to the floor again, because I've delivered Des another message from Madelaine: in ivory and spilling dark down the back of his suit.

Denny's crawling to his feet, droplets of blood falling to the polished floor, thick and floating like mercury berries, not soaking into the varnish. He's smiling, dullness gone from his eyes and with a liberated look, chin up, spreading his shoulders back.

'Jesus, Artie. Well done, mate. Nice one.'

'I've . . . have I? Is he dead?'

'As a fucking dodo,' he says, pushing Des's body off the glass cabinet and putting his boot on his back, next to the knife, which he's nudging to loosen it, with more blood coming to the soaking surface. 'Nice knife, man. Nice knife. What's it say?'

'Don't. Just give it us. Thanks.'

I take the knife, putting it back into the jacket. It's tacky against its sheath, and I feel sick – no pleasure to be found where it ought to be.

'Shit, what's up with Johnny?' asks Denny.

'It's his legs.'

'They'll mend,' he says, matter of fact. 'Best get him outa here.'

'We can't move him.'

'Well, we can't phone an ambulance.'

'Shit.'

'Is . . . is he?' Bianca's at the door, not crying. Not even looking sad, not hanging her head any more.

'Dead?' says Denny. 'Sure is. Who are you?'

'His girlfriend.'

'Shit.'

'It's all right,' she says.

'Jesus, love, I'm sorry.'

'Don't worry. He was a bastard. A fucking bastard,' and she's walking across, to Des's body, taking off her sunglasses. Her eyes are dark and puffed up, going yellow on the old bruise edges. She's gathering up phlegm in her disco face and spitting down onto the back of his head. 'Fucking bastard.'

'You haven't called the police, have you love?' asks Denny.

'No.'

'Good. Look, you come with us, OK? Artie, get a cloth from the kitchen. Clean the prints off everything, and keep the cloth. I'll get her in the car and come back for Johnny.'

'What will I do now?' she asks.

'Anything you want, love,' says Denny.

'For money.'

'Jesus.'

'You wait here,' I'm saying to Denny, getting out of the car and knowing the worst already. No car in the drive. As soon as I open the door I can tell, feel the emptiness of my own echoes.

'Madelaine. Madelaine!'

She can only have been gone an hour or so, but the life has drained out of the house. It's got its new smell back. Nothing's out of place, like she'd left it to make an impression on someone else. I rush upstairs, seeing spaces where her bags had been. I'm checking the surfaces – no note. Nothing to say. Clean break. No paper words to make it worse than it has to be; no more evidence than I've collected already, but equally no sign that she knows: a) I'm on her trail; b) he's dead.

23

I don't know where I stand, with Des's body in a skip and part of Madelaine's present at the bottom of the canal – the blade. I have the handle somewhere safe, somewhere they'll never find. Denny has done the place for prints and any other signs we might have left. He's said not to worry about Bianca, that 'she's taken care of'. He said it with a glint and a smirk that told me he's unlikely to reform, that he'll be a part of the new order.

But that's just the practical side. That's only half the problem. 'He was a bastard. He had it coming.' This is the consensus I am receiving. I know it to be true.

I have killed a man. I have blood on my hands. It was my action: taken with reason, with the knife pre-packed and there just in case what happened happened. It happened in slow motion, when it came to it, in a light made red, coming through the glass, wet stained with Denny's blood. He was a bastard. He had it coming. These things I know.

I have killed a man. I have got blood on my hands – as Cinnamon recognized all that time ago, in the flat beneath the one where I made my killing. I've got fog in my head. Denny assures me 'we'll get away with it'. I don't doubt this to be the case. I have no reason to doubt Denny in such matters. But I can't handle the thought of the questions: in spartan rooms with men in uniforms. They'll break me. I know they will. I'll want to tell them. Share the burden.

I have killed a man. Blood on my hands. Mud in my soul. I want to feel guilty. I want to be ashamed. I want to know that the killing of a man cannot be done lightly. I want remorse, even though I know him to have been an evil man. Even though I am a decent man. I am told this and believe it to be true, but even a decent man cannot be allowed to take another's life and feel nothing.

I have killed a man. He will be on a slab by now. If not now, before long. They will find him and put him on a slab. Men in white coats will come with knives and cut his flesh, through tissue to the bone. They'll pare the flesh from him. They will fillet him for truth.

I have killed a man. He was an evil man but it is still wrong. It doesn't feel wrong, which is wrong. I don't know if I will tell Madelaine. I know that I should know whether or not she would forgive me, but I don't.

I have killed a man whose apartment was adorned with a photograph of my wife. I do not know whether I can forgive her for allowing it to come to be there, for the reasons it was there.

New Year's Eve tomorrow. After all this time it's on me unexpectedly, and I'm alone – a day before I expected to be, and not quite ready. I've got the case packed, with the money wrapped in socks at the bottom. It doesn't feel right taking that much money on a plane and I daren't check if it's legal or not, because it might not be, and where would that leave me?

I've left Denny at the house. We've kind of made friends, and it will keep the place safe, maybe. Also, if Madelaine calls it will piss her off, and the stupid pleasure that the thought of that gave me took me by surprise, came at me like a sort of relief, taking away some of the bitterness of the memory of her framed image in Des's flat. That was the last time I saw her face – looking down at me through her message to him, 'with love', and something fishy, sharp-bladed, between me and the floor.

It's early, and Mum's still in her dressing gown when I get there. She's got old drink vapours in the house, and a watery, vague look that tells me what she was up to last night. I'm going in the front room. Isabella's there, and I remember I let her down, not meeting her the other night. But she's smiling at me, sat listening to quiet music with her back against the radiator and her knees up in her chest. She's taken that part of my guilt away. She's nursing a mug of tea in both hands, looking ordinary in her dressing gown, with her hair ruffled and flat at the back. You wouldn't be able to guess, looking at her like this.

'Hi, Artie.'

'Isabella. I'm sorry about . . .'

'Don't worry about it. You all right? You're limping.'

'It's nothing.'

'You're early?'

'Hmm. I'm going away.'

'Where are you off to?'

'Paris.'

'Great. You didn't say.'

'No. Frankie about?' I ask.

'She's upstairs.' I'm nodding, and getting another smile off her. 'She'll be down in a minute.'

'Good. I just want a quick chat, before I go.' What I don't say, is that I'm here to try to put a part of the past to rights, to get at least a part of my future on a better footing.

'We're off too, tomorrow. Party in London for New Year.'

'Nice.'

'Yes, should be good.'

There's a bang at the door, and in wheels Mum, with a tray on her lap – spilt tea and toast. 'I don't know,' she says, 'can't seem to get people to use back room these days.'

'Maybe you should use this room more often,' I say.

'I prefer back, for myself. What's the case for?'

'Oh, just going away, for New Year.'

'All right for some. Anywhere nice?'

'Not really. Just me and Madelaine.'

'I don't know. You spoil that girl.'

'Not really.'

' 'Course you do. Anyway, I'm off for a scrub. Drink that tea while it's hot.'

'All right.'

'She's nice, your mum,' says Isabella.

'You don't have to live with her.' Frankie is following her gruff voice into the room, coming in with a towelling robe open at the front and making me look away from the dark patch.

'What'd you know about that?' I say.

'Enough.'

'Well I think she's nice,' says Isabella. 'Look, I'm going to make some more toast. Want some?'

'Yes,' says Frankie, taking her place squatting down by the

radiator, pulling the robe together as she sits, and shoving it between her knees, thank God. 'You off somewhere?'

'Paris. Don't tell mum though, she'll worry.'

'All right.'

'I . . . I might be away for a bit. I've, I've . . . sold up.'

'The shop!'

'Sshh.'

'Shit, Artie. You'll have to tell her.'

'I will.'

'When?'

'I don't know.'

'You going to leave her?'

'Who?'

'Mum. In Slipp. She'll freak.'

'I have been here, with her, on my own ever since . . . you know. I think I'm entitled . . .'

'Hey, loosen up. I'm not criticizing,' she says.

'I've had a word with Mary McCafferey. She's going to look in twice a day. And once I've gone, the social will have to do something.'

'She won't go to them.'

'I've got a friend at the council, Denny's going to pay him a visit.'

'That should do the trick,' she says. I smile. She smiles. There's a burst of relief when I see there's something left of old Frankie, proper Frankie.

'I want you to do something for me,' I say, taking an envelope from my bag, 'there's five grand there. I want you to get it to her, fifty quid a week.'

'She won't take it.'

'Say it's from a trust. Say you got it from the Fishmongers' livery. Make something up, just don't let her know it's from me.'

'OK.'

'Thanks.'

'No problem, it's about time you left anyway. You're so set in your ways, Artie.'

'Not any more.'

'Sure.'

'Chalk and cheese, eh?' I say, relaxing.

'Not really.'

'Look at us,' I say.

'Didn't used to be. We used to play all day, remember. Every day. You were my hero.'

'Get away.'

'So big, and strong. Handsome bastard, always were.'

'You used to bully me.'

'I used to hate you,' she says.

'I hated you too.'

'Bullshit. You wanted to be like me, that's all.' She's smiling as she says it. Even though she's a tomboy, and bearded for as long as the chemicals last, she looks pretty when she smiles. When her dimple fissures and her eyes sparkle, like something precious in rock. I've not seen her like this for years, happy. Not since the times we're talking about. As if talking about it can make it come back.

'I used to wish that I had, I don't know, your power,' I say.

'Power?'

'Getting people to do what you wanted. Mum, and Dad, at school.'

'They knew I would hurt them, see – if it came to it. You wouldn't hurt anyone, would you?'

I'm thinking about the body that was above Brenda's flat, with a space in its back where Madelaine's knife fits.

'You left. You hurt us all,' I say.

'I know.'

'You're wrong, about me. About me not hurting anyone.'

'Oh no. No I'm not.'

'You'll see.'

'You two still fighting?' asks Isabella, coming in with a plate of toast piled high, and nestling down next to Frankie.

'Not really,' I say.

'Artie won't argue, not properly. He's scared of losing.'

They've got me sat on the edge of the bath, Frankie and Isabella, and stripped to my waist. Frankie's playing with my chest and shoulders.

'Ooh, wouldn't you just kill for a body like this, Bella.'

'So smooth, so . . . strong.'

'Brawny, ain't he?'

'Look, are you going to do this or not,' I say, referring to the favour I've asked them to do for me, 'and keep the noise down. Mum'll hear.'

'She can come and help,' says Frankie, setting Isabella off in giggles, which are mainly down to what she's smoking, which she says is 'to take the edge off the day'. The window's open and I fear for Mum, who's probably had to put up with no end of hassle since Christmas.

'Just get on with it.'

'All right, all right. What's it to be: a one, two or three?'

'What's the difference?' I ask.

'One's the shortest,' says Isabella, 'really short. Two and three are just short. May as well go for the one.'

'Yeah, come on Artie, go for it.'

'He's got lovely hair. Thick, hmm.'

'OK then,' I'm saying. 'One it is,' and Frankie's got the clippers buzzing, coming up behind me, and tickling my scalp, making me giggle and shiver, setting me on edge with the hair tumbling down in prickly clouds.

It's taking longer than I thought, and my mum's calling upstairs, asking, 'What the hell's going on in there', and all we can do is giggle, making it harder for her to cope.

Frankie's going serious, finishing things off and with her breath in my face, and her tongue poking out of the corner of her mouth in concentration. I can see the individual strands on her goatee, which is thin and wispy in its struggle against nature.

'Stay still,' she says, and I realize, with my hair sticking itchy to my back, that I am beyond the point of no return. I'm becoming unrecognizable, in ways I know I must.

Madelaine has a poem on her wall, in the spare room that became, gradually and without discussion, her study. It's about a man travelling home, along the path he's always taken. It's a forest path and well trodden, and as he makes his way he comes to an unfamiliar and narrow track freshly flattened through bracken. It's a track he's never taken before. He wants to take it, but can't be sure where it will lead. He rests and wonders what to do. After much thought, he takes the new path through the bracken and into a deep glen which is enchanting, unfamiliar. After a mile or so he's lost all his bearings and is overcome by a feeling of both fear and excitement. He realizes that he will never be able to walk along his usual route again and, on coming to that junction of the two paths, be able to take that step into the unknown.

You don't find out if he did the right thing.

'There you go,' says Isabella, holding a mirror in front of me.

'What do you reckon?' asks Frankie, and I watch a new me, a me with the smooth edges gone hard, with eyes that are deeper set – into a strong and threatening head. He moves his mouth.

'Great. I like it. I like it.'

I do, I like it. It fits. It will, given time.

'You'll need some new gear, though,' says Isabella.

'For sure,' says Frankie, in my face again, making me feel like a picture in a gallery. She's looking serious. 'Definitely. What have we got?' she says, with her tongue out again, in concentration. 'Come on,' she's standing up straight from her studious stoop, 'let's finish you off,' and we walk out to our old room, in file with me between them, and my mum watching us, sitting open-mouthed, in her chair that's gliding along rails up the stairs. It spills her onto the landing with a clunk and she says nothing. It's fifteen years since me and Frankie played dressing up. More than fifteen years, but this time it's not a game, and this time it's not Frankie being dressed.

There's an hour and a half until I have to check myself in, at the airport. It's this side of the city and no more than twenty minutes in a cab. I'll order one as soon as I get to the Rainbow, before I finish the last of this part of my unfinished business.

Walking past Blakeley's old shop, I turn quickly to see myself, to catch me unawares like a stranger might, looking the way I might when they catch up with me, the way Madelaine will see the new me before she double-takes and gets shocked. But the window is hardboard, streaked damp and splintering at the bottom where the snow is still lying in a thin ridge. I can't see me. I've let me slip between my fingers. Maybe they won't catch up with me. So I'm turning, to crouch and smile at my new self in the car windows that make me look shorter, more squat than I am, and hard. This is what I could have looked like, all the time, if things had been different.

I'm looking odd. Not just the hair, but the clothes which Frankie and Isabella have given me. To go with my jeans, which they said were 'an old cut, but they'll have to do', I've got a thick cotton shirt, like a smock, with no buttons or collar and coloured in purple and green stripes, flecked with bright yellows and orange. Isabella got it in Nepal and I promised to return it intact, whenever I got back. With it, they've put me in a knitted waistcoat: oatmeal-coloured and oatmeal-textured. It's short, halfway up my back, letting the lap of the shirt trail down in flowing pleats. The girls reckon I look good, 'much better'. I wasn't so sure, but it suits my purposes, and I'm growing to like it. I like the difference it gives me. It makes me feel like I'm leaving something behind, gives a sort of newness and adventure to what I'm doing. Whenever we went on holiday, Madelaine would buy a swimsuit she 'wouldn't dare wear over here'. I can see its appeal now, feeling the rush of escape.

The Rainbow is not busy. It's still early, and the money's being kept for New Year's Eve, but there's a few stood at the bar. I feel less conspicuous now than the last time I came in. Partly because I look as though I'm not from off the hill estate, and partly because it's not really me who's come in, not the me they might think they know.

'All right Ged.'

'All right. Artie?'

'Pint please. And some change for phone.'

'Sure. Bitter?'

'Yeah, great.'

'You . . . had your hair cut. Look different. There you go.'

'Thanks.'

'Phone's over there.'

He wasn't put out to see me. Less unnerved by my being here than last time. I think he even smiled, and now I'm coming back, from the phone, with the cab on its way for me, he's even leaning on the bar, waiting for me to come back.

'How's it going, Artie?'

'Not so bad.'

'Twice in a week, eh? We must be honoured.'

'Just been to see my mum.'

'Sorry about what happened to her other day. The house, you know.'

'Yeah. Some bastards about, eh?'

He's looking embarrassed. Looking sorry. Showing contrition.

'Still, all right now, eh?' he says.

'What?'

'Won't be happening no more, all that shit,' he says.

'What you mean?'

'Well, it'll be different. You've heard?'

'What?'

'Des and Johnny, had a do. Johnny killed the cunt.'

'What? How do you know?'

'Been on the telly.'

'How do you know it was Johnny?'

'Obvious isn't it. Johnny's told us about what happened to his kid. Weren't Denny at all.'

'What's happened to him? Johnny.'

'Oh, they've let him out, from cop shop. In hospital now. No evidence they reckon. Thirty lads from here seen him when it was supposed to have happened anyway. Thirty fucking alibis he's got. You ask me, pigs are happy enough see back of Des anyway.'

'Have you spoken to him?'

'Went round this morning. Bad state he's in. Two bust legs.'

'What did he say happened?'

'You want a short with that? On me.'

'Thanks, go on.'

'Well, he finds out that Des done his Billy – to kick things off so he could break things up on the Nelson. Set it up for himself. So he goes round his flat, posh place in city, and he faces him up, knifes him. Clean as a fucking whistle.'

'On his own?'

''Course on his own.'

'How'd he do it? With two bust legs?'

'Who cares? Fucking hard, Johnny. Fucking hard. Things'll be better now, now he's back. He'll sort it out round here. Everyone's behind him. Boys are up for it, keeping the cunts from Town off the Estate.'

'Cheers.'

'Cheers, Artie lad. You wait, couple of months you won't recognize this place.'

'I hope you're right.'

'You just see. Where you off anyway?'

'What?'

'Case. You off somewhere?'

'Oh, holiday.'

'Nice one. Off to the sun.'

'No, Paris. For a few days.'

'Here's your cab.'

'Right. Thanks for the drink.'

'No problem. Have a good time,' he says.

'Cheers. See you.'

'See you. Oh, Artie. You know where Denny is?'

'No. Why?'

'Someone ought to tell him it's all right now, sorted.'

'He'll know.'

'You say so.'

24

It's just gone twelve – noon that is, and thirty-six hours before the bells chime another year in. The signs to the airport are saying 'four miles', which should be fine, because there's still half an hour before I have to check in and pick my ticket up. Except that we're not moving, haven't been for quarter of an hour.

'What's going on?' I ask.

'Don't know, lad,' says the taxi driver, 'some kind of accident.'

'Is there another way?'

'No. Only one road in, unless we go right round Town.'

'How long will that take?'

'Forty minutes or so.'

'Shit.'

The flight gets me into Paris two hours before Madelaine's.

The next one arrives ten minutes after hers. I've got to get there before her, otherwise I'll be on a wild goose chase. Half an hour, four miles. That's possible, running, but not with the suitcase, and its twenty grand. It doesn't take much to spoil a good day. Doesn't take much to turn an adventure into a disaster. After all this: tracking her without getting caught; sorting the shop out; after I've killed a man and got away with it, it's starting to go wrong. I can taste my just deserts. You can't kill a man and get away with it. Can't just leave like this, the way Frankie did, the way Billy McCafferey tried.

'There you are, lad. Cop cars. I can see 'em up ahead. They're pulling folk in,' he says. 'Looks like a security check.'

'Jesus.'

'I'll phone into the office, see what's going off.'

'Thanks.'

Jesus. I could probably tell him. It is all starting to go wrong.

'Yeah, they're checking everything, both roads. No quicker going the other way.'

'What's the problem?' I'm saying, trying to sound in-different.

'It'll be that murder, last night.'

'Murder?'

'Yeah, near docks. Some businessman knifed. Found him in a skip near the docks. I don't know. Respectable bloke by all accounts. Got them car lots, you know, Christians.'

'Right.'

We're creeping forward, the flashing blue lights getting closer. I can see them pulling cars over, four at a time, with policemen in padded sleeveless jackets leaning in, and others with automatic weapons standing by.

'Jesus, this looks bad,' he says, lighting up a cigarette. I say nothing, starting to feel sick, feeling my tongue going dry, a knotting in my throat and the headrests of the seats in front going blurry and focused, blurry and focused. 'Don't mind, do you? Got window down.' He's checking me in the mirror. I can see him smile as I shake my head, opening my own window, getting some air in. 'Here we go,' he says, starting the car and swinging it over, onto the grass.

'Hey up, Marty,' he says to the policeman.

'Right, Jack. How's tricks?'

'Not so bad. You?'

'All right, so long as you've not got a terrorist in the back there. Morning, sir,' he says, leaning down and looking across to me. My throat tightens and my head goes empty, clueless what I'll say if he asks me a question.

'What's going off, then?' asks the driver.

'Bomb alert.'

'Bomb alert? Jesus. Bloody Christmas, eh?'

'Tell me about it.'

Bomb alert. Thank God.

'Will the planes be delayed, officer?' I ask.

'Wait on, lad, wait on. Do you know him, Jack?'

'No. Picked him up from Nelson Estate.'

The policeman nods, still looking at me, his smile folding downwards with a sucking of teeth when he heard the word 'Nelson'.

'I see. Nelson, eh? What's your address?' I tell him, watching his face go puzzled. 'That's not the Nelson.'

'I've been to see my mum.'

'Can you prove your address?'

'Sure,' I'm saying, taking my wallet out, and handing him my driving licence.

'OK, son. Where you off?'

'Paris.'

'Nice,' he says, 'very nice,' handing back the driving licence. 'Happy New Year.'

'Thanks. Thanks officer, same to you.'

'See you Jack, all the best,' he says.

'Cheers, Marty,' and we're off, onto a clear road with the planes getting bigger and closer.

'Looks like you're going to make it, lad. Long as they don't blow the fucker up,' he says, laughing at his own joke. They say the French haven't got a sense of humour. That, after Slipp, is another thing to look forward to.

'Will we be on time? The plane's not delayed is it?' I ask.

'Passport please, sir.'

'With all the security, you know. Are we still on time?'

'Thank you,' she says, taking the passport. Mine is old and blue, the old British type. Not like Madelaine's, which she renewed last year because she got hers before mine. She had to get a new one for a conference, which she went to on her own, or at least without me.

'We're running a little late, twenty minutes or so. But they'll be boarding soon. Gate six.'

She's looking at the passport, then me. Me, then the passport, with a fixed smile, thick red with flakes of lipstick on her teeth and a dry, plaster complexion.

'One moment, sir.' She's talking into a walkie talkie. 'Yes, if you could come straight away please.' She's peeling a sticky label off its backing and wrapping it round my case handle. 'Did you pack the case yourself?' I'm nodding, feeling my tongue going dry again, wanting a drink, wanting to pass cold water through my mouth, loosen things up. The money in the socks. I should have transferred the money to a bank in Paris, or sent for it later. What, with everything that's happened, everything I've done. To get this close. 'Has the bag been out of your sight since you packed it?'

I feel stupid as I shake my head again, not wanting to speak, let her hear my words crack. An older man climbs over the conveyor belt that takes the cases away. He's come through a door behind the check-in desks, smiling at me from under a peak cap. I've heard stories about what these guys at the airport can do to you.

'Good morning, sir,' he says. I nod at him, feeling my smile crack into pieces before it's even lifted itself. He's taking the passport off the girl, looking at it, then me. Me, then it, flipping the pages over and all the time smiling. 'This won't take a minute, sir.' He nods at the case and the girl stands down from her stool, heaving the case off the conveyor belt and putting it behind her desk. 'Would you come with me please, sir.'

I'm nodding again, trying to get the smile going, but avoiding the girl's look, feeling hot with a sweat rising and my skin pricking against the rough cotton of Isabella's shirt. I follow him, feeling the people around me bouncing around as I put one foot in front of the other, coming at me and away from me on the edges of my vision. He's going through a door, into a room that has a desk, no chairs. I'm into the doorway, hearing him shutting the door behind me, and sealing us in. He's wearing strong scent, spicy.

'I'm terribly sorry, sir. It's just that we're being especially vigilant at the moment.' I let the silence swell, let him break into it, knowing that my muteness can't be helping my cause. 'It's just this photograph, I'm afraid, well . . . the girl thought there might be a problem. I can see it's old. I wonder if you'd mind, it says here that you have a scar, a distinguishing feature. I'm sure you can appreciate, the photograph, well, it doesn't look like you.'

He's holding it out, so I can see my fleshy young face, with long, unstyled waves of hair curling onto my neck. Madelaine always took the piss out of me for it. Said I looked 'so pretty', 'could be a girl'. And here I am now, head shorn and the face looking hard, but not scared any more, lifting up my shirt and breaking into a smile, a real one, flooding wide from the relief that's gushing.

'No problem,' I'm saying, 'here you go.'

'Wow. That's unusual.'

It is. It's a hole, in my side, just under the bottom rib and not much bigger than the eye of a darning needle. But it's a hole nonetheless, big enough to pass string through or stick a pencil into, which, of course, I would do as a party trick during Chemistry or French. Big enough to be worth putting on a passport and getting me into the clear.

'How did you get that?'

'Fencing.'

'Fencing?'

'A sword. Went straight through. I wouldn't let them stitch it. Just grew back like that.'

'Amazing. Sorry to have troubled you, sir.'

'No problem.'

He's got me back to the desk, smiling at me with what I could swear is a lick of his lips, and whispering to the girl, who's smiling and looking at me, showing me her red speckled teeth, and big gums, nodding at what he's saying.

The flight isn't full, and I don't suppose they would have upgraded me otherwise, but it's nice anyway. Crystal glasses, and the champagne coming non-stop, but no excitement from the people. They're travelling first class because it's their job, or they're rich enough not to get pleasure from such simple comforts. I am getting the pleasure, imperfect because I can't share it, or even let it show. I don't want them to think it's too good for me, but not for them.

I'm wishing my mum was here, for the pampering. I take another sip and watch the fields go a smaller patchwork, picturing what she might do with the money. I let a giggle rise, seeing her with chipped mugs of barley wine, in the back room in her dressing gown, telly on and the sounds of kids playing football outside. She wouldn't want to change it though, I don't think. What I've done is best, giving Frankie the five grand, which I really do believe she'll keep for mum, not blow on what she blows her money on. It's due to her, for everything she didn't get, that went to Tommy Jack instead.

Looking down, and watching England haze in cloud, then disappear, I feel all right looking back. There's nothing I could have done that I didn't do, that's how it feels. Except for Madelaine, of course. But that's why I'm here. I'm going to face up to her, find out, and it feels as though I might cope. It really does. Except, that dryness on my tongue, with the policeman in the window and the customs guy in the room. That's how I might cope. It might be. I might choke. So I'm letting the girl with the shiny tunic thighs pour me another glass, and I feel my tongue fizz and the back of my throat go wet and then dry, leaning back and taking the paper on my lap, with its front page story of the senseless murder of a 'hard-working and respectable businessman, a working class boy made good'.

We're an hour late, which is fine. It gives me an hour less to kill before Madelaine gets here. An hour to change money and work out her possibilities. She could get the bus, taxi, or underground. If she goes for the bus or underground, it's simple – just follow her. If she goes for a cab, that's more difficult, so I'm going to line up a cab as soon as her plane arrives, have it waiting for me in case she gets in the queue. Two hundred francs should be enough, and I'm tossing the vocab around, ordering it and second-guessing what the driver might say, and my reply in response while I wait for my case to come along the carousel. Carousel is a good airport word: fun and something everyone can work out. It is what it says it is.

The smells are telling me I'm somewhere new. Tobacco that's stronger and sweet, and the unseen nearness of drains. The tannoy is a jumble of words. I can recognize some, but there's no meaning to what they're saying, and I realize I'm going to struggle with the taxi driver, with my odd request. Every now and then, in the flurry of French, there's an English word, like 'Heathrow' or 'Charles de Gaulle', which isn't English, of course, but familiar – words we might claim as our own, in our own conversations.

The bag's here and I heave it off, overestimating its weight and swinging it into a young man behind me, wearing a brown suede windjammer and smoking a French cigarette.

'Sorry,' I say, my French nowhere near the surface.

'Watch what you're fucking doing,' he says, standing back and dusting ash from his jacket.

'Watch your language,' I say. He hasn't seen me yet, not caught my eye, which he's doing now, with his expression changing as he picks up my accent and sees me.

'Right. Sorry, forget it,' he's saying, turning away in a shuffle. Maybe I am up for this.

They're saying something about 'Heathrow' again, so I leave it, going into the main hall, through customs and looking for an arrivals board.

There's nothing coming on the boards for Heathrow, but they mention it again on the tannoy, so I go to the information desk, where there's a group of people milling round one woman in uniform, who is talking French, with bits of English.

'Do you speak English?' I say to a man in a suit stood at the back of the group.

'Yes.'

'What's happening? Is there a problem with the flights from Heathrow?'

'There's been a bomb.'

'On a plane? From Heathrow?'

'No. At the airport. Bastards,' he says, the words spilling out of the corners of his accent, plummy posh.

'Is there . . . has anyone been . . . killed?'

'Killed? I don't know. They've cancelled all the flights. Bastards. I don't know, bloody Irish, and the French. Jesus.'

There's another woman, in a British Airways uniform walking through the sliding doors so I'm running to catch her. She's smart, with a hat and immaculate French plait and navy overcoat.

'Excuse me, I . . . there's a problem at Heathrow?'

'Yes,' she says, not breaking her stride and walking past the taxi queue.

'Could you tell me, is there . . .'

'I'm off duty.'

'Sorry, but . . .'

'Ask inside. Look, I'm in a . . .'

I've let her go, with her overnight bag rising and falling with her tread.

'My wife, it's my wife . . .' My voice is petering away in cracks, and I can feel my chin tremble. I drop my case and hide my head in my hands, needing to sit down but rigid where I'm stood. This is what it's going to be like, when she goes. Don't let her be dead, though. This isn't what it felt like those times I wished her dead rather than leaving me. I'd rather she lived. Please God.

'I'm sorry.' It's a kind voice with no accent. 'I'm sorry. Look, I've missed my bus anyway. What is it you wanted?' says the uniform woman with the French plait.

'It's my wife, she was coming from London, Heathrow. Is, has anybody been . . .'

'We don't think so,' she says. 'Come with me. The bomb went off in the arrivals area, so it's unlikely she would have been hurt. I can check for you. Wait here. What flight was she on?'

'The three forty.'

'And her name?'

'Madelaine, Madelaine Gill.'

'Fine, I'll be a few minutes. Don't worry.'

'Don't worry,' she says. But I haven't been worrying, that's the trouble. There's a pay-off, there's got to be. Selling the shop, the knife in Des's back, and the running away, Karen Dugg just around the corner – all the truths about Madelaine. Madelaine Gill, for how long, if she's not Madelaine Gill Deceased. I should have taken her passport when I had the chance, if only as a memento, before she reverts to Madelaine Hesketh, which she has been to some people for some time, perhaps all along.

She's coming back with nothing written on her face, no early signs and I can feel the panic coming down again, like a gentle weight, pressing in all around me, laying hands on me – gentle pressure getting heavier, a shortness of breath. I couldn't care less now, about her name. I just want her to be alive.

'There's no list of casualties,' she says. 'It only happened two hours ago. But it wasn't near the terminal for the Paris flights. She'll be fine, they're sure about that.'

*   *   *

The hands are coming off me now. I feel lighter, less full.

'Thank you. Thank you so much,' I say.

'That's OK, really.'

'Do you, I don't suppose . . . will the flight be cancelled?'

Within seconds my expectations were back where they were, tragedy a thing of distant past. I needed details now, to get the plan back, to see her and say all the things I didn't know yet.

'Heathrow is closed down completely. There have been arrangements made, with Eurostar. All passengers for Paris will come by train.'

'When? Do you know when?'

She's smiling, amused. 'There are hundreds of passengers. It depends. It could take a while. At least she's safe.'

'Yes. Yes, you're right. I'm sorry.'

'Josie?' I say.

'Yes.'

'It's Artie.'

'Artie, hi.'

'I, I was wondering, could you, I . . . do you know where Madelaine is, I've got to speak to her, it's urgent.'

'Where are you?'

'Me? Oh, I'm in Town.'

'You sound miles away.'

'Bad line I suppose.'

'Madelaine? She's gone to . . . you know.'

'It's all right, Josie, I know she's in Paris somewhere, she told me.'

'Oh. Oh, right.'

'It's just that I've, I'm doing something with the shop. I've got to get her signature on something. I need to fax her.'

'Oh, right.'

'Do you know where she's staying?'

'I . . . no, I don't.'

'It's all right Josie, we've sorted everything out. I know everything . . . you know.'

'Everything?' she says.

'I just want to send her a fax, all right?'

'Yes, yes I heard you. I don't know where she's staying. She's going for that exhibition, the Picasso thing, you know . . . the stage designs he did.'

'Where?'

'The Orsay. I don't know where she's staying. What's that noise?'

'Got to go.'

'Artie? You all right?'

They must think I'm stupid. As if I'm not an expert on living off scraps of information like that.

25

I wanted to stay near the Madeleine. It's an elegant building, near the Opera. It is not, according to my guide book, what it seems. It looks like a Greek temple but it wasn't built, or even started to be built, until the eighteenth century. They part built it and destroyed it, then part built it again and destroyed it again. Napoleon wanted it to be a monument to his army, a force of destruction. I don't know when they named it 'Madeleine', but in 1814 (which I know is the year before Waterloo, and probably when Napoleon was in exile) Louis the thirteenth decided that the Madeleine should be a church. And so it is, despite its looks. They've named it after the world's most famous whore: Mary Magdalen, who ended up a saint. Now that's forgiveness for you.

According to my taxi driver, (who, after all my fretting, spoke good English when he wanted to), there aren't any hotels by the Madeleine. But he found me a place nearby, in the Place du Marche St Honore. I couldn't really argue with him and it was pouring down, so I didn't have the option of looking around for a place to stay. He had a word with the woman on the front desk, in French, no doubt telling her she could charge virtually what she wanted. I tipped him well anyway and he took me next door, to the Bar Rubis. He introduced me to the owner and his wife, telling them to treat me well – I think. So I bought him a drink, and he accepted, recommending the Calvados, and insisting that I took one with him, and letting me pay for it.

He's left me, here in Bar Rubis, where I've had a plate of cheese and a bottle of wine at a zinc-topped table in the window, watching the office workers drifting in, receiving glasses expertly filled to their brims from the owner, who never stops talking, gesticulating with his free hand. It's a long way from Slipp, which is allowing me to distract myself from the matters in hand; from tomorrow, when I have to go to the Orsay museum and stand in wait for my Madelaine, waiting as long as it takes and still no assurance that she'll come. There you go, I've got myself thinking about it again.

I'm blowing excited and depressed at the thought of it, still not knowing what I'll say and clueless what to expect. Would she know about Des? Was it him she'd been coming with, or someone else? If it was him, would she still come at all, when he didn't show? I could call home, or phone Josie again, but I'm not. I'm ordering another drink – more Calvados, and letting it cut the evening short for me.

*   *   *

It's morning. The hotel room overlooks the old fire station. There are sounds of laughter and people splashing to shelter below. It's nice. It's better than the sounds inside my head. They're coming at me like a breeze, these noises of happy people and rain.

I've been awake for an hour, lying on the bed the way I did last night: wondering what she would say to whatever I might say. Vice versa. Not really daring to think what I might say in the first place, now it's so close, and so far away from where we've been together. It's too close now. I should never have let it come to this. It was one thing to be checking things out, but this is different. I was doing enough not to be taken for a fool. Doing enough to keep her from bringing matters to a head. Until I found that passport. Until I decided not to secrete it, stop her in her tracks, which would have brought everything to a head anyway, only earlier. But that wasn't the start of it, not really. I should never have opened that medical report, or dug and scoured for the postcard. Maybe it goes back further than that. 'Don't marry the pretty ones.'

Eight o'clock. The museum opens at nine thirty, according to the taxi driver. I'll get there for nine, just in case. Get a good spot, where I can see it all. I won't have breakfast, couldn't keep it down. The thought of it brings home that I won't be able to cope if she's leaving me. If she's already left me. So I'm leaning up, and swinging my legs off the bed, feeling the weight of my weakness, and shocking myself in the wardrobe mirror with my reflection. I'm more like the people she mixes with – more like what I think she probably wants, would already have if she hadn't got me too young.

It's a long way from home if it does all go wrong.

This is it. These are the real steps into darkness that Delores O'Brien was talking about. These steps that have taken me past the Madeleine, and the Place de la Concorde, over the

Seine to the railway station they've turned into a museum. Walking into, through, and out of foreign conversations, past people breakfasting behind glass screens, sipping brandy with their newspapers. At least this is exactly what you'd expect of Paris. It really is. A little bit of certainty, but no basis for faith in anything.

Nine o'clock, on the dot, when I get to the museum and I'm not too early. I'm not being too cautious, because there's already a queue. Looks like a school party to me, the way they're splintered into groups that tease each other. They're not bothered about the rain, not letting it spoil their fun – they're even using it to splash and flirt. German by the sounds of it. There's just one couple, in raincoats and huddled under a brolly looking at a book together. They look severe and my guess is they're having an argument, about whose idea it was to come for nine o'clock.

But it wasn't such a mistake, because there's already another party arriving, this time two by two, behind a woman jabbering underneath a brolly she's holding aloft, like a Roman Centurion. They're an old group, individually, (collectively, they're probably as old as a Roman Centurion) with plastic hoods on their lightweight raincoats. And there's more behind them, backing up against a temporary barrier and disappearing round the corner, out of the courtyard and along the pavement that runs alongside the road that runs alongside the Seine. So I'm repositioning myself, moving under a tree at the side of the courtyard to see along the pavement, but it's no use. With the rain and the queue bulging and buckling in raincoats and hoods and hats and brollies, I won't be able to see her when she does come.

I'm joining the queue, so I can wait inside, wait to recognize the way she'll take her coat off, shake her hair dry, rearrange her clothing, and move off to the cloakroom attendant, taking looks with her, looks that will follow mine, imagining what's underneath, what it would be like – to have her.

I've got Frankie's baseball cap on: black with a white X on the front, and a new jacket: leather and black with buttons and lapels and a belt that ties. It's the sort that Frankie said I should get, from the airport, for an arm and a leg. She won't recognize me, not unless she gets up close. I even feel as though I move differently, more confidently, which seems weird given what's ahead, but it's probably down to being anonymous in another person's hair and clothes, in other peoples' country.

Inside, it's perfect – for my purposes. The ticket office is straight ahead – four turnstiles which filter the crowd through in slow-moving, single file. Beyond that is the gift shop, to the left is the baggage desk, and to the right is the ticket desk for the Picasso exhibition. If I know Madelaine she'll come here first, towards my position. I'm in the bookshelves. She'll come my way to get her guide. Then she'll be held up again at the ticket desk. She's bound to come into my net.

Eleven o'clock. I've been here an hour and a half, receiving disapproving looks from humourless cashiers, with an attendant hovering over me. So I've bought a book. A 'how to' book that gets you understanding art. It's by a man called Gombrich, and it might just come in handy later, after today, if things go right.

I'll know soon. It's over now, this waiting game and I feel as though I'm about to burst out of the seams of this new me. At the very moment I need to be still and small and hidden, things are on the move. I feel big and clumsy and out of place, the way I can't afford to be.

She's here, looking brand new, as though it's the first time I've seen her. As though I know nothing about her. She's as bursting with mystery to me as she is to anyone else here. Who is she with? I can't see, can't tell. I don't know what I'm looking for, can't bring myself to take my eyes off her for long enough to check it properly. I'm afraid and excited, being where I shouldn't be, doing things I shouldn't do. Only now, at this moment, can I see that I'm doing the right thing by being here.

She's on her own as far as I can make out. Taking her coat off and shaking her hair free, dropping wet in shorter, thicker waves. Auburn waves, red on the edges under the lights, a new auburn that suits her, suits where she is. She looks just right, and I can see she's got a new dress: long and loose in raw silk. Black and flowing, in ripples from its lightness, but painting out the shapes of her breasts and hips and thighs as it moves – so anyone would be able to trace to what I know about her, about what's underneath. It seems that after all this time, I haven't gained an advantage.

She's coming towards me, with a wave. She's waving at me, almost at me and I duck out of shot, behind a shelf, and looking around to see who she's seen. Someone I might know. It's mainly kids in the gift ship, looking through the poster racks. There's a couple of young men, trendy-looking and bearing knowledge of things around them. They've been here a while, reading through books, as though killing time on a wait. But they're not looking up. There's no-one on the move, moving towards a greeting, but Madelaine's on her way. I'm crouching down, with a book on the bottom shelf, watching her dress flow in and out of view, between shelves and legs, getting closer, almost close enough now to touch. I can hear her voice, nearby, then going away.

'Darling. Sorry, I lost you.'

And it's gone. She's out of range, behind the hubbub. I daren't stand up, not with her so close, so I'm counting to twenty, with a cramp starting in my calf. The old dentist's trick of distracting pains of different types.

'*Monsieur.*'

'Yes,' I say.

'You are English?'

'Yes. *Oui.*'

'*Monsieur*, are you to buy this book?' The attendant's face is coming closer as I unknot the muscles in my legs, rising to see his concerned, weasel face, with a cashier behind. They're talking in French, pointing at me.

'No,' I say, closing the book and looking at its cover, titled in French and a mystery to me. There's a woman looking at me from the cover, in fact she's looking just past me, with dark eyes and pale skin, and fiery auburn hair. She's surrounded by people at a party, but she's looking out of the scene, at something which is distracting her, making her smile, softly. She is enchanted by something.

'*Monsieur, s'il vous plaît?*' he's saying, holding out his hand for the book. Madelaine is nowhere to be seen. I'm twisting around, peering above the crowd, looking for her hair, which I see, then it disappears, see again, and then it's gone, past the ticket desk and into the exhibition. '*Monsieur!*'

'Ah, yes. Sorry. Do you, do you have this, in English,' I'm saying.

'*Oui,*' says the cashier, stepping forward and grabbing the book from me, bending down to replace it and coming back with another, almost identical, which says, 'The Magic of Renoir.' '*Deux cent francs,*' he says, and I'm following him to the cash desk, safe in my new-found knowledge: that Madelaine is secure within the exhibition.

The Picasso exhibition is in the roof, in rooms they've built amongst the iron girders at the top of the building, near the top of the great spread of glass that is big-paned and arcing like a distorted, flattened cathedral. She's in and out of my sights and taking much longer over the exhibits than most of the people. I get glimpses of her taking notes, and referring to a book she's brought with her, talking every now and again to a woman she seems to have befriended, or maybe someone who lives over here, who she knows and lined up when Des didn't show. She's not upset, at least not showing it, so maybe she hasn't heard that he's dead.

I need the toilet. I don't want to go, don't want to lose sight of her, but I'll have to. My stomach is shifting, ahead of the meeting which I'm putting off as long as I can. So I'm taking stock of the situation. Room G, *Parade, 1917.* Madelaine deep in thought, looking up at a gigantic metallic cowboy boot. Her companion has disappeared. She's all alone, and barely anyone else in the room. The perfect time to confront her, to bring an end to delaying the inevitable. So I'm leaving her, with a softness in my belly, low down, as though someone's scooping air from me, like folding a meringue.

I'm following the signs, back down the stairs, taking note of landmarks and turnings, to get me back as soon as possible, so I won't lose her, at least lose track of her. I should have gone up to her, I know that. Gauged her reaction, found out what she knows, where she's staying, if she'll even talk to me or see me while she's over here. But I'm stopping, in my tracks. At the top of the stairwell.

There's the top of a head, turning below me, the colour of the head that Madelaine's been talking to, who is familiar now, now I can see its face from above, squashed features, that become clear as she turns, looking straight at me with a quizzical look that thinks it's recognized me but isn't sure. I dive into a door, a dark room with a video playing and intense faces, with a blade of light on the other side, where I dive out between heavy black curtains, and into another part of the exhibition. I'm disorientated now, unsure of which way to go, but knowing that there's at least two of them for me to find and follow.

It's taken a while, but I'm back on track, got them in my sights and now without a clue how to play it. They talk intensely and when they laugh, they laugh together with bright eyes, really sharing the pleasure. And they touch. Every now and then it'll be a hand on a shoulder with a whisper in the ear, then a giggle, or a nod. And going from room to room, there'll be a flat palm on a hip, or the top of the bottom, guiding and staying too long, or a linking of the arms, a hand on the elbow, and other fond looks exchanged. This, I hadn't allowed for. Not at all. This has blown everything apart, mixed all my feelings.

I'm trying to imagine them together. Really together. Imagine them in my house, her car, at the theatre. In public. Who had seen them? The comments from Frankie and Isabella, how pretty, beautiful, they'd said she was. How many know? How many have seen them and where?

'It's not . . .'

It's an English voice, and not a distinct one, not immediately recognizable to me. Coming out of my thoughts, I see them, opposite me with Brenda's mouth open, and Madelaine caught in a half turn, following Brenda's voice and stopping on me, looking deep into my eyes. There's desire there, I can see it, I'm sure about that. She likes me before she recognizes me, gives me a half smile that's warm before her eyes go wide, before she says my name.

'Artie.'

I've seen what it would be like to be seen by her for the first time. I've seen the look again, the one she showed me all those years ago when she didn't know me.

But it's changing. There's fury building behind her eyes. Scrolling down through her face. Her fists have clenched. I am saved by having done it to her here: in a public place. In the presence of her chosen companion.

26 _____

She's meeting me downstairs, in the Bar Rubis, in half an hour. It feels like a first date, or at least the way I think a first date should feel. Catching myself in the mirror, unawares and viciously shorn, there's definitely a newness to it all, and my first time in Paris too.

There's plenty to go wrong, no shortage of unknowns, which are there to ambush me to no lesser degree than when we said goodbye in the museum, with me feeling small and her looking embarrassed, not short of words, just suppressing them, in front of Brenda, who I'm still not sure about.

'I'm not going to let you spoil this for me,' she'd said, not specifying what 'this' was. But she agreed to meet me, here, and alone, and if pressed wouldn't have been able to deny that look she'd given me, that fresh look, on seeing me new.

I've got her coming at nine thirty, which is late enough to be able to hold onto her until the New Year, with its clean slates and high spirits there to help bale me out, if it comes to that. I've tried preparing, tried a couple of gambits on for size, but I can't get past the floundering that comes with my anticipation of her first reply to my first question. There's no shortage of questions, which I've committed to memory. But you can't do it like that, one after another or all together. And you don't know what the memory's going to do in the heat of battle. I've got to be natural, drop them into the conversation without her getting the upper hand, or storming out. But there's no harm in preparing, which I've had all day to do.

My bottle of wine is three-quarters empty. It's in front of me on the bathroom shelf, lemony in my mouth, still cool and fresh. I think it's good stuff, from the way it's not getting worse. It's made me feel light, but there's still a movement in the bottom of my stomach. When I drink I can feel the wine draining down, sitting there in swirls, like icing on a cake, not settling or soaking. I haven't been able to eat, not since the plane yesterday, so I'm trembly in the knees and hands. But not so bad that I haven't been able to complete my preparations, quicker than I wanted to, still leaving me with thirty long minutes to kill, with nothing better to do than shave again, and run through the list, making sure I know it. They've been with me, these items, for days now. Some of them weeks. They get worse the more you look at them, but I've got to know. I can't go on without knowing. No matter what.

1. What was he doing with a photograph of you?
2. 'Not her sole relationship.' It said it on the form. Who's the other/others?
3. Do you love me?

4. What were you doing in the car with him the other day?
5. Why did you lie to me about the night after your Christmas party?
6. Why aren't you happily married?
7. Why didn't you tell me you were coming away?
7.a. Why do you want to get away from me? (Are you coming back?)
8. What's this new job of yours?
9. He's dead. Did you know?
9.a. How do you feel about that?
10. Why did you do that thing in bed the other night after all these years?
10.a. Did you do it for him?
11. Brenda?

There's arrows everywhere and crossings out. There's no right order to ask them in, so I'm screwing up the paper and filling the clear plastic cup with the rest of the wine, and going to the toilet, again, with only three minutes less to go.

Killing time, I'm back to Plate 87 in my new book. Plate 87 is 'Le Moulin de la Galette', one of Renoir's pieces of Magic. To quote my book, which is quoting Gustave Geffroy: ' "Woman, the modern goddess, in silk, satin, and curves, dressed and ribboned in every colour" is queen of the Moulin de la Galette, the popular dance hall of the working-class families of the district. Here, Renoir was perfectly at home.'

The woman in the picture is beautiful, she is 'animated by Renoir's use of light', by the way he 'pulverizes the forms and changes the young woman's dress into a shimmer of formless matter'. She looks happy enough, but not content. She is enjoying the moment, but looking away, out of the picture, wanting something else.

I'm in Bar Rubis, having checked out the restaurants nearby. I have booked a table in l'Absinthe, just round the corner. I've jotted down the menu and mastered the translation, chosen what I want already. In addition to which, I insisted that the owner had a Calvados with me, so she'll see how well I'm liked, how I fit in, how I can adjust.

The waiting's over, and the preparations have been worthless. I know that now, when I see her coming in through the door, not looking English. I know it when I gauge my reaction, feeling the adrenaline and fear sluice up inside me, flushing around and flooding my head so I don't even know what to say next. I'm not even sure if I can form the shapes with my mouth and send out the air with its messages.

'I need a drink,' she says.

Hard day? Me? Something difficult she's got to say? How can I possibly be expected to pick up the signals and guess why she needs a drink, why she hasn't even said 'hello'. So I nod at the barman, who looks away and serves someone else. My French has gone. I daren't guess what Madelaine wants. I can't even get 'boisson' out, for fear he'll either not hear it or that it'll explode in a shout and they'll all mock my accent, with Madelaine joining in with their laughing, and saying softly, but with perfect resonance, so everyone can hear and understand through their laughter, 'Isn't he a fool? Poor English fool, I've done my best for him, I really have, but he's so vulgar. What am I to do with him?'

'*Pardon, monsieur. Bon soir. Bien. Un café et un cognac s'il vous plait. Non, un armagnac, le mille neuf cent quatre vingt. Non, bas. Oui. Merci.*'

Words, most of which I know. Recognizable sounds but no meaning, except for the magic of the way she's got the barman scurrying around from shelf to shelf showing her bottles, proffering them with a smile that stays, contorting itself, but never waning, and the locals joining in, and talking to her as she shrugs and sees the funny side of what they're saying and she says something else that I can't understand, and which has them in raptures. I don't recognize the sounds this time, said in a slow blur. There's hands shooting across the bar with notes now. Two, three notes, slapping down onto the polished dark wood of the counter, and Madelaine shaking her head and going into her bag, but the barman takes hold of her wrist and says, '*Non, s'il vous plait, s'il vous plait*,' and he lets go of her hand and points into his chest with his palms pressed together and his head to one side. And sure enough, she's shutting her handbag, and saying 'sante', and draining it like a man, and it starts all over again, with the notes slapping on the bar, and the barman banging the bottle back on the counter, making ripples on Madelaine's untouched café.

'Let's go.'

'Go?' she says.

'I don't like this place.'

'You suggested it.'

'It's too crowded.'

'It's fun.'

'I've booked a table, round the corner. It's nice.'

'All right. But you'd better be paying.'

''Course I'm paying,' I say, picking up my coat, and helping her off her stool.

'New coat?'

'Hmm, yes.'

'It's nice.' Nice? Doesn't she want to know why? Tell me it's 'not me', ask what made me get it, be suspicious that it's a present, or at least been chosen by someone not me. Ask me what I've done to my appearance, what's happening to me. Anything that someone who cared the slightest bit would do. 'I think you look good. Love the hair.'

It's not what you want to hear, in the circumstances. You'd think she'd be more angry than this, with my prying. It's unspoken proof that there's something really bad for me to fear, for her to be guilty about. I see a bloodless, civilized end that would suit her more than me, and nothing I can do to prevent it. So I've got her by the arm, and holding the door open, feeling a cold blast come into the warm fug of smoke and heat of the bar. I want to start again, sit down and with no-one butting in.

'*Monsieur.*' Someone's got hold of my coat, tapping me on the shoulder with his other hand and then pointing at the bar, where the barman has got his hand stretching out towards me, rubbing his thumb and middle finger together.

'You've not paid for your drink,' she says.

'I know!' The laughing starts up again, but with Madelaine not joining in, just dropping her head a little.

The restaurant's only a hundred yards from the bar, but a thunderstorm has just started up. The rain is bouncing up off the pavements and wetting us, under the umbrella. We're huddled together underneath it, walking quickly. We wouldn't be mistaken for lovers. She's not linking me, not getting too close, more concerned with the flapping of her skirt, which she's gathered together and holding in a stoop as we go. It looks as though she's cowering away from me. The rain hasn't stopped them at the fire station, where music is coming from inside, with the great doors opened up, and children climbing up onto the engines and grown-ups dancing and drinking, with some young ones running in and out of the rain, splashing in puddles. Two hours to go to the New Year.

The restaurant is packed, not like it was when I booked the table, and the owner doesn't recognize us, not even the name, which he ticks off in his book when Madelaine tells him, after I've faltered. He gets a young girl to take us to a table, wanting us out of the way.

'This is terrific,' she says.

'It's too crowded. Too noisy.'

'It's New Year's Eve.'

'I suppose so.'

'The food looks good. Look at your menu.'

'I'm going to have the sole. They plait it. It comes with a citrus sauce.'

'Have you eaten here before?' she asks, matter of fact, not surprised and thinking only of her appetite as she mouths the French word shapes going down the menu with a finger and saying '*Un kir, s'il vous plaît*' without even looking up as the waiter comes to the table before he's even told us what he's here for.

'*Et monsieur?*'

'What? Oh . . . a beer, to start with, *s'il vous plaît.*'

'*Un bière.* Kronenburg, Heineken, Michelob . . .'

'Anything. Any, just a beer.'

'*Monsieur?*'

'*Quelque chose,*' says Madelaine. I know what she's said, but couldn't come up with it myself, not when I needed to.

'*Merci, mademoiselle.*'

'Are you having a starter?' she asks.

'The *foie gras,*' I say, without looking at the menu.

'Artie! Do you know what they do to those geese to get that stuff. They . . .'

'Of course I know, but it's already there, made. It's in a tin already, or whatever. It would be bad not to eat it after what they . . .'

'If nobody ate it they wouldn't do it to them?'

'You eat meat.'

'Let's drop it shall we?' She's not even looked up as she said it. She doesn't care for what I've got to say, can't imagine that I'd be able to disprove her. She thinks she's saving me from another embarrassment. But all she's doing, by discussing a dead goose and the way it lived and died, is to say that's more important than how we've come to be here. A different kind of slow death.

We're the only couple dining alone and most of the tables have been moved around since earlier, to accommodate parties of sixes and eights, some wearing hats and all looking happy, not caring that much about the food by the looks of things.

'I'm going to have the *terrine de poireaux*,' she says. 'I love . . .'

'Hmm, leek. It's in a mint vinaigrette.' Such is the quality of my research that it makes her head come up above the menu, draws a surprised look on her face, but which turns into a smile, as though she's about to say, 'How sweet. All that work you've put in – for me.' But she says nothing.

'Madelaine?'

'Hmm?'

'We've got to talk.'

'Let's have our meal, hey? Let's enjoy it. It is New Year's Eve.'

The waiter's here, baling us out with the drinks.

'How did you find this place?' she asks. 'The area, I mean. It's very chic round here, all the best shops, and the Opera, and . . .'

'The Madeleine. I'm here because of the Madeleine. You.'

She says, 'Oh, Artie', but she means 'oh shit', which she

says with her eyes going back to the menu, even though I know she's decided.

'It's a church.'

'I know.'

'But it looks like a temple. It looks Greek.'

'It was supposed to have been modelled on the Pantheon,' she says.

'You've been?'

'No. I just remember it, from somewhere.'

'They named it after a whore.'

'Me too, eh?'

'What?'

'My mum must have realized I was going to turn into a right old slapper.' She's laughing. It's not supposed to be funny.

'Don't say that.'

'Lighten up, Artie.'

'It's the bible,' I say. 'You should have more respect.'

'Hey, the Hebrews have got a whore, called Rahab. Any man who pronounced her name ejaculated. Can you imagine? "Hi Rahab. Ooops, sorry."'

'Maybe your mum should have called you Rahab.'

'Artie!'

'Men find you attractive.'

'Women find you attractive.'

'Why are you here?' I say, wading in. I can't lose any more control than I already have.

'I needed to get away, without an argument. Just have a little time on my own.'

'You could have told me.'

'You'd have understood, right?'

'I would. Really. I can see you need a bit of time to yourself.'

'So why are you here?' she asks.

'But you're not by *yourself*.'

'So? It's only Brenda.'

'Only Brenda? Yes, but it wouldn't have been. Would it?'

'Artie? What . . .'

'Not if he hadn't died.' This is too soon. The questions have jumbled, bringing the heaviest to the surface, somehow.

She's saying nothing, just putting her menu down and getting up, wiping her lips with her napkin.

'This is a fine time, Artie, a fine fucking time to bring this up. I'm going to the loo. You can have a think about whether you really want to talk about this.'

I don't. Of course I don't. But it's here. I've uncovered it all now, got almost to the bottom of it. You wouldn't be able to stop now, not here, no-one would. But I've let her get away. I got her here, and I've let her slip away, to compose herself and order the excuses. I should have waited for the food to arrive. That's how I'd planned it.

She's on her way back, but stopping at the bar, talking to the owner and getting a smile from him, getting him to nod in agreement, getting him to go to an optic with a large brandy glass and smiling broader as she swirls it and sniffs, then tips her head right back, handing the empty glass back to him with words that make the smile break out into a laugh and a comment to a waiter who joins in.

'OK,' she says. 'Shall we order first, or do you want to start now? Whatever you want, Artie.'

'Let's order.'

She turns to the bar, and has the owner scuttling across with a raising of her eyebrows.

'*Mademoiselle?*'

'*Oui, pour l'entrée, le terrine de poireaux, aussi le plat degustation. Merci.*'

'*Monsieur?*'

'The foie gras, and the sole, *s'il vous plait.*'

'*Vin?*'

'The Sancerre,' I say.

'I'll pay for the wine. Can I choose?' I'm nodding. What else can I do? 'Le Pouilly Vinzelle.'

'*Parfait, mademoiselle, parfait.*'

'*Merci,*' she says, handing back the menu. The owner takes mine, and as soon as he's gone she leans forward, taking a long drink of the kir. 'Right then. Fire away, at least I'm going to get a decent meal out of you now.'

'You came here to get away from me, didn't you?' I say.

'I came here to straighten things out, to have a rest. That's all.'

'So his death had nothing to do with it.'

'Christ, Artie.'

'You still came here, despite that.'

'I couldn't face it, all right, all those people and the service, everything. I just didn't want to be there.'

'So he didn't mean that much to you?'

'Look, there's no point lying. Of course he did. But that's all a long time ago.'

'A long time? For God's sake Madelaine, it's only two days.'

'Two days? What?'

'I should know.'

'Know what? Artie, what are you talking about?'

'Des, they killed him . . . '

'Des? Des Christian? He's dead?'

'Of course he is, you know he is.'

'Stop messing about, Artie.'

'Me messing about? I'm not the one who's been sleeping with a bloody gangster.'

'Me and Des? . . . You think? . . . Jesus, Artie. How could you?'

'I know everything. I've seen your report, the one from the accident, and the postcard. Relationships, eh? How many others have there been? I saw you on the dance-floor and in his car. I've seen that fucking photograph you gave him.'

'Sshh.'

'I will not . . . oh, thank you, *merci*.'

The *foie gras*, which I've never actually had before, just looks like pâté, with thick bread wrapped warm in starched linen. Madelaine's looks better, the mint dressing whipped thick so it sits round the terrine in two perfect oval pools. The terrine is golden green with the leeks chopped tiny and suspended in the jelly. It's not what I'd expected.

'Let me get this right. You think I was having an affair with Des.' She's smiling, I can see she wants to laugh. Probably hysterics. 'And Des has died? How?'

'How? You know how. You know he's dead.'

'I don't.'

'You said before.'

She's stopped smiling. Gone serious, and breaking open the terrine with a slow and meticulous slice, and dragging it through the dressing. Taking a mouthful and buying time as she chews slowly, takes a sip of the wine.

'I wasn't talking about Des.' She's fixed me with a look, straight into the eyes. I daren't go for my knife and fork, because even if I get it off the plate, my hands will shake and jerk, I'll never get it to my mouth, couldn't swallow anyway. She takes another sip of wine, and picks at the terrine with her fork, looking down, releasing me from her look and saying something quiet.

'It was Bill. Bill was the one.'

'Bill? The one who died. You mean, from Bristol? He can't be. That was . . . that was years ago.'

She's nodding, and upset.

'I'm sorry, Artie. Really. Nothing ever, you know. We didn't . . .'

'You're telling me that you, you had . . .'

'I loved him. I was never unfaithful, Artie. Believe me, I never was, not like . . .'

'All that time ago. All the time we've been . . . Jesus. If he hadn't died, you wouldn't have come back. You've let me be second best, all this time?'

'Honestly, Artie, I would never hurt you. I do love you. I always have, you must know that.'

I want to ask what they did, if they didn't do that. Where they went and what they did. I want to see what she'd wear for him. I want to hear what noises she'd make when she kissed him. I want to know how far he would get with her, what she'd do to him, if they didn't do that. I don't want to know. The more she did with him, the more fake everything we did is proved to be. I want to ask her if that's true.

'All that time. All our time together, when you came to me, at weekends. He'd been . . . Oh God.'

'Artie. I'm sorry. I've never . . .'

'Did he make you come?'

'Artie.'

'Did he?'

'This is stupid.'

'He did.'

'Stop it.'

She's started to cry. No tears, but I can see it rising and

falling in her throat, so I'm stopping, even though I know that she's crying for him: not me or herself.

'It was seven years ago today,' she says.

'I know.'

'I loved him. I really did.'

'I know.'

We've not spoken since. It's getting close to midnight and the restaurant is emptying. They're going into the rain, to be somewhere else for the New Year. I'm watching Madelaine twist and snap and skewer the flesh from the shells that were brought to her on three, tiered beds of ice. Ice, which she tried to break when she offered me an oyster. I got the smile to disappear from her face with a shake of my head. She made the right choice, again. My sole was rubbery, cooked too long, and the sauce was too acidic. Her shellfish looks magnificent on its silver trays, like the cake-stand that Nana would use for her Battenberg and fairy cakes, for her sisters, my great aunts, on Sundays when I'd have to go round.

I've got another bottle of the wine. We're drinking far too quickly.

'Order some brandies, eh?' I say. 'You're better at it.'

She smiles, and does it, rekindling a glint to her eye for the owner, who is hovering by the desk now, with a party to go to, no doubt.

'Well, I won't forget this meal,' she says, smiling. And in the lapsing of that smile, I see that I can't compete. I can't compete with a ghost, dead seven years, and from the glisten in her eyes, the crack in her voice, you can tell how futile it would be to even try. I'm trying to tell myself it's unfair, to compare the real me – dirtied by a thousand arguments, hundreds of petty annoyances – with him, untarnished by virtue of being dead. But it's simpler than that. She doesn't love me as much as she did him. You can see it, even though she's tried her best. I can't bring myself to hate her for it. 'So, you say Des has been killed.'

'Hmm, yes.'

'Doesn't surprise me. Drops me in it, though.'

'Why's that?'

'He'd offered to set me up, us up, if you'd wanted. He wanted someone to set up a theatre. In Amsterdam.'

'It doesn't take much of an imagination to see why.'

'Would you have come? With me.'

'I would have gone anywhere, with you. You shouldn't have to ask,' I say.

'Would have?'

I'm nodding.

'I see,' she says. This time there are tears in her eyes. But I feel dry. I feel empty and blank. Ready to start again, with the rain bouncing up from the pavement and flares lighting up the outline of the fire station opposite in red and blue flashes.

'Can you hear?' I say, turning to trace the noise through the window. The owner's reflection is shuffling across the watery image of the party. There is only us left in the restaurant and the shouting outside getting louder and louder over the music.

'*Dix, neuf, huit, sept, six, cinq, quatre, trois! deux! un! ZERO!*'

'Happy New Year, Artie,' she's saying, leaning across the table, with her eyes closing. But I know it won't be long before someone else will be seeing her that way, so I'm leaning back, just taking her hand in mine, squeezing it softly for the last time and asking for the bill.

'Here, have this. You pay.' I'm handing her one of my bank rolls. Not checking which one, just knowing it's more than enough. Much more, and there's surprise in her eyes for the second time today.

'This is far too much. Artie. Artie!'

But she's behind me now. All I can see is the owner, smiling at her with the bill in his hand, going towards her with a glint in his eye that I don't have to worry about any more.